"You don't have to hide the tears from me, Elizabeth."

The understanding in his voice stopped her in her tracks.

"I know what you are feeling. He was my brother, my best friend. I miss him terribly."

Pain pierced her heart, but David's honesty was an invitation. She turned to face him.

"How do you do it?" she asked.

He left the ladder and crossed the floor. "Do what?"

"Get up each morning? Go about your tasks? Your new job? I can barely breathe."

A look of compassion filled his face. It appeared as though he were about to embrace her, yet just before doing so, he stopped, rubbed his whiskered chin.

"I wish I could take away your pain," David said.

Upon impulse, she moved into his arms. David held her tightly. Elizabeth knew full well the strength and security he offered was only that of a would-be brother-in-law's kindness, yet even so, she soon gave in to temptation.

The same soap… The same shaving balm…

But the added hint of peppermint brought her back to reality. *He is not Jeremiah. He never will be.*

Shannon Farrington and her husband have been married for over twenty years, have two children and are active members in their local church and community. When she isn't researching or writing, you can find her visiting national parks and historical sites or at home herding her small flock of chickens through the backyard. She and her family live in Maryland.

Books by Shannon Farrington

Love Inspired Historical

Her Rebel Heart
An Unlikely Union
Second Chance Love

SHANNON FARRINGTON

Second Chance Love

HARLEQUIN® LOVE INSPIRED® HISTORICAL

Recycling programs
for this product may
not exist in your area.

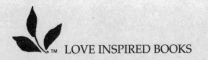

LOVE INSPIRED BOOKS

ISBN-13: 978-0-373-28325-5

Second Chance Love

Copyright © 2015 by Shannon Farrington

www.Harlequin.com

Printed in U.S.A.

For He hath said,
I will never leave thee nor forsake thee.
—*Hebrews* 13:5

For my father, who first inspired my interest
in the Civil War, and my mother,
who has lovingly put up with us both for all these years.

Chapter One

Baltimore, Maryland
1864

David Wainwright stared past his brother's casket to the place where Elizabeth Martin sat. Her beautiful red curls were pulled back tightly in a bun at the base of her neck. Head to toe, she was covered in black. In just a few short weeks the woman would have become part of his family, but not in the way David had hoped.

"I am the resurrection and the life. He that believeth in me, though he were dead, yet shall he live..."

The reverend presiding over the service recited the words of Jesus, but by the look on Elizabeth's face, it appeared she found no comfort in the promise of eternal life. Pale and stunned, she stared at Jeremiah's coffin. By all outward appearances she was the epitome of proper decorum, but the moment David caught her eye he sensed a storm below the surface.

If only you had left well enough alone, she seemed to say. *I'd have given anything for just a few days with him as his wife.*

Grief rolled through him in more ways than one. The loss of his brother was like a knife to his soul, and the sight of Elizabeth's pain cut him just as deeply.

I'm sorry, he wanted to say. *So sorry for everything.*

She returned her focus to the minister, but David's thoughts remained in the past.

Little had he realized when he first met her that his life, and that of his brother's, would be changed forever. Elizabeth was a Baltimore belle, born and bred. Like many other women from her city, she had volunteered to serve as a nurse following the battle of Antietam. Scores of wounded soldiers, Union and rebel alike, had come to Baltimore's US Army General Hospital for care and processing. David and Jeremiah were a pair of soldiers from Boston who had been assigned as stewards in the place. Elizabeth had worked in the ward alongside David. Jeremiah served next door.

Her Southern sympathy revealed itself from time to time, mostly in expressions of relief whenever she learned of rebel victories on the battlefield. As a Union soldier and the son of an abolition-preaching minister, David found that troubling. Then he learned Elizabeth's loyalty was more to an older brother named George, who had enlisted in the rebel forces, than to the actual Confederacy.

Her devotion to her secession-supporting family member, however, had cost her the position at the hospital. For, when a rebel prisoner escaped, Elizabeth and several other Baltimore volunteer nurses were accused of assisting him. She was found innocent of the charges but was forced to leave the hospital for refusing to sign an oath of loyalty that would have demanded that she cut off all contact with her brother.

It had been a dark day when she left David's ward, but worse ones were to follow. Shortly after her dismissal, Jeremiah had announced he was courting her.

Why didn't I speak up then? David couldn't help but think. *Why didn't I do something? Surely my brother would have respected my wishes if I'd told him that I'd fallen in love with her.*

Three weeks later Jeremiah had proposed. He and Elizabeth had planned to marry immediately. David had done his best to speak then. He remembered every detail of that conversation.

"You can't marry her," he'd insisted.

"Why not?"

"Well…this war."

"I will not reenlist," Jeremiah had announced. "I've done my duty. I'm going to marry Elizabeth."

"But you would marry her before your service is through? Why, you barely know each other."

"We will have a lifetime to get to know each other. I love her. She loves me."

The pain that statement had inflicted was more than David could stand, but he did not let his brother know that. "But surely you want what is best for her," he'd said.

"Of course I do."

"Then consider what *could* happen. If you married her before your service in the army is finished…"

Jeremiah had quickly dismissed his misgivings. "They have kept us in the same hospital for the past two years. There is no reason to think they would change our posting now. It's already November! We'll be out the first of January."

"But you can't be certain of that. You have no guarantee the army will keep you here in Baltimore until your enlistment ends. They could extend our service. What if we are sent to the battlefield?"

"Then I will do my duty."

David didn't doubt his brother's courage, and that was exactly what had frightened him.

"For her sake, don't be selfish, man! Think of her! Will you run the risk of making your new bride a widow? And if there is a child, would you leave him fatherless? Where will that leave her? I'll tell you— with the memory of a short-lived love and the lifelong responsibility of rearing the consequences!"

He may have been crass, indelicate for certain, but Jeremiah saw his point and he'd postponed the wedding. For David, however, it was hardly a victory.

Sitting here now before his brother's casket, his own words pounded repeatedly in his mind. *Don't be selfish, man! Think of her...*

He had told himself he had acted for Elizabeth's protection, but he realized now he had spoken for his own well-being. Deep down David knew he could not bear the thought of her belonging to another man, even one as good and as God-fearing as Jeremiah.

But a man without the courage to proclaim his own intentions has no business disrupting another's.

The minister continued on, talking of Jeremiah's unselfish nature, how he'd ministered to sick soldiers, many of whom considered him the enemy. David's guilt grew.

I am the older brother. I was supposed to be looking out for him. That's why I enlisted in the first place. I should have encouraged him to marry Elizabeth when he wished. I had no idea he would succumb to pneumonia just days before our service in the army ended.

He chanced a glance in her direction. She was staring

straight at the coffin. Her chin was quivering, but she was trying desperately to maintain control.

The last thing on earth he'd wanted to do was hurt her, and yet that was exactly what he had done. He had stolen what precious little happiness Elizabeth could have had. He'd stolen it from Jeremiah, as well.

The casket was closed. A bone-rattling chill, one even colder than the dreadful January weather, shivered through him. The minister offered a final prayer, and when it was over, David and his fellow mourners stood.

Across the way, Elizabeth did the same. She wiped her eyes, tucked her black-trimmed handkerchief in the cuff of her sleeve and prepared to greet each of their guests. David was confident she would do so with respect and grace, no matter what she may be feeling inside. She would execute the duties of this day. He would do the same.

In a few hours he would place his brother's casket on the northbound train. When he reached Boston, his family would then conduct a second service at their home, followed by internment in the Wainwright plot. All honors would be paid to Jeremiah for his service to the Union.

In the weeks to come David would help settle his brother's affairs, then do his best to reenter civilian life. In all likelihood he would never see Elizabeth Martin again, but he knew what he had done to her and his brother would haunt him for the rest of his days.

Elizabeth mustered her strength and stood. She'd told herself she could get through this. She *would* get through this. Her determination, however, was immediately tested as Jeremiah's older brother approached.

Elizabeth had managed to avoid him all morning, but now there was no escaping his presence.

The sight of David made her heart squeeze. He wore the same blue uniform, had the same dark, wavy hair and lean yet muscular build. Were it not for the neatly trimmed mustache and chin whiskers, he could have easily been Jeremiah's twin.

What can I say to him? What can he possibly say to me? Even if he were to apologize, he could never undo what has been done.

She would never forget the day her fiancé came to tell her the wedding would be postponed.

"You want to wait until you finish with the army?" Elizabeth had asked.

"I spoke with David and he had a good point. One never knows what the army may do. I shouldn't want you to be carrying our child if I am sent to battle…"

Elizabeth had blushed ten shades of crimson. How dare David discuss such intimate details of her and Jeremiah's life! Her embarrassment had only been surpassed by the fear invoked by the validity of the statement. The thought of Jeremiah leaving the safety of the hospital, of him lying wounded in some blood-crusted field, had made her tremble. Her beloved had immediately realized her distress and taken her in his arms.

"Come now, don't think of such things… Besides, you know that hospital can't get along without me. Why, I heard a rumor that next week they are planning on making me chief of surgery!"

The words had been so ridiculous that she'd laughed.

But the merriment could not last for long.

A cold, wet November had brought sickness to the hospital. The army had suspended all liberty passes as pneumonia and other ailments ravaged the wards. Jeremiah had soon fallen ill himself. Elizabeth, frantic with worry, had begged to tend to him. She knew the hospital was short on nurses and her help was surely needed, but because of her brother's involvement in the Confederate army, and her refusal to disavow him, she wasn't permitted to step foot on hospital grounds.

It hadn't been until dear old Dr. Turner, the physician she had once served, pleaded her case to hospital command that she'd been allowed to see her fiancé. David had come to fetch her the night Jeremiah lay dying. By then he'd been too ill to recognize her, let alone speak.

Elizabeth had held his hand those final hours and watched helplessly as he'd slipped into eternity. Her faith had slipped away that night, as well. She felt cheated, in every sense of the word. Cheated by God.

Cheated by him...

David stood before her quietly. His eyes were as blue and clear as Jeremiah's had once been. Elizabeth didn't want him anywhere near her, but she forced herself to display customary courtesy. She had to focus on his chin whiskers in order to keep her voice steady. "David, I must thank you for your assistance... I appreciate your willingness to allow a funeral here in Baltimore."

"It was the least I could do," he said. "Considering..."

Her heart squeezed again, and she was grateful he didn't finish the sentence. Instead of claiming the place beside her, he moved to the far end of the receiving line, putting Elizabeth's mother, Jane, and her sister, Trudy, between them. Her mother tugged on her hand. Elizabeth knew it was both a gesture of comfort and direction.

"It is time, Beth," she whispered.

Turning to the left, Elizabeth began the difficult task

of greeting her guests. All of her closest friends had gathered—Julia and her husband, Samuel Ward, Sally Hastings and Rebekah Van der Geld. Even Emily and her new husband, Dr. Evan Mackay, had come. They had arrived by way of the Washington train early that morning.

Dr. Mackay was first in line. "Your fiancé was a good soldier," he insisted, "and a fine Christian man."

Both the compliment and the man's presence brought a quiver to her chin. Elizabeth fought hard to keep control. Jeremiah had once served in his ward. Dr. Mackay was skilled in treating lung ailments, and Elizabeth had no doubt her fiancé would have survived his illness had this particular physician not been transferred just weeks before to the hospital in Washington.

"May God comfort you in your loss," Dr. Mackay added.

She had been told by others previously that He would, but so far she was still waiting.

Emily then moved to embrace her. "Don't concern yourself with anything in the kitchen," she whispered. "The girls and I will see to everything."

"Thank you," Elizabeth managed. She *was* grateful for her friends' assistance, as well as for the food they had supplied. *A proper funeral demands a proper meal. Today should be a day of dignity and respect.*

As Emily and her husband moved to her mother, Elizabeth glanced to her left. The queue of mourners stretched throughout the darkened parlor. She willed them to disappear. She did not want their condolences. She did not even want their prayers. What she wanted drove an ache so deep through her body that she feared for a moment her knees were going to buckle. She wanted Jeremiah back.

Get a hold of yourself, she commanded. *You must not cry.*

She tried to steel her resolve by reminding herself she had but only a few more hours to endure, then she could retreat to the solitude of her room. There she would not be forced to make polite conversation. She could be alone.

"This world will not be the same without him," she heard Dr. Mackay say to David.

The finality of her fiancé's death seemed to wrap her in a tight-fitting shroud. *It is not just these few hours I must endure*, she realized. *It is a lifetime. I will never again hear the sound of his laughter, feel his kiss upon my lips. I will never claim his name as my own or hold his child in my arms. My dreams have died with him. I will mourn his loss the rest of my days.*

When the last person had paid their respects, Elizabeth very quickly left the parlor. David wanted to follow after her, but he didn't dare. He knew she'd prefer to be alone.

As her mother gently laid a hand upon his arm, David turned. The lines around her eyes were far too many for her years. Worry and sorrow had deeply etched their mark.

"Why don't you go to the kitchen?" she suggested. "Get something to eat."

"Oh, thank you, ma'am, but I'm not that hungry."

"You must keep up your strength."

She was concerned for his health, as were many of the ladies here today. Several had been volunteer nurses and apparently thought *his* welfare was in jeopardy. One had asked if he had enough warm clothing for the jour-

ney north. Another if he'd been showing any signs of
chills or respiratory illness himself.

David assured them all that *physically*, he was fine.

To please Mrs. Martin, he went to the kitchen and accepted the piece of fried chicken that Miss Sally Hastings laid upon his plate.

"How about a slice of raisin pie?" she asked.

David doubted he could even handle the chicken. "I'm
certain it is delicious but…I don't think so…"

Miss Hastings must have understood, for she smiled
sympathetically. David knew she had recently lost a
brother herself. "I'll set aside some food for you to take
on the train," she promised.

He thanked her politely and then moved to the dining area. As he stepped into the once elegant room, he
couldn't help but notice some of the flocked wallpaper
was peeling. In another corner, a piece of crown molding was loose. With Elizabeth's father having passed
four years ago and her brother somewhere south of the
Potomac, the absence of any male presence to maintain
the house was beginning to show.

David wondered why Jeremiah had not seen to such
things before falling ill. *I suppose he and Elizabeth had
far more on their minds than household repairs.* Shov-
ing the thought aside, he scanned the faces in the room.
His fellow mourners were gathered in tight groups of
conversation. Hushed whispers drifted about. Most of
the words centered on his brother and Elizabeth.

At the far end of the room several hospital physicians
had collected along with a few members of David's regiment who, like him, had completed their enlistment and
were about to return home. Though he appreciated their
presence, he had no desire to speak with any of them at

the moment. The only person with whom he did truly wish to speak did not wish for him to do so.

Claiming a spot on the window ledge, he tried to force down the chicken. He soon felt nauseous and wondered if it was the chicken or the thought of Elizabeth remaining in perpetual mourning.

"I wanted to thank you."

Dr. Evan Mackay's voice broke in to his thoughts. David looked up to see the Scottish-born physician once again standing before him. He quickly stood and reached for the man's outstretched hand.

"I am humbled that you selected me as one of the pallbearers."

All the other men David had chosen had each expressed the same sentiment. They considered it an honor to provide final escort for one of their comrades.

"You are soon leaving for the train station?" the army physician asked.

David checked his watch. It was nearly three o'clock. "Yes. Within the hour."

Dr. Mackay nodded, then glanced quickly about, as if what he were about to say was to be held in strict confidence. "I would advise against Miss Martin accompanying the body to the station."

"Why is that?" David asked.

"I don't believe she is up for the task. My wife is with her now." He leveled his gaze. "You should go to her."

"Go to her?"

The Scotsman nodded. "See for yourself."

Though the man was no longer David's superior, the instinct was still there to follow his commands. Especially since David knew the order was surely given out of concern for Elizabeth, for the doctor's wife and she were close friends. Still, he balked.

You're the physician and family friend. If she is having difficulty in some way, what can I do? She doesn't want to see me. It isn't my place.

Yet Dr. Mackay stared at him as if it were. David then realized, with Elizabeth's father dead and her brother away at war, *he was* the closest she had to any male relative. As much as she may wish for him to leave her alone, it was his duty today to look after her.

Handing the physician the plate of chicken, David walked toward the parlor. The light was dim. The house was shuttered, and many of the windows were draped in black. The fires were lit, but winter's chill still invaded every space. Appropriately, the place felt like a tomb.

Rounding the corner he found Elizabeth seated before his brother's casket. Mrs. Mackay was beside her.

"But you know we must," he heard her say.

Seeing Elizabeth's head bowed, her shoulders shaking, pierced David's heart. She had held her composure for so long, but here in the final moments it was crumbling. Quietly he approached. Tears streaked her face, but her eyes were as sharp as steel.

"No, David. Not yet. I won't let you take him."

She thought he had come to begin the processional. Now he knew why Dr. Mackay thought it unwise for her to go to the train station.

She cannot bring herself to say goodbye.

He knelt before her. "Elizabeth, I want to…help."

"Haven't you done enough already?" Her voice was barely above a whisper, but he clearly heard the anger. "You caused this!"

Guilt and grief rained down upon him. He felt torn

between allowing her privacy and remaining with her. He foolishly chose the latter.

"Elizabeth, I'm sorry... I never should have interfered."

"If you had left well enough alone, he would have married me. Things would have turned out differently. I know they would have. We would have been...so..."

Happy, he thought.

Anger gave way to anguish. Great sobs shook her entire frame. Mrs. Mackay immediately took Elizabeth in her arms and tried to soothe her. Frozen in his place, David wished there was something he could do to ease her pain.

"I loved him!" Elizabeth cried.

"And he, you," Mrs. Mackay whispered. "No one on this earth could have loved you more."

That isn't true, David thought. *That isn't the whole story*. Suddenly he wanted her to know why he had done what he did. He wanted to tell her he'd been in love with her from the moment she first walked in to his ward. His mind told him the confession would bring relief to him, but he knew for *her*, it would only bring more pain. So, he kept his mouth shut. Just like he had done every other time she was near him.

By now her cries had drawn the attention of the entire house. Her mother, sister and her other friends soon surrounded them. Trudy looked at him, her expression a mixture of embarrassment and pity. "Don't worry, David. We'll take care of her."

"No," Elizabeth cried.

"Let him see to Jeremiah," Miss Hastings insisted. "It is what is best."

"No..."

"Come with us, Elizabeth," Mrs. Mackay gently urged.

The women pulled her to her feet, escorting her to the staircase. He watched helplessly as Elizabeth disappeared in a swirl of hazy black crepe.

"David," he then heard her mother quietly say, "perhaps it would be best if you now see to your brother."

"Yes, of course."

He did not have to search far for the other men. Elizabeth's cries had drawn each of them to the parlor, as well. In quiet reverence the pallbearers took their places alongside Jeremiah's casket. David claimed his position at the head of the processional, his body and mind now numb.

Jeremiah's flag-draped coffin was carried through the front door, the barren garden and out to the street. Carefully it was placed in the hearse. The pallbearers and remaining men then formed a line behind the black-adorned carriage. All of the women had elected to stay behind. David wondered if they were still surrounding Elizabeth. Were they offering words of comfort to her, words he could not give? Words she would not accept from him?

He glanced toward the upstairs windows. Part of him wished to return to the house, seek her out, if only to say goodbye. The rest of him knew it was better this way.

Just then, Mrs. Martin stepped from the porch and embraced him. "God keep you, David," she whispered. "May He ease your troubled heart."

"Ma'am," he said, "I wish there was something I could do…"

"I know you do, son, but there is nothing to be done.

Return to your home, and may God keep you from any more sorrow."

Not knowing what else to say, he respectfully kissed her cheek, then directed the men to move. The processional made its way through the slush-covered streets toward the train station. As they passed through Monument Square, carriages halted. The citizens of Baltimore removed their hats out of respect for the fallen Union soldier, although in all probability many of them had advocated secession. Honoring a life took precedence over politics this day, yet the gesture offered David little comfort. He wondered how many more funerals this city would witness before this war was over.

At the President Street station, Jeremiah's casket was loaded on to a freight car. His fellow soldiers offered a last salute, and the men of Baltimore, their final condolences. David then boarded the northbound train, solemnly claiming a seat.

Within a few moments he heard the whispers around him. Though the mood was still somber, his fellow Massachusetts comrades were speaking of what they would do when they reached Boston. David tried to focus his thoughts forward, as well, reminding himself that he also was going home.

But I am returning alone...

The car lurched forward as the train began to roll. The coal yards, docks and military fortifications soon gave way to snow-covered fields and ice-encased forests. Glass-like icicles dangled from bare tree limbs. He tried to focus on the peaceful scene outside his window, but his thoughts kept returning to the anguish Jeremiah had suffered in those final hours. David had been powerless to do anything to help him.

Elizabeth's words sliced his soul. "You caused all this!"

If he could turn the clock back, he would, and this time he would not allow his personal feelings to interfere. He'd swallow his heart and stand beside his brother as he kissed his bride, content to be Elizabeth's brother-in-law.

But it is too late. Jeremiah is gone, and Elizabeth will never forgive me.

His hands began to tremble. How was he to handle returning to Boston? How could he face his family? His parents had not even the luxury of saying goodbye. His sister Clara's difficult delivery of her first child had kept them from making the journey to Baltimore. He knew his mother and father would not blame him for Jeremiah's passing. Their telegram had confirmed it. Though they were heartbroken, they accepted their son's death as "divine will."

They will do their best to be grateful for the years Jeremiah was alive, for the memories they have of him. They will encourage me to do the same.

The memory of Elizabeth's tear-streaked face, the look in her eyes, once more crossed his mind. His parents had each other. Clara had her husband, Patrick, and their new baby.

But who will comfort Elizabeth and her family? Who will encourage them?

As the train chugged northward, he thought of all the things he had seen in her house that required tending. There was woodwork in need of repair, squeaky hinges to be oiled. *Seeing to such things would not ease her pain, but it would keep her house in running order...*

He shoved the thought aside as quickly as it came,

telling himself any idea of returning to Baltimore was foolish. *My interference would not be a comfort to her. I would only add to her grief, and she to mine.*

He told himself she had friends, a church family that cared for her. Surely they had noticed what he had. *They will take care of such things. Why, if I know Dr. Mackay as well as I think I do, the man has probably already issued orders for someone to complete the tasks.*

He never wanted to see Baltimore again. He wanted to forget the suffering he had witnessed and experienced there, yet the thought of returning nagged him for miles.

I have my old job waiting for me back at the Boston Journal. *Lord willing, I will use words to shape my country's future, not bullets.* The train crossed the Susquehanna River. Workers were busy harvesting ice. By the thickness of the blocks it looked as though spring would never come.

But it will come, David thought, *and the fighting will resume. More men will be wounded. More men will grow sick. More men will die.* With the exception of the Pratt Street Riot, the city of Baltimore had witnessed no battles, only the aftereffects of them. But what if all that was about to change? *What if the rebels advance into Union territory? The fortifications around Washington are strong, but what if they circumvent the defenses of the Capitol, setting their sights on Baltimore instead? Who will protect Elizabeth, her sister, her mother?*

If David's brother had married her, he would have brought Elizabeth back to Boston. Jeremiah had told him he would have convinced her family to come, as well, at least until the war was over.

She will never leave Baltimore now. Especially not

to visit a place that will remind her of things that can never be.

David shifted uncomfortably in his seat as once again he was reminded of his duty. *My duty to see to her welfare does not end with the funeral. It is for as long as this war lasts, or until her own brother returns, whichever comes first.*

He knew what he had to do, and he knew how hard it was going to be. Even so, his mind was made up. He would travel to Boston and bury his brother with honors. Then he would return to Baltimore to look after Jeremiah's heartbroken bride. After what he had done, he owed them both at least that much.

Chapter Two

Elizabeth stared at the ceiling, just as she had every day for the past two months. Trudy had brought up a light breakfast of tea, toast and marmalade, but Elizabeth left it untouched. She could not stomach food. All she wanted to do was go back to sleep. In her dreams, she lived happily ever after.

But there is no happily-ever-after.

The words of the church matrons repeated over and over again in her mind. She'd caught their whispers before she'd made such a fool of herself at the funeral.

"Such a tragedy…so young…but the best thing *she* can do is go on with her life. Find herself a new beau."

Elizabeth winced and rolled to her side. She did not want to get on with her life. Had she actually been married to Jeremiah, society would have granted her a full year of heavy mourning. But as a fiancée, she was not afforded the same right. Somehow the pain was supposed to be less. *Time is moving on. I'm expected to do so, as well.*

Friends and neighbors hinted at such by their constant visits to the house. They wanted to chat with her, take her on some sort of outing. Trudy and her mother were forced to receive them as Elizabeth simply could not. Not an hour passed that she didn't spend in tears. Crying was simply a way of life now.

"Oh, Beth, I know it is hard," her mother said repeatedly, "but you must seek God's strength. It was the only way I survived your father's passing."

Elizabeth tried, but she had no more prayers to offer. *I prayed for Father, but he still died. I prayed for my country, and yet war still came. I prayed George would not have to leave, but he did.*

Like so many others, her brother had been caught up in the states' rights fervor that had gripped Baltimore after the riot on Pratt Street. When the Confederacy declared independence, President Lincoln had called for soldiers to force the seceding states back into the Union. Finding the thought of firing upon their fellow countrymen appalling, most men from Maryland, including George, ignored the call. Men from Massachusetts and Pennsylvania, however, answered it expediently. Summoned to Washington to protect the capital, they'd passed through Baltimore one fateful April morning.

As the Northern soldiers had marched to the southbound trains at Camden Street, a small group of citizens gathered around them at Pratt Street. Who started what, the world would probably never know, but insults were exchanged from both sides. Rocks and bottles, in the hands of the locals, began to fly. The Massachusetts men then opened fire. When the musket smoke cleared, eleven Baltimoreans were dead, along with four Northern soldiers. Countless more on both sides had been wounded.

In the days that followed, the federal army seized control of the city. They'd closed newspapers that held any hint of Southern sympathy, arrested anyone suspected of disloyalty to the Union and instituted martial law.

Outraged, Elizabeth's brother, as well as many other men from her Mount Vernon neighborhood, had slipped out of the city by night and joined Confederate regiments. They'd promised to soon return and deliver Maryland from federal tyranny. Though heartbroken to see him go, Elizabeth had then supported her brother's decision. She'd loathed those Northern soldiers occupying her city.

Then I fell in love with one. And I prayed for him, as well...

Swallowing back her sobs, she rolled to the opposite side of her bed. Sunlight was pushing its way through the shutter slats, testifying that it was now well past noon. Her mother had met with a local businessman that morning in regard to selling what was left of the family silver.

Elizabeth sighed. *I should have accompanied her instead of lying about. As the oldest daughter, even if it is only by a matter of minutes, it is my duty. I shouldn't be leaving all the housework for Trudy, either.*

She forced herself to rise and put her feet to the floor. Going to the washbasin, Elizabeth splashed water on her face, then stared into the looking glass. Her cheeks were hollow, her color pale and sickly.

What would Jeremiah think if he saw me like this?

She tried to ignore the pain the thought provoked, but it was no use. Her tears got the better of her, and she sank to the bed once more.

David had been back in Baltimore for three days and still couldn't bring himself to make his relocation known to Elizabeth's family. Mindful of his duty, though, he passed by their house at least twice each day from the far side of the street and witnessed the coming and going of many friends.

There was little going on with the war at present. The March rains had kept both armies axle deep in mud and unable to fight. All, at least, appeared to be well and safe in Baltimore. David couldn't shake the feeling, however, that he was supposed to stay.

He'd sought employment in the only area that truly interested him. He'd gone to the *Baltimore Sun* and a host of other local newspapers, but no one seemed much interested in hiring a man who'd spent most of his time before the war fetching coffee and sandwiches, or covering the few cast-off assignments the feature reporters didn't want. Then he came to the *Free American*.

The large brick building not far from Monument Square looked impressive from the outside, but the appearances were deceiving. David stepped inside only to discover the paper occupied just a small portion of the structure. The publisher, a man by the name of Peter Carpenter, served also as the executive editor, the editorial director and a host of other things. It was a struggling publication to be certain, but they were hiring.

I need a job, he reminded himself. *And I need one here in Baltimore. If I am careful with the money I saved before the war, I can get by on meager wages, at least for a while.*

"So you're looking for work," Carpenter said.

The man was older than David, midthirties perhaps. He was curt, to the point, with a military-like manner that reminded David of the officers he'd once served under.

"Yes, sir. I am."

"Reporter?"

"Yes, sir."

"You got any experience?"

The moment David mentioned he'd held an entry position at the *Boston Journal*, Carpenter asked to see some of his work. It wasn't much and it certainly wasn't very exciting, but the man looked intrigued. David held hopeful expectation.

"You serve in the army?" Carpenter asked.

"Yes, sir. I spent much of the time of service right here in Baltimore." He told him about the hospital.

The man's eyes narrowed. His forehead furrowed. "Then you know the lay of the land. Politically speaking, that is."

"Yes, sir." David was well aware Baltimore was a divided city. Immigrants and other newcomers favored a strong federal government, but many of the older established families still advocated strong states' rights. As a Union soldier he'd received his share of derogatory remarks from those who supported the South.

David wondered what view the man before him subscribed to and what position his paper took. *He can't be too sympathetic to the South, though. The city's outright pro-Southern papers have all been closed. But does he lean too far in the opposite direction?* Fearing suspension, many publications now painted the federal government in such a glorious light, it was simply unbelievable. David believed wholeheartedly in the preservation of the Union, but he also believed in freedom of the press. He was impressed when Carpenter then said, "Notice the sign on the door says the *Free American*. You can't have a free America without a free press. I don't care which army occupies this city, or who is vying for control of the statehouse. Here we stick to the facts. We don't bury or sugarcoat them, and we don't try to make the local leadership something they are not." He paused. "If you can check your own political agendas at the door, the job is yours."

David's heart skipped a beat. "Thank you, sir." Then suddenly fearing a return to coffee and sandwiches, he asked, "What exactly is the job?"

"You'll be handling local news and features."

He could feel the grin tugging at his lips.

"You'll report directly to me," the man said, "and you can start immediately."

As excited as he was to take pen in hand, *immediately* was a little too soon. There was another matter to which David must tend, even though he dreaded doing so. *I need to visit Elizabeth. I can't put this off any longer. For, once I begin reporting, I don't know what my schedule will be like.*

"Sir, I appreciate that, but given that I've only recently returned from Boston, I've a few matters I must see to first. Would tomorrow suffice?"

Carpenter squinted. "Why were you in Boston? I thought you said you'd spent your service here."

"I did." He explained his brother's passing and then his return home. He didn't tell him why exactly he had come back to Baltimore. He hoped the man would not ask. David wasn't certain what he would say if he did.

"My condolences," was all Carpenter said. "I should have noticed the black armband. See to what you must. Tomorrow will suffice."

"Thank you, sir."

"Before you go, though, let me show you about."

Carpenter reached for a cane that was hooked to the back of his chair. David hadn't noticed it until now. The man rose somewhat awkwardly from his seat. Knowing his newest reporter was curious, he said, "No. It isn't from the war. I was born this way."

David nodded but didn't say anything. He followed the man as he hobbled toward the newsroom. The space was clean and well organized but much smaller than what David had been used to in Boston. A half dozen or so desks were scattered about. Only a handful of men claimed them.

"Gentlemen," Carpenter announced. "Our newest reporter, Mr. Wainwright. He comes to us by way of the *Boston Journal*."

The men nodded their respect. Their publisher/editor then pointed to each one, starting with an older gentleman wearing spectacles. "This is Mr. Collins, business manager. He handles our advertising and circulation."

David acknowledged him.

"Mr. Russell covers local events. Mr. Detwiler, foreign news and finance. Mr. Ross, cultural events and daily humor." To which Carpenter then added, "The ladies seem to like him."

David wasn't certain if the comment was made in regard to the man's articles or looks. He did not ask, however. He was still too busy taking in his surroundings. There were no artists, no copy editors, no other reporters present.

Perhaps they are in another office or out on assignment, he thought. *Surely this isn't everyone.*

"Well, that's about it," Carpenter said, as if he'd read his mind. "For now, anyway. Oh, and I forgot to tell you,

you'll also be handling whatever comes in over the wire concerning the war."

David gulped. So he was to cover national news, as well? It was sink or swim. *I wanted a chance to write,* he thought. *It appears I have one.* "Yes, sir. Thank you."

At that moment a boy, who couldn't have been more than sixteen or so, came into the room. He handed Carpenter a proof copy of the day's edition. Evidently the man saw to that job, also.

"And this is young Mr. Keedy, our assistant," he said.

David shook the boy's hand. Keedy was wide-eyed, and innocent-looking, much like David had been before the war. *God willing, the suffering will end before this young man comes of age to serve,* he thought.

Carpenter dismissed Keedy, then motioned David toward the staircase. "Our press is this way…"

The moment David smelled the ink and paper, his excitement stirred. *This is what I was meant to do.*

Given the limited number of news staff, he half expected to find an old-style flatbed press churning out today's edition. Much to his surprise, however, the *Free American* boasted a decent-sized rotary press, a Taylor Double Cylinder, in fact. It was a little worse for wear but functional. David wondered if Carpenter had acquired it from one of his competitors who'd recently been closed down.

A handful of typesetters and pressmen were busy preparing the machine, their over sleeves and fingers stained black. Carpenter introduced each of them, then motioned for David to return to the stairs.

"You change your mind?" he asked, as though he feared David had. "Want to try your luck at the *Sun*?"

David chuckled but did not let on that he'd already been there *and* been turned down. "No, sir," he said.

"Good. Before you go, I've got some work I want you to take with you. Notes and outline are all in order. Just write the piece after you settle your business. It won't take long." From his coat pocket he pulled out a folded set of papers, handed them over.

So you'll have me start immediately after all, David thought, but he wasn't the least bit put out. Rather, he was intrigued. "What is this?" he asked as he quickly perused the notes.

"The city provost marshal, Colonel William Fish, has been arrested on charges of fraud and corruption. The man and his accomplices allegedly made a business out of arresting innocent citizens, accusing them of being rebel spies and whatnot, then interceding on their behalf."

"For a price," David guessed.

Carpenter nodded.

"I see." It was exactly the kind of thing that made David feel so strongly about returning to Baltimore. There was already the risk of a rebel invasion. Elizabeth and her family shouldn't have to fear the predations of unscrupulous, greedy bureaucrats, as well. David was again pleased to see his publisher had the courage to cover such a story, even if it would cast a shadow on a member of the Union army.

"I'll have this on your desk first thing tomorrow," he promised.

The man nodded matter-of-factly, then hobbled toward the staircase. "Eight a.m.," he insisted. "Sharp."

"Yes, sir."

His own inexperience, coupled with the workload,

was going to make his job here at the *Free American* a challenge. Keeping Elizabeth and his brother out of his thoughts while doing so was going to be an even bigger one. Even so, David had a feeling he was going to like working in Baltimore.

Leaving the paper, he returned to his room at the Hotel Barnum. The location worked well for his purposes, for the establishment was a fixture in Mount Vernon. This placed him in Elizabeth's neighborhood, as well as close to the newspaper.

Sitting down at a small writing desk, David looked over the very detailed notes and outline Peter Carpenter had given him. Colonel Fish's court martial was to take place in the next few weeks. If convicted, the man would be sent to prison in Albany, New York.

It was a straightforward, simple assignment. Although he wanted to dive right in, he didn't. *I can take care of this tonight*, he thought, and he forced himself to leave pen and paper behind.

Feeling much more uncertain than he had knocking on Peter Carpenter's door, David approached Elizabeth's house. The wreath on the front door and the black crepe that had draped the windows at the time of his brother's funeral had been removed. In the garden, crocuses were in bloom and the daffodils were just beginning to flower. Spring had come, yet David wondered if winter still held Elizabeth in its icy grip.

Drawing in a deep breath, he stepped to the porch and rang the bell. Trudy greeted him. Her eyes flew open wide the moment she recognized him.

"David!" she said, quickly hugging him. "What a surprise! Oh! It is so good to see you!"

He chuckled slightly. It was nice to know that someone had missed him. "Hello, Trudy. It is good to see you, as well."

Stepping back, she happily ushered him inside. "Come in! Come in!"

She was an exact duplicate of her sister in features, yet whereas Elizabeth carried herself like a queen, Trudy was more like an excited child.

"It is so strange to see you out of uniform," she then remarked.

It was still strange to him, too. He'd looked forward to the end of his service, but little had he known he would put away his blue wool for a black suit of mourning.

"The coat looks nice," she said. "Have you come to Baltimore on business?"

He wasn't certain how to answer that. It didn't seem right just to blurt out, *I'm here to look after you and your family.* "Business in a matter of speaking, I suppose."

"May I take your hat?"

"Yes. Thank you." As she laid it on the table behind her, David realized just how fast his heart was beating. *Any moment Elizabeth will round the corner or appear at the top of the staircase. What will I say to her?* He wasn't one who had trouble with words, except when it came to her.

"I'm afraid Mother isn't here," Trudy said. "She's out on business herself, but she should be home very soon. Please, come visit for a while."

He balked. She had not mentioned Elizabeth, but even if she was here, that meant the ladies were alone. "Perhaps, I shouldn't…"

Trudy cocked her head and offered that delightful, innocent grin. "Don't be silly. You are no stranger. You're family. Mother will be pleased to see you."

Yes, he reminded himself. *Family. Elizabeth's would-be brother-in-law.*

She motioned toward the parlor. David stepped forward and drew in a shallow breath. The furniture had all been returned to its original position, but the setting from the funeral remained raw in his mind. He still had trouble believing his brother was actually gone. Some days he expected him to appear, as if returning from a long journey.

But he isn't coming back. I buried him. His coffin was right there. I sat here...and she...she sat there... Her face flashed through his mind. He forced the memory of her heartbroken expression aside.

"Shall I fetch you some lemonade?" Trudy asked. "You must be thirsty after that long train ride."

He knew he should be honest, and he felt himself redden. "Actually, I've been in Baltimore for several days."

She blinked. *And you are just now coming to visit?* her look said. It was quickly replaced, however, with a smile. "Well, I imagine you must be thirsty, anyway. I'll fetch you a glass."

"Thank you, Trudy. I would appreciate that."

She scurried for the kitchen. The moment she had gone, the floorboards above his head creaked. David swallowed hard, for he knew exactly who was treading overhead. Had she heard his voice? Was she now on her way to see him?

Will she be pleased to find me here?

He suspected not. Silently he prayed God would give him both guidance and grace to handle whatever was coming. He claimed a chair beside the fireplace, only to immediately stand. Trudy had returned with the lemonade.

"Oh, please," she insisted, "sit."

She handed him the glass, then a plate of freshly baked scones and afterwards took a seat opposite him. The creaking overhead had stopped. David kept one ear cocked toward the staircase but heard nothing further. Apparently Elizabeth wouldn't be coming down anytime soon. He wasn't sure if he was troubled by that or relieved.

Trudy seemed to know what he was thinking. "Elizabeth is upstairs," she said, "but I'm afraid she won't be joining us."

"I see," was all he could think to say.

There was a long pause. When Trudy bit her lip, the hair on the back of his neck stood up. "What's wrong?" he asked.

She hesitated, making him all the more concerned. "David, please, don't say anything…but…I'm worried about her. You saw how she was at the funeral."

Not an hour went by that he didn't think of that. The memory of her cries still cut him to the core.

"It has been two months and she will not leave the house. She barely steps foot outside her room. Julia and Sally come almost every day, but she will not receive them. She hardly even speaks to me or Mother."

David's heart ached.

"I'll tell you the truth," Trudy continued. "I have never seen her this way. When father passed, she grieved, of course, but she attended to mother faithfully. And when George left for the war, she stepped up and tried to fill his shoes."

"She kept busy," he said.

"Yes."

That was how she'd managed at the hospital when

she was troubled. Whenever one of the wounded had died, she'd immediately taken to changing the bed linens, preparing for the next man.

"She won't eat," Trudy said. "Mother and I are at a loss as to how to help her."

Tears filled her eyes. David reached over and took her hand. "Don't cry, Trudy. We'll think of something."

Hope now flickered across her face. "*We?* Will you be staying in Baltimore for a time?"

"Yes. Indefinitely, as a matter of fact. I have taken a job with one of the local newspapers."

"Oh, David, that's wonderful! You are an answer to prayer!"

He wasn't so sure about that, but her eagerness encouraged him. "I'll be here, and if you, your mother or Elizabeth have need of anything, do not hesitate to ask."

She didn't. "Will you come for supper this evening?"

"Supper?"

"Dinner, as you say up north."

He knew to what she was referring, and although he greatly appreciated the invitation, he wasn't certain it would be wise to accept. True, he'd just told her he'd do anything to help, but he'd been thinking more along the lines of household repairs, assistance with business transactions.

If Elizabeth isn't even receiving her closest friends, what makes Trudy think she'd be willing to endure a dinner with me?

"I know what happened between the two of you," she said.

David dropped her hand immediately and sat back in his chair, wondering just what exactly Trudy knew. *Have my feelings for Elizabeth been obvious? Does Elizabeth know, as well? Is that why she was so angry with me?*

"I know you convinced Jeremiah to delay the wedding. Despite that, I believe your presence could be a comfort to my sister. She always spoke very highly of you."

"I don't believe she thinks very highly of me now."

Trudy shook her head in protest. "As dreadful as the circumstance are…you acted in her best interest. A baby is more than a *keepsake*. And in times like these…" Knowing she'd said far too much, she then blushed. "Forgive me. I don't normally go about discussing such things. It's just that…well, as I said before…you are *family*."

Why did that word cut him and yet console him at the same time? "I am honored that you think of me that way, Trudy. Still…I regret what I did."

"We all have regrets, David. I regret encouraging her to volunteer for the hospital in the first place. I suppose a body can only take so much suffering. I think her having watched all those other soldiers die makes Jeremiah's death all the more difficult."

"I believe you are correct."

David didn't know what to say next. He wanted to make Trudy feel better in some way, but he didn't know how. He wanted to make up for what he had done to Elizabeth but had no idea where to even begin.

"Will you then come?" she asked. "For supper?"

He drew in a breath. He still wasn't certain it was such a good idea, but he knew he had to do something. He wanted to be there for Trudy's sake, if nothing else. "What time should I arrive?"

Her face brightened. "Around seven."

"Seven it is, then." Though it pleased him that he had made her happy, it was her sister's smile he most wanted to see.

Elizabeth heard the front door shut. Wanting to apologize to her mother for not lending whatever assistance she could, she hurried for the staircase. Trudy was in the foyer. She had a happy look on her face, so Elizabeth assumed the silver had brought a good price.

"Did Mother's meeting go well?" she asked.

The look faded to a more cautious one. "I don't know. She hasn't returned yet."

"I thought I heard the door."

"You did. It was…David."

"David?" Elizabeth blinked. *"David Wainwright?"*

"Yes."

She felt the blood drain from her face. "What was *he* doing here?"

Trudy stepped toward the staircase and leaned against the banister. "He has returned to Baltimore. Apparently he's taken a job with one of the local papers, although he did not say which one."

Oh, no, Elizabeth thought. *That means today's visit more than likely will not be the last. Why would he come back to Baltimore? He always said that when his enlistment was over he would go back to his job at the* Boston Journal.

She pondered for a moment. Perhaps Trudy had misunderstood. Perhaps the Boston paper had sent him here on assignment. *If that is the case, then he will not be in town for very long. I can simply avoid him.*

Trudy still held the rail. She now looked rather sheepish. "I invited him for supper tonight."

Panic spread over Elizabeth. "Supper? Oh, Trudy, what were you thinking? I can't sit across the table and make polite conversation with that man!"

"*That man?* Beth, he's family, and I believe he is grieving as deeply as you. Perhaps even more so. He regrets interfering. He told me so himself."

Indignation tightened Elizabeth's jaw. *He may indeed regret what he has done, but it doesn't change anything, and it doesn't make the thought of supper with him any more bearable.*

"You could be a help to one another," Trudy insisted.

"I don't see how."

"You could be a comfort to each other. You could also be a comfort to Mother. I know it will do her good to see him."

Elizabeth seriously doubted she or David could benefit from the presence of *each other*, but Trudy had a point. Their mother liked him. She always had. When Elizabeth had worked at the hospital, Mother had often visited the wounded men. She would bring fresh bread and flowers to cheer them. While some of the Northern soldiers did not wish to be bothered with the local civilians, David had always treated her mother with courtesy and respect. As a result, she thought very highly of him.

And if she knew how I spoke to him at the funeral, she would be severely disappointed in me. Embarrassment burned her cheeks as she remembered her words. *I told him he could not take Jeremiah away. I told him it was all his fault. He must have thought me mad.*

She knew she should apologize, and not just for the lunacy of trying to postpone the unavoidable. He was not responsible for his brother's death.

Even if Jeremiah and I had married when we wished,

our marriage would not have held back the inevitable. He still would have been a soldier. He still would have been working in that disease-infested hospital. He still would have taken ill.

Trudy was waiting patiently at the bannister. Her words echoed through Elizabeth's mind.

He is grieving as deeply as you...perhaps even more so. He regrets what he has done.

She still didn't like the idea of his company, but she did need to apologize for her behavior at the funeral. *And if spending the evening discussing his new job or whatever else he is now involved in will lift Mother's spirit, I should do my best to comply.*

"For Mother's sake, then," Elizabeth said.

Trudy offered her a gentle smile. "I'll help you dress, if you like. I'll roll your hair for you."

Elizabeth appreciated the offer. Tonight's supper made it impossible for her to go about in her gown and morning robe or even a cotton wrapper, but the thought of putting on that black taffeta dress again made her tremble. She had not worn it since the funeral.

In tune to her thoughts, Trudy moved toward her. "It's only David, Beth. He won't be expecting witty conversation."

Nor will he offer it, she thought, for he had always been a quiet man, seemingly content to observe life rather than participate in it. So unlike his brother. "He probably won't stay long, will he?"

"No. Probably not."

By the time the supper hour approached Elizabeth was properly dressed, and Trudy had managed to roll her mangled mass of unruly red curls into a low conservative bun.

"Shall we now go downstairs?" her sister asked.

Hiding a sigh, Elizabeth complied and followed Trudy to the dining room. Their mother had set the table with their finest dishes, minus the silver. The wall sconces were glowing. A vase of freshly cut daffodils was on the table. Trudy fingered one of the bright yellow petals and smiled once more.

"I picked them earlier this evening," she said. "They just opened."

"That was kind of you," Elizabeth said.

Her sister was well aware that daffodils were her favorite flower. She appreciated the gesture, but all she could think of was the last time there had been food and greenery in this room.

We covered the table with pine boughs. People hovered about speaking in whispered tones. David kept staring at me, looking as though there was something he desperately wished to say but could not bring himself to do so.

The kitchen door creaked, and her mother stepped into the room. Elizabeth noted her face looked a little brighter than it had the past few weeks.

"The table looks lovely, Mother," Elizabeth said.

Jane Martin set the soup tureen on the table, then kissed her cheek. "I am pleased that you approve."

The doorbell rang, and Elizabeth's stomach immediately knotted. She knew exactly who was now standing upon her front porch. Since Trudy had run to the kitchen to fetch the bread, Elizabeth's mother urged *her* to the door.

"That's him, Beth. Please, welcome him while I see to the last of the food."

Her knees felt weak. She had no idea what she was going to say when she opened the door, but forcing her feet forward, Elizabeth went to greet him.

Chapter Three

Elizabeth slowly opened the door. Even with the civilian clothing and chin whiskers, his resemblance to his brother stole her breath. *The same nose, the same forehead, the same smile.*

David appeared to be just as taken aback by the sight of her.

Yes, she thought. *I look dreadful.*

Being too much of a gentleman to actually say such a thing, he quickly removed his hat. "Hello, Elizabeth."

"David…"

He hesitated, as though he wondered if he should greet her with a kiss of the hand or a brotherly peck on the cheek. He did neither. He just stood there, the awkwardness between them very apparent.

Finally, she had the presence of mind to step back and invite him inside. As he crossed the threshold, she offered to take his hat.

"Thank you," was all he said.

Elizabeth laid it on the table and tried desperately to think of something to say to him. It was no use. All her thoughts revolved around Jeremiah. Just when Elizabeth felt tears gathering in her eyes, her mother stepped into the foyer. She cheerfully embraced David.

"How good it is to see you again. Trudy tells me you have taken a job with a newspaper here in Baltimore."

His face brightened. "Yes," he said. "*The Free American.*"

"Oh? I'm not familiar with that one. Is that one of the penny presses?"

He chuckled slightly at her mother's question. "We aim to be a penny press, but I suppose as of now we're more a *halfpenny.*"

"Well, with you there, no doubt it will grow to be as big as…as…" Her mother was searching. "What was it you and Jeremiah were always reading?"

"Harper's Weekly."

"Yes. That was it."

Elizabeth winced at the mention of Jeremiah's favorite paper. David even pronounced it the same. *Hahpuh's Weekly,* as if there were no *r*'s in a Massachusetts man's alphabet. "Congratulations," she managed, forcing herself to enter the conversation. "I supposed, though, you would return to your position in Boston. You mentioned that quite often when we worked together."

The smile he had given her mother faded. A look of uneasiness took its place. "My job at the *Journal* was only as an assistant," he said. "I didn't get to do much writing. Here I will."

"I see." She tried to think of something else to say but came up empty.

After another long pause, her mother directed them toward the dining room. "Well, won't you join us, David? Everything is on the table."

"Yes. Thank you."

They moved to do so. Trudy also welcomed him with a hug, while Elizabeth stood silently by. As soon as her mother offered David the seat at the head of the table, however, it was all she could do to keep from crying out. *No! That's Jeremiah's seat!*

He had claimed that position on the very last evening they had dined together. Elizabeth could remember every detail. *He* had been the one to ask the blessing. It was *his* fingers that brushed hers when the serving dishes had been passed. Now David said Grace and offered her bread and butter. The pain cut so deep it was all she could do to remain at the table.

"Tell us about your reporting," Trudy insisted. "Have you been given any interesting assignments?"

He told them about an article on the former provost marshal, but Elizabeth was only half listening. What route the conversation then took she could not say, but all of a sudden she heard David ask, "Have you heard from George?"

Elizabeth looked up just in time to see her mother and sister exchange hesitant glances. Evidently certain that David's question was one of brotherly concern and not a reporter's inquisition, her mother then answered.

"I've not heard from my son since the summer."

"Not since Gettysburg," Trudy added.

"I'm sorry to hear that," he said.

Elizabeth's eyes returned to her plate, her throat even tighter than it was before. Her brother's letters had been few and far between since he'd joined the Confederate army, but he had always managed to send word. The more time that passed, however, the more fearful she became. Over six months had gone by, and she had no idea where he was currently or what battles he may have been involved in. Julia's brother Edward was now a prisoner of war. Sally's brother Stephen had been killed. Elizabeth could not escape the thought that something terrible had happened to George, as well.

For if harm could befall a soldier at even a safe posting such as Jeremiah's, what horrors could the front lines bring?

"I pray for him daily." David's voice broke into her thoughts.

She looked up once more to find him staring straight at her. He may have been a member of the opposing army, but Elizabeth clearly noticed his concern and could not doubt the honesty of his words or his intentions. Sympathy was written all over his face.

I suppose that is something we have in common, she thought. *He, too, knows what it is like to worry about a brother.*

David then looked back at her mother. "Forgive me if this is too forward, but I have noticed there are things around this house which need…tending. I should like to be of assistance to you, until George is able to return."

Elizabeth didn't know what to think of that offer. It was considerate indeed, but she didn't wish to have him make a regular appearance. It was simply too hard.

"That is very kind of you, David," her mother said, "but you are our guest…"

"Please, do not think of me that way. I should like to do my part. As Trudy reminded me earlier today, we are family."

Her sister nodded, and her mother smiled appreciatively. Clearly they welcomed his presence.

Why is he doing this? Elizabeth wondered. *Why would he wish to return to Baltimore, given all that*

*has taken place here? Why would he leave his family
and his business opportunities in Boston for a paper as
small as the* Free American, *no matter how much writing he may be able to do?*

Trudy's earlier words passed through her mind. *"He
is grieving as deeply as you. You could be a comfort to
one another..."*

Then it made sense to her. David had left Boston because he could not sit at his own family table. He could
not view Jeremiah's empty chair.

A wide array of emotions rushed through her in that
moment. David's voice, his face would be a constant
reminder to her of what could never be, but Elizabeth
knew her sister was right. He was grieving as deeply as
she, and Elizabeth wouldn't wish that pain on anyone.
*If oiling a few squeaky hinges and having a bite to eat
with us now and again will help him cope with his loss,
I can hardly say no. After all, Jeremiah would want his
brother to be looked after.*

As if reading her thoughts, her mother urged her with
a hint of a smile. Elizabeth drew in a quick breath, then
looked to David. She tried to sound calm, but her voice
was shaky. "I believe we will accept your offer of assistance, only if you will accept an open invitation to dine
with us whenever your schedule permits."

"Thank you, Elizabeth. You have no idea how much
I appreciate that." His face had visibly brightened, and
for a moment he looked almost happy.

The hour was not late, but David knew he should go.
He could tell the evening had been difficult for Elizabeth, and he did not wish to prolong her pain. She had
done her best to manage polite conversation, but it had

clearly been a struggle. For him it had been, as well. The moment she'd opened the front door, a rock had lodged in his throat that he could not swallow.

The sight of those hollow cheeks and vacant eyes cut him deeply. Her grief had been apparent at the funeral, but the weeks since had levied an even harsher effect. Her skin was as pale as New England snow, and those green eyes of hers held no promise of spring. As they walked to the foyer so he could take his leave, he searched desperately for something encouraging to say. All he could come up with was a promise to return tomorrow or the following day to oil the hinges on the kitchen door.

She nodded quietly, and thanked him.

"I noticed there is a sizeable oak limb on the parlor roof," he then said.

"Yes. It came down a few weeks ago during an ice storm."

"I'll see to that, as well. Some of the roof tiles may have been damaged. If they have, they'll need to be repaired before the next rainstorm."

"I'd appreciate that."

The tension between them was so thick that you could cut it with a knife. As uncomfortable as he was, though, he believed he was doing his duty. His father, although he knew not David's true feelings for Elizabeth, had encouraged him, as well.

"Looking after those ladies is the Christian thing to do," he had said. "There is no guarantee that young Mr. Martin will ever return from battle."

And if he does, David thought, *in what condition will he return?*

He'd served in the hospital long enough to know how

many veterans, rebel and Union alike, would return in wretched condition. Scores would be legless, armless, others half-witted or unable to comprehend at all.

They return as helpless as they were in infancy. They can no longer care for their families. Their families must care for them.

He wondered if Elizabeth thought of such things. Did she fear that fate for her brother? Had she ever confessed such fears to Jeremiah? Had he been able to comfort her?

The thought of his brother holding her tight, kissing away her tears, made David's chest burn, but he forced the image away.

I have no right to think of such things. I came to protect her, to lend a hand in practical matters, as any decent male relative should.

When they reached the front door, Elizabeth asked about his sister. "Has Clara recovered? Is the baby strong?"

Trudy had asked the exact same question at dinner. *Elizabeth must not have been listening.* "Yes," he replied once more. "Both mother and son are doing well."

She tried her best to smile. It wasn't a very convincing one. "I am pleased to hear that. I imagine that is a great comfort to your family. What did they name him?"

David swallowed hard. "Jeremiah."

Immediately her eyes clouded, and it was only then that she asked about the burial. David delicately told her the details. Her chin quivered when she learned the band had played his favorite hymn.

"'What a Friend We Have in Jesus,'" she whispered.

"Yes."

He was hesitant to give her what he'd been carrying in his vest pocket, uncertain how she would respond, but taking a chance, he withdrew the handkerchief. A ragged gasp escaped her throat when he unfolded it and revealed the lock of his brother's hair.

He stumbled through his words. "I thought you would like to have it…perhaps for…a…piece of jewelry…"

Brooches and pins made from a loved one's hair were common art forms where he came from. David suspected the trend was practiced here in Baltimore, as well, for Elizabeth quickly accepted what he had offered, pressing the handkerchief to her heart.

"I never asked him for a lock of his hair because I did not want to think that something terrible could happen. And yet…"

Tears squeezed past her eyelids. David ached to hold her, but he didn't dare. He knew no matter what repairs he made to her home, he'd never be able to repair the damage to her heart.

"Elizabeth, I'm sorry—"

She looked up at him with those sorrow-filled eyes. "It is I who owe you an apology," she said. "I shouldn't have spoken to you the way I did at the funeral. It was wrong. Please, forgive me. It's just… I miss him so much…"

"I know you do." He swallowed back the lump in his throat. "And you need not apologize. You were to be his bride. You've done nothing for which you need feel ashamed." Elizabeth now stared at the floor.

"I should have asked this from the beginning," he said. "I want to be of assistance to your family, but in doing so, I want to respect your wishes. Please, answer my question honestly. Does my presence trouble you? Would you rather I keep my distance?"

She was still clutching the handkerchief to her heart,

only now with both hands. David couldn't help but notice the engagement ring she still wore on her finger. He braced himself for the rejection that was surely coming.

"No," she said finally, looking up. "I appreciate what you are trying to do. It's just…you remind me so much of *him*."

He knew she meant that as the dearest of compliments, but the words were still hard to take. He picked up his hat. "I'll see you sometime tomorrow," he managed, and with that he turned for the door.

Elizabeth stood in the foyer for a few moments after David had gone, still holding the handkerchief close. It smelled like peppermint drops. She was not surprised, for David always kept the candy in his pockets. Elizabeth had often seen him munching on them at the hospital.

Words could not express what his gesture and the acceptance of her apology meant to her. She would indeed have Jeremiah's hair made into a memorial brooch as soon as she could afford to do so.

She turned for the kitchen. Although Elizabeth would rather seek solitude, there were dishes to be washed, and she did not want the burden to fall to her mother and sister yet again. But being the expedient workers they were, the task was already complete by the time she stepped into the room.

Did I really spend that long conversing with David? It didn't seem so. "I'm sorry, Mother," she quickly said. "I'd intended to help."

Her mother smiled at her, as did Trudy. "Oh, Beth, you have already been a help," she said. "I am so thankful that you invited David to join us. I'm certain he appreciated that greatly. Did you see how his face lit up when you did so?"

"I did." But the look hadn't lasted long. The moment they were alone, his troubled expression had returned. She understood. Her heart was just as heavy. She showed them the handkerchief with its precious contents.

"That was very thoughtful of him," her mother said.

"Indeed," Trudy said, laying aside her dish towel and reaching for the lamp. "I shall enjoy having him about. I hope he will come often."

Elizabeth then thought of something she had not before. "Mother, I am sorry, I did not even think of the hardship this may bring. The extra food to prepare, the extra expense..."

Jane Martin kissed her daughter's forehead, like she had often done when Elizabeth was a child. "We will make do," she said. "I, like Trudy, shall enjoy having him about."

Elizabeth wished she could feel the same, but she didn't. There wasn't anything she enjoyed these days. Life was not something to be celebrated; it was something to be endured.

"Come, join us in the parlor, Beth," Trudy then insisted. "I'm going to play a few hymns. Your voice would benefit my playing greatly."

But Elizabeth told them she didn't feel much like singing. Instead she went to her father's library. Her sketchbook was lying on the desk, and although she had not touched it in weeks, tonight for some reason she felt a pull toward it. Picking it up, she claimed a nearby chair. Her father had given her the book when she was sixteen, shortly after visiting a gallery showing in New York.

As a child Elizabeth had always been interested in art,

and when she became older, her interest grew. She had been so taken with the works of Thomas Doughty and others from the Hudson River School that she wished to copy the quiet, serene landscapes they had painted. She'd spent hours trying to emulate what she had seen, views so lifelike that one could almost expect to step right into them. There was nothing, however, even remotely realistic about her landscapes. Still, her father had encouraged her to continue.

"You're a talented young lady, Beth, but perhaps landscapes aren't your strong suit. Why don't you try something like those sketches you see in the paper?"

She'd been intrigued by the suggestion, and so her father saved the newspapers. Elizabeth made careful study of the sketch artists' lines, their use of perspective and shading. She'd copied drawing after drawing, everything from the local politicians' portraits to the political cartoons poking fun at then President Buchanan.

Her work had improved, and soon she was capturing everyday life in the household.

She fingered through the drawings of her father, her mother, of Trudy and George. *Our life was so happy then*, she thought.

Turning from those early efforts she came to the more recent pages, ones she'd done from memory, or from her imagination. There were numerous sketches of George marching along some distant battlefield. There were soldiers from the hospital, as well, the ones that haunted her dreams. The drawings had been her offerings to God, prayers of a sort when her mind was too troubled to formulate words.

Then she turned to the final sketch, the one she'd desperately poured out just before David had come to fetch her the night Jeremiah died.

Dark wavy hair, that clean-shaven chin, the dimples when he smiled...

When she'd first met Jeremiah she hadn't known she would fall in love with him. Back then he was simply David's brother, just another steward she occasionally worked alongside. She'd had no idea he had taken notice of her until after she had left the hospital.

One day in late October, her church had held an afternoon tea. The event was an opportunity for courting couples, and those who soon hoped to be such, to spend time with one another while properly chaperoned. Since neither she nor her sister had been presently interested in any particular beau, they'd agreed to serve the tea.

Jeremiah had attended the event along with a few other Northern soldiers who had managed a day's liberty. Most of the men had socialized with the unattached Baltimore belles seated at the tables, but Jeremiah had made no effort to do so. He'd simply stood quietly against the wall, drinking his tea. Repeatedly he'd approached Elizabeth asking for more. By the fourth cup she'd suspected he had taken an interest in her, but with little more than a *thank you, Miss Martin* each time he departed, he'd obviously lacked the courage to make his intentions known.

She'd found his persistence, however bashful, absolutely charming.

By the fifth time he'd come to the table, it was all she could do to keep her smile in check.

"More tea, Private Wainwright?" she'd asked.

"No," he'd then said. "In all honesty, I have never really cared for it."

She'd blinked. "You certainly gave a good impression up until now."

A pair of dimples, along with the most handsome smile she had ever seen, emerged. "A good impression is exactly what I hoped to give."

Elizabeth had burst into laughter, and he did, also.

Sorrow sliced her soul as she remembered the scene. She ran her fingers over the paper. Oh, how she longed to touch him, to hear his voice, feel his arms tighten around her. *Now all that I have is this portrait and a lock of his hair.*

Her stomach rolled. Knowing she was about to be sick, Elizabeth laid aside the sketchbook and ran for her room.

Although David's assignment was simple, it was a struggle to complete his article on the provost marshal. It wasn't because he couldn't read the notes Peter Carpenter had given him or turn words into sentences. It was because thoughts of Elizabeth kept invading. The task took much longer than it should have, but he somehow managed to pen the necessary lines and even catch a few hours of sleep before meeting his editor the following morning.

"Well, you're punctual," the man said. "I'm pleased to see that."

David appreciated the remark, but he hoped Peter Carpenter would be pleased with more than just his management of time. He held his breath as the man perused his work.

"Fine, fine," Carpenter said, and he laid it aside. "I've got another assignment for you. I'm certain by now you've heard that the people of Maryland will soon decide whether or not they wish to end slavery."

"Yes, sir."

Lincoln's Emancipation Proclamation, which had taken affect well over a year ago, had not freed slaves in the border states. Since that time Maryland abolitionists had been pressing the politicians to rectify that. The present state constitution insisted slavery would exist for all time. Having just won elections in the fall, a new crop of legislators promised to write a revised governing document if the people of the state so wished. The vote was to take place in early April. If enough of the population voted to outlaw slavery, the legislators promised to see it done.

"I want you to cover what's happening with that," Peter said. "Talk to the newly elected delegates here in Baltimore. If we can manage it, I'll send you to the statehouse in Annapolis."

Covering a story from the statehouse! David's excitement perked. That was a far cry from fetching coffee and sandwiches in Boston. "Thank you, sir. I would like that."

Carpenter nodded. "In addition," he then said, "I want a series of articles showing the thoughts of the voters, the opinions of both sides. Tell me, who are the faces of slavery? Who are the owners? Who are the slaves? How will the proposed changes impact this state, morally and economically?"

The opinions of slaves? David liked that idea, but he wasn't so certain he'd find many willing or able to sit down for an interview. He mentioned his concern.

"No. No. Of course not. That's not what I'm getting at," his editor said. "You are not a Maryland man, therefore you have an outsider's perspective. Write what you observe day to day. If people will talk to you, then by all means…" Carpenter paused, squinted shrewdly. "I don't know where you stand on this issue…"

David was honest. "I oppose slavery, sir."

His editor offered a curt nod. "Well, to make no bones about it, I hope it's outlawed once and for all." Leaning forward in his chair, he then pointed his finger at his newest reporter. "But I'm not running some two-bit press backed by rich, anonymous abolitionists from up north. Don't editorialize this. Your job is to tell the facts. Let the readers decide for themselves how they will vote."

"Yes, sir."

Even with the man's stern warning, David could barely contain his excitement. This was exactly the kind of writing he wished to do. He wanted to report on issues that would make people think, cause them to look at life from another's perspective. He hoped to challenge readers not only to become better citizens of this nation but of the Heavenly one, as well.

Carpenter shuffled the stack of papers on his desk as though searching for something. David waited to see if there was something else.

"You don't sketch, do you?" the man asked.

"Sketch? No, sir."

"Pity. That would really add to your series. At present, though, I can't spare you an artist."

David kept his grin in check. *That's because we haven't got one*, he thought. *Anyone worth his salt is at the* Sun.

Still shuffling through his littered desk, his editor gave him a time line, then waved him away. "Any question or concerns, see me immediately."

"Thank you, sir."

Carpenter's motion stilled as he then looked up. "And it's Mr. Carpenter or Peter," he said. "You can drop that *sir* business. You're not in the army anymore."

"I apologize. Old habits are hard to break."

"Well, see that you break that one."

"Yes—" David caught himself. "I'll do that."

Carpenter eyed him for a moment, then went back to his work.

When David left the office that afternoon he could hardly wait to tackle "The Faces of Slavery" assignment. But there was another assignment now to be completed. With a sigh and a prayer, he went to visit Elizabeth.

Elizabeth turned the dirt in the backyard. The ground was still a bit muddy, but it was time to get in the lettuce and other spring vegetables. She chopped the shriveled remains of what she had planted last fall. It felt good to work, to unleash some of the pent-up energy she'd been carrying, but once spent, there was left a void.

She was determined to shake off the black cloud hovering around her, to not let it keep her from completing her task. *I will accomplish this. I told Trudy I would. The garden has to be planted. At the rate the money is draining, we will need it.*

She continued on, hoeing, scattering seeds, patting down the dirt. The job took quite some time, but that was not an inconvenience. In fact, she welcomed it. It gave her a good excuse for not attending the sewing circle. Trudy had been asking her for weeks now, but Elizabeth just couldn't bring herself to go.

Every Friday for as long as she could remember, her neighborhood friends had gathered for tea and needlework in each other's homes. Currently they were meeting in Julia's home. The group was always busy with one project or another. At the beginning of the war they had knitted socks for their brothers' regiment, then later crafted more when many of those same men became wounded prisoners.

But did any of our efforts accomplish anything? All the socks, all the prayers... Most of those men have died. Elizabeth sighed. Her seeds now buried, she tossed her hoe aside and stared Heavenward. Thick, gray clouds were gathering. She couldn't tell if the rolling late-March sky held the promise of spring's gentle rain or a return to winter's chill. After taking her tools to the lean-to, she headed for the house. She peeled off her muddy shoes and soiled pinner apron at the back door, then went into the kitchen to wash her hands. Her mother was standing at the table, stirring a pitcher of lemonade.

"Thank you for getting the seeds in, Beth. It will be so good to have fresh greens again."

"I apologize for not getting them in sooner."

"You have done it today. That's all that matters."

Elizabeth appreciated her mother's kind understanding. "I planted more rows than last year," she said.

"That was probably wise. I suppose with David now joining us, we will need them."

The unmistakable sound of hammering then filled Elizabeth's ears. "He is here already?"

"Yes. He arrived just a little while ago. I tried to get him to sit for a spell, being as he'd just put in his first full day at the newspaper, but he was insistent upon getting to work."

Elizabeth was not surprised. It was his nature to put duty above pleasure. Jeremiah had been the same way.

But whereas David always conducted his duties in a most serious fashion, Jeremiah had found humor in everything.

The hammering continued. "Bless his heart," her mother said. "He has already oiled all the first-floor hinges and seen to the loose molding in the dining room. He must have found more in the library." She poured a glass of the lemonade. "Will you take this to him? I am certain he must be thirsty."

"Yes, of course," she said with more eagerness than she actually felt. As she started for the library, her mother called after her.

"And invite him to attend church with us on Sunday."

"Yes, ma'am." Elizabeth knew the invitation was an effort not only to bring David into their particular fold but to lure her, as well. She hadn't attended church since Jeremiah's passing. After what had happened at the funeral, she could not face her fellow congregants. She still could not get through an hour without crying. She knew she'd never be able to last an entire service, especially with David beside her.

I could barely manage supper time.

As she walked toward the library, she mentally prepared to face him. *I'll give him the lemonade. I will invite him to attend church with Mother and Trudy, then I will leave. I will not focus on the family resemblance. I will not cry.*

The hammering had stopped. The moment she crossed the library threshold she discovered why. David was seated in the chair that she had occupied last evening. In his hands was the sketchbook. She hadn't remembered leaving it there until now.

Panic seized her. "Please, don't look at that!"

Startled, he immediately stood. "It was lying on the chair," he stammered. "Forgive me, I...couldn't resist."

Elizabeth quickly handed him the glass of lemonade, and he passed the book to her. He'd been studying the picture of Jeremiah. She pulled the portrait close, hiding it from view.

"I didn't know you could draw," he said.

"It's not something I share."

"You should. You have talent. You captured him perfectly."

His compliment surprised her. David wasn't one to offer gentlemanly flattery. He had always been a man of few words, but that was because he weighed them so carefully. Elizabeth slowly lowered the sketchbook, staring down at the picture. He stepped a little closer.

"My guess is that's a *Hahpuh's Weekly* in his hands."

"Yes."

"My brother wouldn't read anything else." He offered her a smile. Elizabeth tried her best not to think of Jeremiah's handsome dimples, but she was certain David had a matching pair beneath his mustache and chin whiskers. Her throat tightened.

"Mother wishes to invite you to attend Sunday services," she announced.

"Oh? Well, thank you. I would be pleased to attend services with you."

"Not with me," she quickly corrected. "With Mother and Trudy."

The sentence hung in the air for several seconds.

"Oh," David said finally, looking somewhat disappointed. He took a swallow of the lemonade. For whatever reason, Elizabeth just stood there, sketchbook once again pressed to her chest. After another moment of awkward silence, he told her about his newest assignment.

"My editor wants me to do a series of articles on the slave vote."

Her stomach immediately knotted. She knew he and Jeremiah had strong convictions concerning the subject of slavery. Their father was a well-respected Boston minister who preached against the institution repeatedly. *What would he and his family think if—?* She pushed the thought aside and tried to focus on what David was saying.

"Peter wishes for me to tell all sides of the story. Even that of a slave's perspective. I can hardly wait to do so. It could be an opportunity to influence the future for good." His excitement was building with each phrase. Elizabeth had rarely seen such emotion from him. He had always been so somber, so subdued at the hospital.

"You know," he then said, "good sketch artists are always in demand. In fact, we are in need of a few at the *Free American*."

Sketch artists? She wondered where the conversation was going.

He took another sip of lemonade. "Why don't you come with me while I gather information for my articles? Draw a few scenes. I'll pass them on to Peter. If he likes them, not only will he print them, but you'll be paid for your work."

Elizabeth blinked, unsure she'd heard correctly. "You're asking me to accompany you? To work with you? As an artist?"

He nodded and smiled.

He thinks my drawings are worthy of publication? A rush of heat filled her cheeks. To say she was honored was putting it mildly, for Elizabeth had once dreamed of being a sketch artist. *But surely his editor will think differently.* "That's very kind of you, David, but I hardly believe *I* am qualified."

"Elizabeth, I do have *some* experience in the newspaper business. I have seen sketches before. I wouldn't have suggested it if I didn't think you were good enough."

The gentle certainty with which he spoke caused her to actually consider the idea. *We could use the money. And I wouldn't be copying someone else's sketches. I'd be doing my own.* The thought was both thrilling and terrifying at the same time.

David must have sensed her fear. "Tell you what," he then said. "Forget showing them to Peter for now. Just come with me. Give it a try. If you don't enjoy yourself, what have you really wasted?"

He made it sound so intriguing, so inviting, like a pleasant outing in the sunshine. Allowing her time to think on it, he set the now empty lemonade glass on the table and returned to the ladder at the far corner of the room. Soon he was back to hammering the crown molding.

For a moment Elizabeth watched him work. The cuffs of his sleeves were open, the fabric rolled up an inch or two, revealing strong, muscular forearms. Suddenly the thought struck her that she had never seen Jeremiah in anything but a federal uniform. How handsome he would have been in a pressed white shirt, silk vest and dark pair of trousers.

Tears sprang to her eyes. She could feel the black fog rolling in. As wonderful as David's offer to sketch was, she knew she must decline. It was obvious she could not accompany him about the city. She knew she had to leave the room, lest once more she make a fool of herself in front of him.

"I appreciate your kindness, David. Really I do. But...I can't... Please, excuse me." She turned for the door.

"You don't have to hide the tears from me, Elizabeth."

The understanding in his voice stopped her in her tracks.

"I know what you are feeling. He was my brother, my best friend. I miss him terribly."

Pain pierced her heart, but his honesty was an invitation. She turned to face him.

"How do you do it?" she asked.

He left the ladder and crossed the floor. "Do what?"

"Get up each morning? Go about your tasks? Your new job? I can barely breathe."

A look of compassion filled his face. It appeared as though he were about to embrace her, yet just before doing so, he stopped and rubbed his whiskered chin.

"I try to remember where he is," he said. "I try to remember there is no sickness or war in Heaven. I know he's happy there, and one day, I will see him again."

Elizabeth wanted her fiancé to be at rest, to be happy, but she wanted to be happy, as well. She wanted Jeremiah here with her.

"I wish I could take away your pain," David said.

Upon impulse, she moved into his arms. David held her tightly. Elizabeth knew full well that the strength and security he offered was only that of a would-be brother-in-law's kindness, yet even so, she soon gave in to temptation.

The same soap...the same shaving balm...

But the added hint of peppermint brought her back to

reality. *He is not Jeremiah. He never will be.* Stiffening, she stepped out of his embrace. "Forgive me," she said.

He took half a step back, too, and cleared his throat. Embarrassment colored his cheeks. Elizabeth felt it, as well. She wondered if David knew what she had been thinking. If he did, mercifully, he did not say. He hitched his thumb over his shoulder.

"I'm going to take this here *laddah* and see to those tiles on the roof."

"Thank you," she managed, though her face was still afire. She offered to refill his empty glass.

"I'd appreciate that." Ladder in hand, he moved toward the door. Just before leaving the room, however, he stopped and looked back. "By the way, my brother would be proud of that sketch. I'm certain of it."

She looked down at the image in her hands. *If only he had lived to see it.*

Chapter Four

David did as he had promised and carried the ladder outside. His heart was still pounding from the moment he'd held her. Elizabeth had come to *him*. He wanted that. He wanted to soothe her fears, be the strength she needed, the place where she found comfort.

But it isn't me she is seeking.

He'd known the moment he'd heard the soft sigh escape her lips and felt her sketchbook pressed between them. Elizabeth was courting a memory. He shouldn't have allowed it, for her sake and his. The instant his arms had closed around her, the desire to kiss her had been strong. He couldn't help but wonder if she would have permitted him to do so.

You cad, he thought. *She would slap your face if she knew what you were thinking. Perhaps she should. That would end this foolishness here and now.*

He realized he was going to have to keep his distance from her. He would have to keep up his guard.

But just how am I going to do that?

He popped a peppermint drop into his mouth and bit down hard. Leaning the ladder against the front of the house, he then climbed to the roof. Careful inspection revealed two slate tiles were cracked, four were loose and several others were missing altogether. David craned his neck to view the tree spread out above him. There were other limbs that looked as though they would come down given one hard Maryland thunderstorm, but he wouldn't see to them today. The clouds at present indicated the imminent coming of steady rain. The roof needed to be repaired, lest the Martin women wake to an ugly stain on their parlor ceiling.

He removed the oak limb. Perhaps the family had some spare tiles in the lean-to. If not, David would have to cover the roof until he could get new ones. He tried to keep his mind on the task at present, but it kept drifting to her.

Elizabeth's drawings had surprised him. He had not known of her artistic abilities, and he suspected Jeremiah hadn't, either, for his brother had never spoken of them even though he'd talked about her incessantly. Her work was as good as, if not better than, much of what David had seen in the papers. Many sketch artists could capture action, but she could convey the emotion. Love, laughter, pain, honor, he'd seen it all in the faces of her family members and the wounded soldiers she had drawn.

If Peter wants the series on the slave vote to be personal, Elizabeth could certainly do that. Her talents could help shape this state for the better.

But David couldn't help but wonder if it was really the people of Baltimore he wished to benefit or himself. He reminded himself that there was no reason to worry about that now. She had, after all, declined his invitation, and he could tell by the sorrow in her eyes she didn't have plans to change her mind anytime soon.

He descended the ladder and went to the lean-to, only to discover there were no tiles on hand. David did manage to find some oilskin cloth, so he covered the damaged portion of the roof. He was just about to put the ladder away when the front door opened. Elizabeth stepped out to the porch. In her hands was the promised glass of lemonade.

"How's the roof?" she asked.

He told her. She paled when he said he would have to purchase the tiles.

"David, we—"

She stopped, but he knew exactly what she had been about to say. *We can't afford it.*

He wanted to reassure her. "Elizabeth, you needn't worry. I'll see to the repairs."

Her eyes widened in momentary relief, but the look quickly faded. "That's very generous of you, but I can't ask you to do so."

"You didn't ask. I offered. I know the financial situation at present is difficult."

She blushed.

"Elizabeth, there is no shame in your family's position. You aren't the first woman to run low on funds because the war has lasted longer than anyone expected. Sadly, you probably won't be the last."

"I'll come up with the money to buy the tiles myself. It will just take me a little time."

"You haven't got time. All it will take is one thunderstorm, and you'll be facing serious water damage."

"I know." She bit her lower lip. "I just keep thinking George will be home soon. And when he returns to work…"

Even if the war ended tomorrow and her brother came

back abled-bodied and clearheaded, David doubted a Confederate veteran would be able to simply slip back into his previous life. Too many employers feared the mark of *disloyalty* and the consequences it would bring. Businessmen would be careful about who they associated themselves with as long as the US Army occupied Baltimore. He didn't tell her that, though.

"Tell you what," he said instead, "let me see to the repairs for now, and your brother can settle up with me when he is able."

David had no intention of actually making claim on any bills, but she didn't need to know that, either. His suggestion seemed to please her. A look of appreciation filled her eyes. He tried not to think more of it than he should.

This is to be my business, he reminded himself. *Roof tiles, loose molding, trimming tree limbs. Nothing more.* "I'll pick up the new tiles tomorrow when I finish at the paper," he said.

She nodded. "Thank you, David. I appreciate your kindness. I know Mother and Trudy do, as well." Then, offering to take the now empty lemonade glass, she turned and went back inside.

David returned as promised the following afternoon to repair the roof. After seeing to it, he quickly took leave. Elizabeth's mother tried to get him to stay for supper, but he politely declined. Elizabeth was relieved that he had. After crying and falling into his arms yesterday, she preferred to limit the contact between them.

"I've an assignment for which I must prepare," David explained to them. "An interview tomorrow with state delegates Nash and Van der Geld."

Elizabeth knew the two men were bitter rivals. One supported slave owners' rights, the other immediate abolition. She wondered how David would manage such an interview. "Are you interviewing them at the same time?"

He chuckled slightly. "No. I am smarter than that. It is to be separate interviews. If not, I doubt I'd get any questions asked. They'd be too busy arguing with one another."

The thought crossed her mind that she could capture delegate Van der Geld's likeness in a sketch quite easily. Elizabeth knew him personally. He was the father of her friend Rebekah. She dismissed the idea, however, as quickly as it came. She couldn't cover the slave vote, for more reasons than one.

"I hope all goes well for you," her mother then said to him. "I'm certain it will make for a nice article."

David smiled. "Thank you. I suppose then I'll see each of you on Sunday. I'm looking forward to the service."

As he left, Elizabeth breathed a shallow sigh. Once more she had been reminded of her shortcomings. David might be eager to attend worship, but she most definitely was not. Crying at the church service would be even worse than breaking down at the funeral. Elizabeth wasn't certain how she would manage to excuse herself from worship again this week, but she was counting on the fact that her mother would be so pleased with David's attendance that she would be willing to accept Elizabeth's excuse to stay home.

Sunday dawned, however, and her plan came to naught. When her mother called her to her bedside, Elizabeth knew something was wrong. Jane Martin often suffered from headaches, and a particularly painful one had struck her that morning. Hoping to ease her discomfort, Elizabeth quickly gathered fresh water and a cool cloth to lay upon her mother's forehead.

"Shall I ask Trudy to fetch Dr. Stanton?" she asked.

"No. That isn't necessary. The medicine never really helps, anyway. I just need to rest. The pain will pass in time."

Elizabeth knew from past experience that what her mother said was true, yet she still felt helpless. She hated watching her mother suffer, just as she'd hated watching those soldiers at the hospital.

"It is such a shame," her mother said. "I so wished to be in church this morning."

Elizabeth could hear the disappointment in her voice. "Church will still be there next week. You can go then."

"But David promised to come. He was so looking forward to it."

Elizabeth glanced at her father's watch. Her mother wound it every night and kept it ticking by her bedside. According to it, David would be arriving shortly.

"Perhaps Trudy may still accompany him," Elizabeth offered. She had no sooner said the words when her sister entered the room. Elizabeth took one look at her and knew she'd be staying home, as well. Clutching her lower abdomen, Trudy was as pale as could be.

"I'm sorry, Beth, but I am indisposed. I'm afraid I won't be able to make it to services today, either."

Oh, no, Elizabeth thought, for she knew exactly what was coming.

"Beth, dear," her mother said, "will you then be kind enough to accompany him?"

A rock lodged in the back of Elizabeth's throat. Her

heart began to race. *I can't face the congregation! I certainly can't do it with him at my side, not when everything he does reminds me of Jeremiah!* "I think, given the circumstances, David would understand. There is always next week."

"No," her mother said, mustering more strength than Elizabeth thought she had in her at present. "He should not be alone. He needs his family. It is important that *you* be there. I want you to go."

It was not a wish. It was a command, and while Elizabeth wanted to plead her case, list all the reasons she could not step inside the church building, she would not do so. She would not go against her mother's wishes, especially when she was ill. Elizabeth would obey if for no other reason than to bring this conversation to a close so Jane could rest.

"Very well," she said, leaning over and kissing her mother's cheek, "I will go."

Despite her pain, Jane Martin smiled. "Thank you, dear. I appreciate that."

Elizabeth tried to muster her strength, but inside she was quaking. The only way she managed to dress and roll her hair was by telling herself she wouldn't *actually* have to leave the house. *Surely when David learns that mother is ill and Trudy's indisposed, he will decline my offer to accompany him.*

She was waiting in the foyer when he arrived. She told him the story straightaway.

"I'm sorry to hear that," he said, concern evident on his face. "Shall I fetch the doctor?"

"No. Thank you, though. Mother said that wasn't necessary. She simply needs to rest. Trudy is going to look after her."

"Oh? Then you and I will still be able to attend church?"

Now is my chance, she thought. *I will tell him no. Surely he will understand, given the circumstances.* But then she remembered her mother's insistence. The only way out of this was for *him* to decline. Elizabeth chose her words carefully. "Do *you* still wish to attend?"

"Yes," he said. "Very much so."

She was trapped. Biting back her dismay, Elizabeth did her best to make certain her voice was steady. "Very well. Please, give me a moment to fetch my bonnet and gloves."

"Certainly."

As she turned for the staircase, her knees were wobbling.

David paced about the foyer, waiting for her return. He told himself there was no reason to feel nervous. He had spent plenty of time with her before.

We worked together every day at the hospital. Surely I can come up with enough conversation on the way to and from church. I certainly won't have to speak during it.

Elizabeth came down the stairs, having donned a pair of black gloves and an equally drab bonnet. He wasn't dressed any more colorfully, and, given the pain that still raked his soul every time he thought of his brother's passing, he didn't want to be. Elizabeth, however, looked even more grave. *Black dress, black cuffs, black collar, black shoes.* He longed for the day when her heart would feel light enough to wrap itself in the colors of life.

The conflict inside him intensified. He missed his brother terribly and yet at the same time wanted Elizabeth to lay his memory to rest.

"Thank you for waiting," she said.

Though he knew for his sake he should not offer his arm to her, his parents had raised him to be a gentleman. Escorting a lady was proper. *If I don't do it, she will think something is wrong. She may think I am angry with her for coming to me.*

Anger was the farthest thing from his mind.

So he offered his arm. The moment she touched him, he felt his heart quicken. He tried to remember who he was. He was here to protect her. He was here for her assistance, nothing more.

He could feel the tension in her grip as they made their way up the sidewalk. David knew she was nervous, this being her first time in public since the funeral. He was nervous for her, as well. How would she respond to their fellow congregants when they greeted her? How would he?

They continued up the street. The sunlight filtered through the cherry trees, and blossoms floated on the breeze. It was a glorious God-given day, yet Elizabeth walked with her head down, looking as though she were being led not to worship but to her execution. David stopped. He could not stand to see her in so much pain.

"Do you want to go back?" he asked.

She gave her head a shake, but it was so slight that David couldn't tell if it was a yes or a no. Elizabeth let go of his arm, then laid her hand across her narrow waist. Evidently she was struggling to breathe.

God, help her.

"I know I must do this," she said.

"You don't have to do it for my sake."

She shook her head again, this time more definitively. In the distance the church bell tolled. "Mother says I *should* be in church. I know she is right, but the thought of…"

When she didn't finish her sentence, David tried to encourage her. How he longed to know what she was thinking. "The thought of?"

She drew in a ragged breath. "The thought of facing them frightens me."

"Facing who? Your friends?"

She nodded, bit her lip. "What am I to do if they ask me how I am? What am I to tell them?"

"The truth." Even as David said that, the accusation fired back at him. *You're a fine one to speak of such things.* He tried to focus on what she was saying.

"That isn't the answer I'm supposed to give."

"What do you mean?"

"I am supposed to say, 'My faith is sustaining me.' That 'God's grace is sufficient.'"

And obviously it wasn't. Or at least she didn't think it was.

"I can't say that."

"Then, don't," he said.

Elizabeth blinked. "Don't?"

"If they truly are your friends, they will understand. Haven't they each known hardship and loss, as well?" If he remembered correctly, one had lost a brother at Gettysburg, and another had a brother who had been taken prisoner of war.

She sighed, lowered her chin. Cherry blossoms dusted her bonnet, brightening the drab fabric with a smattering of pink. "They handle it all so much better than I," she said. "They are constantly knitting socks, baking bread, praying for sick prisoners and slaves."

"And don't you do the same? Jeremiah told me of the

items you collected on behalf of the Christian Commission last fall, and I saw how many times you prayed with those men at the hospital."

Her expression hardened, yet her chin quivered. "A lot of good that did."

Now he realized what this conversation was really about. This had nothing to do with her friends. It had to do with God. She thought He had abandoned her. His heart ached. *Lord, please give me the words...*

"I prayed so hard, David. My family prayed. My friends prayed. And yet…"

"War still came." He drew in a breath of his own, understanding exactly what she was feeling. He had prayed, as well. So had his brother. Their father had even held prayer meetings at his church, patterned after the ones started in New York City.

In the wake of the financial collapse of 1857, Christians had gathered each day on their lunch hour to ask God to bring about a spiritual awakening in this land. With the poor economy and the prospect of a war between the states looming, they had realized the problems of this nation were too big to solve on their own. They had cried out to the Almighty for help. They had repented of their known sins, had tried to live in peace with their neighbors.

They had done the same in Baltimore, but the results were not what Elizabeth had hoped for. Tears pooled in her eyes. "It doesn't matter how many prayers we offer or how many socks we knit," she said. "The fighting still continues. Everyone I love dies."

"We all die, Elizabeth. It's the world we live in. The thing is being prepared for it. Perhaps that's the difference those prayers made. How many soldiers went off to war scared at the prospect of their earthly future but certain of their eternal one?"

She looked at him with those sorrow-filled green eyes but said nothing. How he wanted to help, but, oh, how he wished his brother was here. Jeremiah had his doubts like any other Christian, but once he'd determined to take a matter on faith, he never wavered. David wasn't so strong.

"We can't stop praying just because our prayers aren't answered the way we hoped, Elizabeth. We have to have faith. We have to believe that God is at work, that He has a purpose, even in the suffering."

"Why did you become a soldier, David?" she asked. "Were your reasons the same as Jeremiah's? To preserve the Union, to make it *as it should be*?"

It was a reference to freeing the slaves. "To be quite honest, I joined to preserve *my brother*. I enlisted because *he* did. I didn't want to fight. I was never more relieved than when the army handed the two of us bandage rolls instead of muskets."

He hadn't intended on saying that last part. He'd never told anyone such a thing before. As far as everyone back home in Massachusetts knew, he'd wholeheartedly been willing to sacrifice his life on the altar of his country, without reservation. *But now she knows differently*, and lest she think him a copperhead or, worse, a *coward*, he tried to explain.

"As for slavery, I believe the same as Jeremiah. It is a man's duty to look after the downtrodden. But hearts won't be changed by the point of a bayonet. They'll only be changed by the truth of God's Word. That's why I'm so eager to cover this vote on the state constitution. If

I can convey His principles, I believe I can make a difference."

"My brother thought he was going to make a difference." Her voice sounded very far away. "After what happened on Pratt Street, he feared Washington would jail anyone who disagreed with the idea of an all-powerful federal government. He believed it was his duty to stand up for the rights of his state, even if he didn't agree with all of the current laws." Her chin quivered once more. "He thought God would be on his side."

If David had a dollar for every man in the war who believed the same, he'd be a wealthy man. Yet Union soldiers died alongside rebels, and abolitionists with slave holders. "If you're looking for a way to reconcile God's presence in all of this, Elizabeth, I can only offer you one answer. We are sinful people. We do terrible things, and yet in spite of that, He loves us. He gave His son to die for us, to pay the penalty for our wrongdoing, so that one day we may be with Him in a place where there is no more suffering."

Tears trickled down her face. For one second he almost reached out and brushed them away, but remembering his place, he handed her his handkerchief instead.

"As dark and as difficult as this life is," he said, "God is still at work. He promises us that He will never leave us, never forsake us."

"Is that promise enough for you?" she asked. The question was an honest one, an aching for truth. He could see the struggle on her face, the struggle to believe. "Is God, Himself, enough for you?"

He paused. David knew what would happen when he died. He had never doubted God's promise of salvation. He had done his best to make peace with the cost of this war, with his brother's passing. He believed it was his duty to return to Baltimore. He was thankful to still be part of Elizabeth's life.

But he wanted more.

"No," he admitted. "At times He's not. But I don't believe that's because of any lacking on His part."

She sighed, but he couldn't tell if it was one of resignation or relief.

"Thank you," she said softly.

"For what?"

"For being honest. You have always told me the truth. I appreciate that."

Not always, Elizabeth.

His heart was pounding. Once more he searched for the appropriate words, only to realize he had none to offer. *But it isn't my words she needs*, he then thought. From the pocket of his sack coat he pulled out a small soldier's Bible. "I want you to have this."

"I can't take your Bible."

"It's not mine. It's *his*."

Immediately she reached for it.

"Read it, Elizabeth. It will help."

Her hands trembled as she pressed the frayed, tattered scriptures to her heart. In the distance the church bell continued to chime.

"It's your choice," he said. "If you wish to return home, I'll take you."

She looked toward her house. David was sure that was the direction she'd choose. She surprised him.

"No," she said. "I'll go with you to church."

"Are you certain?"

She drew in a hesitant breath. "Yes. Mother wishes for us to do so. But, David…"

"Yes?"

"Will you stay close to me? The thought of facing everyone still frightens me."

The fact that she would even wish for him to do so warmed his heart. "I promise. I'll stay with you."

And with one hand on his elbow and the other holding Jeremiah's Bible, Elizabeth took her first tentative steps forward.

Chapter Five

By the time they stepped into church, the service was just about to begin. Worshippers were already seated in their pews. Elizabeth felt the weight of their glances as David led her down the aisle. She could hear their whispers, and although she could not make out the specific words, she was certain the congregants were speaking about *them*.

Clutching her beloved's Bible close, she and David claimed their place in her family's pew. After the customary hymns and prayers, Reverend Perry took to the pulpit and began to preach. Elizabeth tried to listen but soon became more interested in Jeremiah's Bible than the actual sermon.

She had given up weeks ago trying to read the Scriptures. The pages always blurred. The words jumbled together so that she couldn't even remember what she'd just read, let alone find any comfort in it. The pages of Jeremiah's Bible, though, were frayed, well worn. It appeared her fiancé had studied them repeatedly. Had he also battled fear and uncertainty? Did he struggle to believe, as well? Or had he accepted without question the sovereign hand of God in life and death?

Elizabeth did not know. There were so many things she did not know about him, so much she had never been able to ask. Glancing at David, she wondered what he might be able tell her. She knew he and Jeremiah had been close. *Surely they must have talked about such things.*

At present, David's attention was fixed solely on Reverend Perry. Elizabeth couldn't tell if he was simply concentrating on the sermon or was lost in thought himself. His forehead was furrowed, and he was crunching hard on a peppermint drop.

She turned her attention back to the Bible. Reverently she fingered through the pages, hoping to find some notation or marking, anything that might offer further insight into her beloved's thoughts. She found one in the book of *Hebrews*, and the feeling of connection to him made her heart squeeze and yet leap with joy at the same time. Jeremiah had underlined a particular verse in Chapter Thirteen. Elizabeth examined it carefully.

"...for he hath said, I will never leave thee nor forsake thee... The Lord is my helper, and I will not fear what man shall do to me."

The word *never* had been circled.

"I will never leave thee..."

Elizabeth gasped as the words sank in. David immediately turned to look at her. Lest he fear she was ill or on the verge of causing a scene, she quickly pointed to the verse. He had admitted that at times he felt as if God was distant. The same thoughts must have plagued Jeremiah, as well, or why else would he have marked such a verse?

David offered her a sad yet gentle smile, and as soon as the service ended he said, "I see you found his verse."

Elizabeth read it out loud. *"I will never leave thee nor forsake thee..."*

He nodded slowly. "Elizabeth, Jeremiah had his share of doubts and unanswered questions, as well, but instead of dwelling on them, he took them straight to God."

Knowing that gave her a small measure of comfort. For if two upstanding, abolition-subscribing minister's sons still fell prey to fear and doubt, perhaps she was not so far off course that she could not return. *I have never doubted that God exists*, she thought. *I just don't know where He has gone.*

David looked as though he were about to say something else, but he did not have the opportunity. Julia, Sally and Rebekah had come running. Elizabeth drew in a quick, shallow breath as she and David both stood.

Julia hugged her immediately. "I am so pleased to see you," she said. "I have missed you so."

"We've been praying for you," Rebekah said. "Both of you."

"Yes," Sally added, embracing Elizabeth, also. "I know how hard it was for me after my brother died. I couldn't come to church for weeks. I couldn't even face the sewing circle. It was just too difficult."

Elizabeth had forgotten that. David caught her eye.

See, he seemed to say. *They aren't any different than you or me.*

She breathed fully for the first time since the service had ended. Her friends' kind understanding, coupled with David's quiet presence, calmed her heart. The inquisition she feared had not come. Julia, Sally and Rebekah were most gracious. Not one of them asked how she was feeling. They seemed to already know.

Julia then asked about her mother and Trudy. Elizabeth explained what had happened.

"Oh, dear," Julia said. "My mother suffers from those headaches at times. Is there anything I might do? Why don't I bring you some soup this evening and some fresh bread?" She must have seen the hesitancy on Elizabeth's face, for Julia then added, "I promise only to bring the meal. I won't stay to wash the dishes, clean the kitchen or anything else."

She offered her a smile, and Elizabeth felt one tugging at the corners of her own mouth. She appreciated Julia's generosity and the fact that her friend was willing to respect her privacy.

"Thank you," she said. "That would be very kind."

David again caught her eye. His look told her she had just done a good thing.

Julia turned to him. "We are so grateful you have returned, David. Trudy tells us you have been most helpful."

Indeed he has, Elizabeth thought, and although it was still a test of strength to be on *his* arm, she was thankful he was with her.

After Elizabeth's friends had gone, David led her home. If someone had asked him what the sermon had been about today, he couldn't have answered. All throughout the service he had been distracted. His mind kept imagining what might have been if only he had spoken up when he had the opportunity.

We would be sitting in my father's church, in my fam-

*ily's pew. Her hand would brush mine as we stood to
sing. My ring would be on her finger.*

There was one on her hand now. David remembered
all too vividly the day his brother had asked him to accompany him to the jewelry store.

"No," David had said crossly, "I don't want to spend
my only day's liberty shopping."

Jeremiah, however, had been persistent. "Come on. I
need your help. You know how important this is. I want
to make certain I get something she will like."

So he'd swallowed his heart and gone. Jeremiah had
succeeded, for Elizabeth treasured her pearl engagement ring.

David's heart squeezed. Everything within him
wanted to go back to the day he had convinced his
brother to postpone the wedding. He wanted them to
be happy, and yet still inside him the battle raged. *He*
wanted to be the one to make her happy.

But that can never be.

Her tender voice pulled him back to the present.

"I appreciate you staying beside me when the girls
came to speak to us."

Her beautiful sunset-red hair was overshadowed
by that drab black bonnet, but her eyes seemed a little
brighter than before. For that, he told himself, he should
be thankful. "I promised you I would."

She nodded slightly. "I want to thank you again for
Jeremiah's Bible. I promise I will continue to read it, although it may take me a while. My concentration isn't
what it used to be. I can't seem to comprehend much
more than a verse at a time."

"I can understand that."

"You can?"

"Yes. I have had the same difficulty."

She offered him a questioning glance. "Then how is it you are able to concentrate on your work?"

"Work is different. It's—" He shrugged. "Well, I don't know, exactly. It's just something I seem to lose myself in."

The look of curiosity settled to a knowing smile. "You always wanted to be a newspaperman, didn't you? I remember the conversations we'd have in those rare times at the hospital when the workload was light."

They had talked about what they would do when the war was over. She'd eagerly awaited her brother's return. He'd spoken of Boston. Elizabeth would listen to his descriptions of the city with great interest. He cherished every one of those moments. It did his heart good to know she remembered them.

"Yes," he said. "I've wanted to write since I was a boy. I feel like it's what I'm meant to do. It may sound silly, but it is almost as if I feel God's pleasure when I write."

"It doesn't sound silly. I see the excitement in your eyes when you talk about your work, especially the series of articles about the upcoming vote."

"I imagine at one time sketching must have brought you similar enjoyment."

She looked surprised. "How do you know that?" she asked.

"I saw it in the portraits. You have God-given talent, Elizabeth. You are a fine artist." He wanted to renew his offer for her to accompany him while he covered the slave vote, but he did not dare. He wouldn't push her into doing something she was not ready for, or try to coerce her into spending time with him. His compliment had drawn a pleasant color to her cheeks. That was enough. He considered it a victory just to see her smile.

Elizabeth appreciated his words of praise. She hadn't picked up a stick of charcoal since Jeremiah's passing, but David was right. Sketching had always brought her enjoyment, a measure of peace. In those moments of watching faces take shape on paper, God seemed close.

She missed Him as much as she missed Jeremiah.

"I will never leave thee or forsake thee..."

Even before Jeremiah died, Elizabeth hadn't been able to formulate thoughts into prayers for a very long time. But she had been able to do so with her drawing pencils. Could she once again find God in the pages of her sketchbook? She didn't know.

But perhaps...

They continued toward her house. She asked about his interview with delegates Nash and Van der Geld.

"It went well," he said. "The article on both is to appear in tomorrow's edition."

Elizabeth nodded. "The vote on slavery is, what, two weeks away?"

"Less than that."

"And if there are enough votes, the institution will be finally outlawed?"

"Unfortunately, no," David said. "At least, not yet. This first vote is only to give the legislators permission to rewrite the state constitution."

"Oh. But if they are given permission, then they will outlaw slavery?"

"If they can agree on how it should be done."

She sighed. "That could take months."

"Unfortunately, yes, and then the people will still

have to vote on whatever changes are made. That probably wouldn't happen until late summer, maybe even fall."

"Are you to write an article for each day until then?" Elizabeth asked.

"Only until the April 6th vote, for now."

"How does that work, exactly? Are you assigned a specific subject for each day?"

"No," David said. "At least not for this series. Peter is leaving that up to me. He wants me to show all sides of the issue. I would like to present the slaves' viewpoint in my next article, but I don't have anyone particular in mind as of yet. I may start with the master's perspective—perhaps one of the local textile merchants. I'm not certain."

Why she asked her next question she was not sure, yet out it came. "Have you hired an artist?"

David blinked. A hint of a grin emerged on his face. "No, we have not," he said. "Why do you ask? Are you reconsidering my offer?"

Elizabeth swallowed. For a moment she was about to respond with a firm *no*, but the look on his face was so pleasant that she could not bring herself to do so.

"I'm not certain…"

The grin shifted to a gentle smile. "That's a safe answer."

Indeed, Elizabeth thought. She was torn. For although she was apprehensive about taking pencil in hand again, she did so wish to try, and she hadn't wanted to try anything for months. S*itting at home is accomplishing nothing. And if he is only covering a few textile merchants tomorrow, I need not fear.*

"I'm not saying I would like to offer any sketches to

your editor, but I would appreciate the opportunity to draw. I think…it may help."

He nodded thoughtfully. "Your idea is a capital one. You needn't doubt your ability, but have no fear, I won't try to persuade you to submit anything to Peter if that is not your wish."

She appreciated his graciousness. "We will simply have ourselves an outing."

"Yes. Simply an opportunity to take pencil in hand."

That I can manage. "Are you certain, though, I would not be a hindrance to you?"

"Of course not," he said decidedly. "I should be *very* pleased to have you accompany me."

Pleased. Even after all the foot dragging I've done. "Thank you, David. I appreciate that."

"It is my pleasure. I am expected at the paper first thing in the morning, but after that I will head out. I should be around to collect you, say, ten. Will that be acceptable?"

"Yes. Quite."

They had arrived at her front gate. She asked if he would like to come inside for a bite to eat, but he declined. "I don't want to impose, especially with your mother feeling ill." With that he lifted his hat and smiled. "Until tomorrow, then."

Elizabeth thanked him once more for his kindness, then she turned for the house. Trudy was just coming down the staircase when she stepped inside. Her color was better than it had been previously.

"How are you feeling?" Elizabeth asked.

"Much better, as is Mother. She is dressing and will be down shortly."

Elizabeth was relieved to hear that.

"Where is David?" Trudy asked. "Could he not stay for dinner?"

"I invited him but he declined. He said he did not wish to be an imposition."

Her sister smiled. "He is such a considerate man." She then noticed the Bible. "Did he give you that?"

"Yes." Elizabeth explained to whom it had once belonged.

"Oh, how gracious of him. Did you see the girls?"

"Yes. They were most kind, as well. By the way, Julia is bringing soup tonight."

"Wonderful. Dare I say that it looks as though you enjoyed the service?"

Elizabeth wouldn't go that far, but she was relieved to have finally faced her friends. She told her sister so and then mentioned her and David's planned outing.

Trudy squealed with excitement. "Oh, how wonderful, Beth! You have wanted to be an artist since we were little! Oh, wait till Mother hears of this! My sister is a sketch artist for the *Free American*!" She turned, ready to run upstairs and tell the news. Elizabeth stopped her.

"I am not an artist for the *Free American*," she corrected. "It's only an outing. Just an opportunity to draw. I won't actually be showing anything to David's editor."

"Not yet," Trudy said with an impish grin. "I knew spending time together would be good for the two of you. You can help each other heal."

Heal? Elizabeth knew Trudy meant well, so she did not say anything contrary. Yes, David was sympathetic and considerate, and she appreciated this opportunity to accompany him, even if it was for experience alone. His presence had indeed been a comfort this morning as she took her first tentative steps back into life.

But it is still a life without Jeremiah.

She might learn to pray again. She might reenter society. She might even eventually get through a day without crying, but deep down, Elizabeth knew her heart would never heal.

Chapter Six

William Fish, the former provost marshal of Baltimore, had been convicted of his crimes and was on his way to a federal prison camp in New York. David finished up the article, then handed it over to Peter.

"Good," the man said. "This will be front page, tomorrow's edition."

David smiled to himself. *Front page.*

"Where are you headed now?" his editor asked as he picked up another reporter's work and began to read.

"Out to cover the slave vote."

The man stopped reading. "A reminder," he said pointedly. "Whichever side you choose to feature first, make certain you keep your opinions out of it."

David nodded. "Don't editorialize."

"Exactly. You will have to be extra vigilant because you've just profiled delegates Nash and Van der Geld. The latter, you know, is one of those *Unconditionals.* Just the mention of the word is enough to make some men's blood boil."

Unconditionals were members of the National Union Party, and they now occupied a sizeable portion of the statehouse. While not every Unionist in Maryland believed loyalty to the federal government should come without question, the party had garnered votes in the previous election by making abolition a major plank. People who would have otherwise never voted to support candidates committed to strengthening the power of Washington were willing to lay down some personal liberties temporarily for the sake of outlawing a cause they so detested.

David, of course, wanted slavery to end and the country reunited, but he didn't want the principles of freedom and democracy this nation had been founded on to be shredded in the process. He hoped that the more moderate politicians would keep the Unconditionals in check.

"Some readers will try to peg you," Peter said. "They will speculate which side you represent. Tell the truth and tell it passionately, but do so in context, with sensibility and without bias."

David understood. Politics could overshadow freedom. If he didn't write carefully he would lose the opportunity for people to see the viewpoint of the slave.

With that warning, he left his editor's office and returned to his desk. He gathered his journal and hat, then headed outside. As eager as David was to begin, the responsibility weighed heavily upon him. For one split second he wished he was back in Boston, fetching sandwiches and covering subjects no one cared to read about, anyway.

Give me courage, Lord. Give me the right words.

He also needed more direction. Yesterday he had considered starting with a master's perspective, telling the effect the end of slavery could have on his business.

Today, however, he felt he should clearly begin with that of the slave.

But where will I find a man or woman currently enslaved, brave enough to talk with me?

He stepped to the edge of the street. Baltimore was bustling on this early-spring morning. Buckboard wagons delivering goods to and from the harbor jockeyed with carriages of all shapes and sizes. While David waited for them to pass, he glanced at his watch.

I promised to meet Elizabeth at ten, but I had hoped to at least have a plan before doing so.

And with that, he knew what the real problem was. It had nothing to do with the Unconditionals or the slave-supporting voters. Elizabeth wasn't even with him, yet already she was a distraction.

She was waiting in the foyer when he arrived, sketchbook in hand. The black dress bore witness to a woman still in mourning, but the white collar and cuffs showed her first attempts at moving forward. Uncertainty filled her eyes, but she offered him a timid smile.

David swallowed hard. Why did she have to look so beautiful?

"Are you ready?" he asked, hoping she did not detect the nervousness in his voice.

"Yes. I believe I am."

Her bonnet was lying on the table. He offered it to her, then held the sketchbook while she tied a bow beneath her chin.

"Where are we going?" she asked.

He said the most logical location he could think of. "The harbor."

She blinked, cocked her head slightly to the side. "You aren't going to the textile mill?"

"I have changed my mind," he said. "I feel as though I should start with the slave's perspective after all."

"I see." Now it was she who sounded nervous.

"Don't worry," he said, thinking she feared difficulty sketching a new subject. "Remember, this is just an outing. There is no pressure to perform."

She nodded, but the look on her face told him she wasn't entirely convinced of that. Even so, she slid her delicate hand into the crook of his elbow. David was surprised at how quickly he was becoming accustomed to having it there.

Perhaps this wasn't such a good idea, he thought, but it was too late to do anything about it now.

Elizabeth said very little as they walked down Charles Street. David took the opportunity to try and gather his thoughts. By the time they reached the waterfront, however, he was no closer to an article than he had been when he'd left the paper.

It wasn't for lack of material.

The harbor was as busy as always. Nets of fish and crates full of cargo swung to and fro as workers saw to the various goods. Scattered about were bales of Southern-grown cotton, shipped from plantations and ports now under control of the US Army. The bales were awaiting transport to the various local mills where the raw material would be turned into shirts, hospital bedsheets and other items needed for the Union. Negro laborers, both free and bound, mixed with sailors and soldiers in blue.

Somewhere here there is a specific story to tell. I will find it. I will put it together. But at this moment, with Elizabeth on his arm, he was having great difficulty putting any thoughts together that did not include her.

Notes, David reminded himself. *All I need at this point are notes. The article can be written tonight, when I am alone.* In order to have notes, though, he had to have a specific subject, and he still didn't have one.

Elizabeth was surveying the surroundings with a look of great interest—the most interest, in fact, that he'd seen her show in quite a while. "On whom should I be focusing?" she asked.

He removed his hat, scratched his head. There was no point pretending any further. "I confess, I don't really know. I don't know where to start."

She offered him a compassionate smile. That made it even worse.

"Who do you see when you stand here?" she asked.

You, was his first thought. "A lot of choices," he said.

"I suppose, then, the challenge is for us to find the best choice." Eyes roving, she counted off the details, "Let's see…there are two laborers by that cart. Over by the crabbing vessel are—"

Abruptly, she stopped.

David realized where she was looking. To the left of where they stood they could see Union Dock and the General Hospital where they had worked, the place where Jeremiah had died. His heart squeezed.

I'm such a fool, he thought. *I shouldn't have done this.*

Elizabeth's jaw twitched as she struggled to keep her emotions under control. "Perhaps, we should try down past the steamship."

She turned before he could even offer his arm. David stepped quickly to catch her, for one of the sailors, a scruffy-looking rogue with a tuft of black chest hair, was giving her the eye.

"I think we should head back toward Mount Vernon," he said.

She did not disagree. Features still taut, she immediately turned her back on the murky, dark water. David's guilt, as well as his frustration, was great. The clock was ticking, a deadline looming, and so far the only thing he had accomplished was to upset Elizabeth while dragging her along on a very fruitless excursion.

Then it struck him that perhaps they were going about this the wrong way. Instead of seeking out a subject, they should allow the subject to come to them. "Why don't we head over to the park," he said, "and see what comes our way?"

"If you think that will help."

That was just it. He didn't know what would help.

The late March sunshine was strong, but it did little to warm Elizabeth's heart. Sorrow had once again wrapped her in its icy shroud. Determined not to break down, she allowed David to lead her back to Monument Square. He was just as heavyhearted as she. She could see it in his eyes.

She wondered if the day would ever come when the two of them could think of Jeremiah without feeling pain. She suspected not. Her mother still deeply missed her father, and he had died four years ago.

I suppose grief is something we must learn to live with.

Reaching the square, they claimed a bench beneath a budding shade tree. She chose one end, he the other, and the sketchbook lay between. Neither of them said anything for a very long time. Elizabeth stared out at the green grass, but from the corner of her eye she saw David bow his head. He appeared to be praying.

She wondered who he was praying for. For himself? For her? For them both? Elizabeth was relieved he had not asked her to join him. She didn't know what she would say to God, especially with David listening in.

She turned her attention to a robin hopping awkwardly a few yards before her. By his movements, Elizabeth guessed him to be injured. She felt sorry for him, perhaps even felt his pain.

He can no longer fly.

"I apologize for that business at the harbor," David then said. "That was poor planning on my fault. Please, forgive me."

He took off his hat and raked his fingers through his dark waves. Watching the painfully familiar gesture, Elizabeth winced.

"Everything I do reminds you of my brother, doesn't it?"

That was true, but the difficulty did not lay with him. He was worried about her, and she felt terrible for distressing him so. *He has work to do, important work, and I am only getting in the way. I shouldn't have come, especially now that he is seeking to write about a slave.*

"This is my fault," she said. "I hinder your work."

He quickly tossed his hat atop her sketchbook and leaned a little closer. A look of determination filled his face. "No," he said. "No."

"I can see it in your eyes, David. I know I bring you grief. It's no wonder. I was to be his wife. You and I would have been family. Now we are only..." She searched for an appropriate word. *Strangers* did not fit, for they were more than that, yet *friends* didn't seem right, either.

"Elizabeth, we *are* family. We always will be." His voice wavered slightly. "I will be honest. At times when I look at you, I am distracted. I do think of him."

"Then perhaps we should go our separate ways. You have deadlines to meet—"

That determined expression remained. "You don't need to concern yourself with that. I promised you that I would look after you, and your sister and mother. I intend to keep that promise, and I want to do what I can to encourage your artistic talent, whether you ever seek publication or not."

His tone was quiet, yet firm. Deep down, she appreciated his certainty, his persistence. He had already been an encouragement to her, just in the fact that he thought her work was worthy of publication. That compliment had brought a spark of life to her heart, one she realized she needed to hold on to.

She told him that.

"Then let us bear with one another," he said. "Faults and all."

As difficult as it was to be near him, she did not wish for him to leave. David was the last link to her beloved. "Agreed," she said. "But what will you do now about finding a subject?"

A look of quiet confidence filled his face. "I have asked God for help with this article. If you don't mind, I am going to sit here on this bench until I receive it."

His matter-of-factness almost made her smile. It certainly made her curious. Elizabeth wanted to see if his request would be answered.

"I don't mind waiting," she said.

He offered her a smile, then took out his notebook and pencil. Both of them settled back on the bench.

Twenty minutes or so passed, most of it in silence. David stared across the square, expectantly waiting, watching. Her eyes swept the area, as well. Just a few yards in front of them, two little girls in striped dresses were playing the Game of Graces. One jumped happily when she caught her friend's ribbon-trimmed hoop on the edge of her stick.

Then Elizabeth spied them. Pulse quickening, she reached for his arm. "David, look!" Two Negro boys, one lean and lank, the other shorter but just as thin, were shouldering a large sack of grain. They were heading north on the street before them.

Elizabeth had seen them the same moment as he. *These are not freedmen's children earning a pittance of a paid wage*, he thought. *These are the faces of slavery. Eight, ten years old perhaps...rag shirts, torn trousers and make-do burlap shoes.* "Yes!" he immediately said to Elizabeth. "Yes!"

She had already opened her sketchbook. At once her pencil was moving, capturing the boys' basic outlines. David scribbled down their descriptions, their clothes, their gait, the size and weight of the sack of grain they carried.

"I know them," she said.

"You *know* them?"

"Of them, at least. Elijah and Elisha. They are brothers. I don't know why I didn't think of them before."

His pulse quickened. "Where are they headed?"

"I'm not certain. Somewhere up Charles Street."

She grinned at him, mischievously. "You want to follow them, don't you?"

"Yes." In fact he felt compelled to do so.

"Go," she urged. "Gather what information you can. I'll wait here for you."

He jumped to his feet only to then freeze. *I can't just leave her here.* There was no telling who was lurking about. She was a woman in obvious mourning, but that hadn't stopped the swarthy sailor from eyeing her. And in spite of the black fabric, she didn't look as if she was mourning now. That grin was growing wider by the minute. Her pencil practically danced across her lap.

"Come with me," he said.

"I can't come with you! We would look like a parade. We'd scare them, and you'd never get a story. Go on. I'll wait for you here."

He knew she was right. *But still...*

"I'll be fine," she insisted, reading his thoughts. "It isn't as if I've never been to the park by myself before. I used to come here lots of times to sketch. Besides, there is a policeman keeping watch just yonder. Go. Is this not what you prayed for?"

He knew it was, and in more ways than one. The excitement in her voice fueled his confidence. "I won't be long."

She nodded, eyes now following the children. "I'll be right here when you return."

Leaving her beneath the shade tree, David hurried to catch up with the two little boys. Despite the heavy sack, they were moving quite quickly up Charles Street. Just as he reached them, they stopped. David halted as they set down the grain.

The younger boy was struggling with the load.

Though David's immediate instinct was to help the child, he knew he could not intrude. Right now all he could do was shadow them. Pulling out his watch, he pretended to inspect the chain. From the corner of his eye he studied them.

Sweat was trickling down the youngest boy's dark face. The older one tried to offer encouragement.

"C'mon 'Lisha. Almost there."

The littlest one bravely shouldered his share once more. When they resumed walking, David did, as well. He followed them the distance of another three blocks, right past Elizabeth's house. They then made a turn to the left and crossed two more streets. When they came to a blacksmith shop, David hung back while the boys went inside. He stood in front of a nearby tobacco store with a window full of pipes and pouches, recording what he'd seen so far.

When the children emerged, David waited for them to pass, then headed on. The delivery having been made, their pace was even more hurried. He had to walk quickly in order to keep up with them and be privy to their conversation.

"I'm hungry," the little one said. "Can we stop at the church?"

"No church. Have to git back 'fore Master Wallace takes fire."

David didn't know why the boy wanted to stop at the unnamed church. He'd have to ask Elizabeth. Perhaps she would know. He did however understand the *take fire* phrase. If these slave children were tardy, they would suffer their owner's wrath.

Indignation rumbled through him. For all the talk freedom politicians and wealthy abolitionists were spouting, why was it taking a vote long after Lincoln's Emancipation Proclamation to decide the fate of boys such as these?

For a moment he wished Peter had assigned him an editorial so he could express his feelings on the subject. *Boy, would I express them...*

He followed the children back as far as the park. They then continued toward the harbor. He wanted to go on after them, but he didn't want to leave Elizabeth unattended any longer. She was still at her post, scribbling away. She was so absorbed in what she was doing that she failed to notice him even when he came up alongside her.

David leaned closer for a peek at her sketch. The boys were smack center on the paper. Tattered caps shaded their faces. Already she was adding details to their ragged hemmed trousers and threadbare shirts.

"Excellent job," he said.

Startled, she looked up, only to then immediately throw her hands over her work, as if she never intended anyone else to view it. He hoped that would not be the case.

"You scared me," she said.

"Sorry." He sat down beside her. "I know I said I wouldn't pressure you concerning submission, but if you continue to draw like that, I'll be hard-pressed not to."

A humble, irresistible blush filled her face as she then examined the work herself. "Do you really think it could be good enough for your editor?"

Did he? He most certainly did, but he couldn't resist teasing her just a bit. "Well, I'm not really certain about this thing here." He pointed to a pair of long skinny lines, obviously only an outline for something more to come. "That's a terribly large lamppost."

Her lips shifted to a slight pout. "That's a tree, silly." She motioned across the street. "That one. There."

He squinted, then looked down at the sketch once more. "Ah, well, perhaps once you add the leaves…"

She swatted him playfully. David was thrilled. For a few moments Elizabeth had forgotten her grief. There was no war, no sickness, no death weighing on her heart or her mind. She was doing what she loved, and it showed. The brightness in her eyes nearly stole his breath.

She looked again to her drawing. "I can't remember if they were both wearing burlap shoes. Do you know?"

"They were."

She then pointed to the boys' faces. "I set their caps down over their eyes like that because I thought it unwise to make them recognizable."

David blinked. "Recognizable?"

"Was that not a good idea?"

"It's a capital idea. We *wouldn't* want anyone to recognize them. It could be dangerous for them if their pictures were published. But…does this mean, then, that you're actually going to let Peter see the sketch?"

She bit her lip. Her color and her confidence drained before his eyes. David wanted desperately to encourage her.

"You know, when I first started at the *Journal* I jumped at any story tossed my way. But then, while trying to complete it, I often got sidetracked by my own thoughts. I started thinking, who am I kidding? I'm not a *real* reporter. I don't know half as much as those other men."

Elizabeth's green eyes widened with interest. "Were you afraid they would laugh at you?"

"Yes."

"Did they?"

"A time or two. But I survived. I learned from it. I kept at it."

She drew in a breath. "And now you are the feature reporter for the *Free American*..."

He didn't say anything to that. He just let her come to her own conclusion. Elizabeth looked down once more at the work on her lap. "Would this really be helpful to you?"

"Most definitely. More people will notice the article that way. Sketches command attention."

"But are you certain *this one* is good enough?"

"It will be when you finish it."

The slightest grin tugged at her face. *Come on*, he wanted to say. *Give it a try. What have you got to lose?*

"Well, if you really think this will be good enough... then I'll finish it. But will *you* deliver it to your editor? I don't believe I'd have the courage to face him."

"I would be honored to do so, Elizabeth." David could barely contain his excitement.

In spite of her fears, she was willing to try. He was so proud of her that it was all he could do not to reach for her hand. Partners they were, and for one brief moment David allowed himself to think, *That's my girl*.

An anxious excitement made Elizabeth's fingers twitch, so much so that she could barely hold her drawing pencil. David had agreed to deliver the sketch to his editor. Her thoughts raced concerning what that could mean.

*If accepted, I would be a real artist! I'd even be paid!
Mother would certainly appreciate that!*

But there was something even more heart pounding
than the prospect of publication. David had told her he
had prayed for guidance. Little Elijah and Elisha had
crossed their path at just the right time, and both David
and she had sensed immediately it was *their* story that
needed to be told. In capturing their likeness, Elizabeth
had felt that gift of fulfillment, that peace she'd been
missing so long.

She'd been wondering where God was. Could it be,
despite her anger, her disappointment, her lack of faith,
that He was still beside her? Jeremiah's verse drifted
through her mind. *I will never leave thee nor forsake
thee...*

Her fiancé had believed God worked with a purpose,
that even suffering could be used for good, when part of
His plan. David believed that, as well. He even believed
his life could be part of that plan. He'd found purpose
in writing, in encouraging freedom. Was it possible she
could find purpose along a similar path, only with a
sketchbook instead of a reporter's journal?

Her heart was thumping wildly. For the first time
since Jeremiah's death, Elizabeth felt a sense of antici-
pation, a feeling that there was something in this life to
still look forward to.

Beside her, David was now quietly thumbing through
his notebook.

"Were you able to collect enough information for your
article?" she asked. "If not, I know where the boys may
be headed, or at least where they will end up."

A look of eagerness filled his face. "More information is always good. What can you tell me?"

"Well, Elijah and Elisha are owned by a dry goods merchant on Light Street. Wallace, I believe, is his name. He has owned the children since at least the time the war began."

David nodded. "They mentioned him. How do you know these boys?"

"From Sam and Julia."

"Sam and Julia? Your friends?"

"Yes. It was they who met them first, during the noontide prayer meetings. Sam and Julia manned the refreshment table the first few months of the war. They gave the boys cold water and something to eat each day when they came by while making their deliveries."

David then told her how Elisha had asked to stop by the church. His older brother had told him no. Elizabeth was not surprised. "Sam and Julia have tried repeatedly to redeem the children, but Wallace won't hear of it. The man has a bit of a temper. They have had to be extremely careful since the failed attempts."

"Any attempt to show kindness to the boys, he perceives as a threat to steal his 'property,'" David said knowingly.

"Yes."

She watched his jaw tighten. Elizabeth had never seen anger on his face before, but she clearly saw it now. She could also hear the disgust in his voice. "I hope the people of this state will finally realize how brutal the institution of slavery is. I hope the slaveholders will answer for their crimes."

Every bit of excitement she'd felt previously vanished. Guilt took its place. *If only I'd realized how brutal slavery could be before I'd—*

"I'd like to get a look at this man," David said. "You say his shop is located on Light Street?"

"Yes."

"Well, since we are no longer in danger of looking like a parade, why not pay him a visit?"

You want me to come with you while you visit that slave owner? Elizabeth swallowed. Part of her wanted to go. She wanted to see this merchant for herself because she knew him only by what her friends had told her. She wanted to see Elijah and Elisha, as well, see if there might be some way she could help them.

Memories of the past, however, slammed the door on that idea. *What could I do to help them?* "Why not?" Elizabeth stammered. She'd meant the words as a question, but David apparently heard them as a statement. He smiled happily, and quickly slipped his pencil and journal in the pocket of his frock coat.

"Thank you," he said. "Two sets of eyes are always better than one."

Oh, dear... How could she tell him no now, especially when he thought she would be able to contribute to his investigation? Reluctantly she placed her sketchbook and pencils in her satchel, and they started back in the direction of the harbor.

"Is there anything else you can tell me?" he asked. "I didn't even think of it before, but you probably know people in your very neighborhood who own slaves."

Elizabeth gulped. She knew she should tell him about her own experience. *But I never told anyone that! Not mother or father, not even Jeremiah!* The idea of revealing to David that which she had not even shared with her own fiancé seemed disloyal.

Elizabeth thought quickly, hoping the uneasiness she

felt wasn't showing in her voice. "If you want to learn more, you should probably speak with Sam and Julia. They could tell you much more about Elijah and Elisha. I'm certain they are aware of other stories, as well, since they are involved with the local abolitionist society."

"Would they mind a visit from me?" he asked.

"I don't believe so. In fact, today might be a good time. Sam arrives home early on Monday afternoons."

"I'll visit him then, after we visit the merchant. I could meet you back at your house when I'm finished. Will that will give you enough time to complete your sketch?"

"Yes. I should have it completed by supper time." Or at least she hoped she could, for now she had her doubts. Her past history was nagging her, but as they walked steadily toward Light Street, Elizabeth convinced herself that David need not know of it.

The past is the past. He doesn't need to know any of it in order to complete his present article. There have been enough secrets shared between us already.

When they arrived at the dry goods store, a bell on the back of the door signaled their entrance. The man behind the counter, middle-aged and apron clad, looked up.

"Help you, sir?"

The words were courteous, yet David detected a hint of arrogance in the shopkeeper's tone. In addition he'd ignored Elizabeth's presence altogether. For the sake of gathering more information, he let it pass, for now.

"Yes," David said. "Half a pound of coffee." If funds were as low at the Martin home as he suspected, the ladies probably hadn't enjoyed the wartime delicacy in a while.

The man nodded and set about filling the order. Elizabeth moved to the large barrels lining the wall, giving the stores of oatmeal, beans and flour a good look. As she did, David glanced about the shop. He could hear a bit of shuffling coming from the back room. He wondered if it was the children. Elizabeth then caught his eye. She must have been thinking the same.

He had tucked away his journal, but her satchel was still on her arm. David hoped that she would not say or do anything to alert the merchant as to their true identity. *I should have said something to her before we came inside.* He was certain posing as sweethearts would garner more information with much less suspicion than a reporter and a sketch artist could.

The shopkeeper laid the small sack of coffee beans on the counter and asked if there would be anything else.

David looked to Elizabeth. "What would you care for, *dear?*"

She blushed but was quick to realize the purpose for his ruse. Her eyes fell upon the glass jars on the shelf above the counter. They were filled with candy and other items. "Some peppermint drops would be nice."

He allowed himself a smile. *So she's noticed my penchant for them.* "Wicked good," he said and turned back to the merchant. "A small sack, please."

The man squinted, surely wondering why David was supposedly proclaiming the candy both *evil* and wonderful in the same breath. "You're not from around here, are you?" he said.

David realized the mistake he had made. Wallace had picked up on his accent and use of Northern phrases. He couldn't risk being pegged as a Boston abolitionist, so he tried to smooth things over. "No. I'm from the north originally—but I like it here." It was the truth, after all. He liked his job. He liked being near Elizabeth. If the merchant chose to believe he enjoyed living in a slave state, as well, then so be it.

Wallace took down the jar of peppermints. Upon closer inspection David could tell there wasn't enough candy there to fill his order. He waited to see what would happen next. Sadly he wasn't surprised.

"Boy!" the man barked. "Get out here with more peppermint drops!"

Elizabeth again came up alongside him. She stood quietly by as the older child emerged with a small box of candy. The shopkeeper angrily snatched it from him.

"Next time I tell ya to fill the shelves, you do it! You've kept this gentleman waiting!"

The slave child hung his head.

"Go on," the merchant then commanded. "Finish the stock in the back—but mind you, you ain't gettin' any supper."

David inwardly winced as the child scurried off. Elizabeth had watched the scene unfold with a stone-faced expression. He hoped he'd done the same. Though he wished to tell the man what he truly thought, David held his tongue. *I may need to return here for further investigation. I mustn't burn my bridges by alienating the man.*

"Don't know why I bother with him or that brother of his," the merchant mumbled.

Yes, you do. Cheap labor. "They give you trouble often?" David asked.

Wallace rolled his eyes. "You know how they all are. They ain't worth their salt."

David's mouth soured, but he played on. "How do you keep them in tow?"

"Hunger is usually a powerful motivation," the man said with a laugh.

David did his best to laugh as well, but the sound turned his stomach. "And when it isn't?" he asked.

Wallace simply grinned, as if mistreating a human being was a form of pleasure. David's anger burned, but he maintained his guise. "Well, you might not have to suffer with them much longer, if the abolitionists have their way with the upcoming vote," David commented.

"There's ways around that."

Just what do you have in mind? "Really? How so?"

The merchant's raised eyebrow told David it was time to back off. "What do I owe you?" he then asked.

Wallace gave him a price. David counted out the money and handed it over while Elizabeth played her role exceptionally. She acted as if she was much more interested in the peppermint drops and coffee than anything else.

David hoped he'd done half as well. He desperately wanted to know more. He wondered just how Wallace would handle turning loose his "property" if the vote to end slavery carried. If the Maryland legislature followed the example of the District of Columbia prior to the Emancipation Proclamation, the merchant would be compensated monetarily for the children's release. Considering the fact that the sum was bound to be low and given what Wallace had said earlier, David doubted the money would be enough to compel the man to follow the new rule of law.

I wouldn't put it past him to sell his slaves secretly to someone in a territory where Emancipation does not apply. David's jaw tightened as he thought about all the other slaves in Maryland facing the same possibility.

Their business now complete, at least as far as the present was concerned, he and Elizabeth stepped outside. As soon as they turned the corner on to Charles Street and were a safe distance from the dry goods store, she spoke.

"I saw shackles."

He stopped, looked at her. "You saw *what*?"

"Shackles." She was visibly upset, and her voice was quivering. "When I was standing by the oatmeal barrel I could see inside the back room. I saw two sets of shackles, just the size for two little boys."

His stomach rolled. "Are you sure of it?"

She nodded with certainty. "I have seen such things before."

No doubt she has, being a citizen of this state. "So that's how Marylanders keep their slaves in line. They starve them, then they bind them." David didn't know what he felt more, disgust or desperation.

Elizabeth said nothing else.

As they walked on, he thought again about his plans to visit her friends. If Sam and Julia were involved with the local abolitionist societies, then it was possible they were also involved with the Underground Railroad. David knew they'd never admit to it if they were, especially not to a reporter, but he wanted to make certain they understood the danger these boys were facing. David wasn't usually a man to condone breaking the law, but Elijah and Elisha needed to be rescued, the sooner, the better.

Chapter Seven

After seeing Elizabeth safely to her house, David walked a few blocks north of her neighborhood to the home of Sam and Julia Ward. When he knocked on the door, the man welcomed him inside.

"David, how nice to see you. Do come in. To what do I owe the pleasure?"

"Elizabeth suggested I pay you a visit."

"Oh? It was nice to see her back in church." He invited David into the parlor. A stack of books littered the settee. Sam quickly moved them to a nearby table, then offered him a place to sit. "I apologize," he said with a sheepish grin. "Julia has taken our daughter Rachael over to visit Sally for the afternoon. I had seized the opportunity to read."

"I'm sorry to interrupt."

"Not at all." He claimed a chair across from him. "What can I do for you?"

David explained that he was here on matters of business, both official and unofficial. He told Sam about the series of articles he was writing, the material he was looking for. "It is important that I show all sides of the slave issue," he said.

Sam was more than eager to assist. "I know of plenty of people you could interview—former slaves who would be willing to tell their stories, ex–bounty hunters. I also know of one man who has just recently had a run-in with the more radical element. He's a guard at the slave pen. He was severely beaten."

David cringed. Despite the man's despicable occupation, he didn't wish for anyone to be treated so mercilessly. "I'd like to learn more of this man's story. It certainly shows the violence that slavery can provoke on both sides."

"Indeed," Sam said.

David took down his name, as well as the others that were mentioned. Sam even offered to set up the interviews. "Thank you," David said. "That would be most helpful."

"You're quite welcome. I'm happy to do anything I can to help stress the importance of ending the slave industry." Sam paused. "I assume that is the *official* business."

"Yes."

To make certain the man knew his *unofficial* business was strictly off the record, David put away his journal. Sam looked most interested to know where this conversation was headed, so David got right to the point.

"I am concerned about two slave children," he said. "They are brothers. They are held by the dry goods merchant on Light Street. I believe you know them."

Sam's eyebrows rose. "Elijah and Elisha?"

David nodded. "Just so you know, I *am* doing a story about them, centering on the hardships slave children face. They, however, will not be named, and specifics about them and their particular master will not be given."

"Good."

"Elizabeth tells me you and your wife have made attempts at their redemption."

"We have, but Wallace won't hear of it."

David knew he must tread carefully. One didn't go about openly asking questions concerning the Underground Railroad, not if he wanted to actually learn anything. "With you being a member of the abolitionist society, you are probably aware of activities that sometimes take place when redemption attempts have failed."

Sam said nothing, but the look on his face told David he knew exactly to what he was referring. David hurried to explain. "I say this not because I am investigating any such activities but because I am deeply concerned for Elijah and Elisha."

"I, too, am concerned," Sam admitted. "That's why I'm eager to see this vote take place. If a new state constitution is drafted—"

"That's just it. Even if the people of Maryland vote to end slavery, more than likely the process of actually changing the law will drag on for months. There is no telling at this point what provisions a new constitution will make, especially for children. Many of the more moderate politicians favor apprenticeship."

Sam clearly understood that matter, and he shook his head sadly. "The slave owners would keep control of them until they come of age. Supposedly they would be required to teach the children to read and write, but I have my doubts."

"As do I. We could also be looking at compensation, then release," David said, but he explained his concerns that Wallace may not be satisfied with the sum promised him.

"I don't want to see those boys sold off secretly to a place where the Emancipation Proclamation is not being enforced," Sam said.

David nodded. He thought once more of the shackles, the lack of food. He asked Sam if he was aware of such things. The man confirmed Elizabeth's testimony, adding that he'd seen the bruises on Elijah's and Elisha's wrists firsthand.

After that, neither of them said anything for a few moments. The gravity of the situation weighed heavily upon them both. By now David suspected the man did indeed have connections to the Underground Railroad, but he did not address the possibility directly. Obviously, at least up until now, Sam thought it best to deal with the children's release in a strictly legal manner.

David understood completely. Just the notion of advocating an *illegal* act went against everything he'd ever been taught. An honorable man, a soldier, a Christian *followed* the law. He did not break it.

And if the law is unjust, he seeks to change it.

That was what he was striving to do with his articles, what Sam Ward wanted, as well. *But something must be done quickly. Elijah and Elisha's very lives are at stake. And knowing what I do of Sam Ward, he isn't going to beat the dry goods merchant to a pulp while rescuing those children.*

"I say all this to stress the urgency of the situation," David explained. "I would not place trust in the constitutional process alone. If the vote passes, Wallace may take matters into his own hands while he still has the opportunity. If there is *anyone* who may be able to help *expedite* the boys' freedom, I believe now is the time. And," he then added, going out on a limb perhaps, "if I can be of assistance in any way, please, do not hesitate to ask."

Sam still said nothing, but David was certain he had made his point. He stood and shook the man's hand. "I am most grateful for the *official* information you have given me," David said. "I will do my very best to make readers aware of the magnitude of the upcoming vote."

"God be with you," Sam said.

"And with you." With that, David took leave.

The sunlight which had previously flooded the library floor had given way to the long shadows of late afternoon. Elizabeth was so sickened by what she had witnessed at the dry goods store that the only way she had managed to complete her sketch of Elijah and Elisha was by offering up each movement of her pencil as a wordless prayer for their well-being. She hoped God would hear it.

The thought that He'd listen to a prayer of David's seemed much more likely. In him Elijah and Elisha had an advocate. He'd known from the beginning how cruel slave masters could be.

She wondered what would happen if she told him everything. Sins could be forgiven, yes, but they weren't easily forgotten, at least from the human perspective. *Would he understand? Would he say we all make mistakes? The important thing is learning from them?*

She thought of how many times he had said that to her when they worked together in the hospital. Elizabeth had often had trouble with medical procedures. Her fingers fumbled, and at times the sight of blood made her nauseous. More than once David had to come alongside her to assist her in some task. *Yet never once did he lose his patience with me, nor did I feel condemned. Perhaps it would be the same now. Perhaps he would understand.*

Sighing, she picked up her charcoal stick. The foreground of her picture needed just a bit more shading. She had just gotten the drawing to her liking when David walked in. A pleasant expression filled his face.

"Still hard at work?" he asked.

"I've just finished."

"Well done, partner."

Partner. She liked the sound of that. "How was your visit?" she asked.

The smile faded from his face. "Productive, yet disturbing. Sam confirmed what you saw."

When he told her of the markings on the boys' wrists, her heart sank more deeply in her chest. "I hoped I had been wrong about that," she said. "I hoped there was some other explanation."

"What other explanation could there be?"

Elizabeth didn't answer that. She held her breath as David gave her sketch a good once-over. His smile returned.

"This is beautiful," he said. "Absolutely beautiful."

She exhaled. "You really think so?"

"Indeed I do. After having heard the boys' conversation firsthand, I was going to focus on their fear of disappointing their master and the consequences thereof. You captured that without even knowing." He pointed to the drawing. "Look here. See the sense of hurry? There is hunger on their faces, but it's clear they know there will be terrible consequences for slowing even for a moment to receive kindness from a charitable soul. I can't, of course, tell the details of the church bread table. If I did, I would give away their identity."

"But," Elizabeth said, guessing where he was going, "if you are careful you can still convey their hardships while protecting their anonymity."

"Yes." He pointed again to her sketch. "I like what you did here with adding the extra storefronts. No one will recognize this as Monument Square. It could be anywhere in Baltimore."

"Thank you. It seemed like a good idea."

"It was a capital idea."

Even with his compliment, her uncertainty lingered. "David, what if your editor doesn't approve?"

"Of the story?"

"Of the sketch."

His voice was firm yet gentle. "Elizabeth, I wouldn't worry. But should either of us run into difficulty, let us agree to take Peter's suggestions under advisement and try again."

Try again. How many times had he said that to her at the hospital?

"Thomas Nast had better watch out," he then said. "You'll soon have his job."

Elizabeth blushed at the reference to the famous *Harper's Weekly* artist. He was one of her favorites. In fact she kept two of his sketches, *Christmas Eve 1862* and *Emancipation*, tucked inside her sketchbook. "I should think I have quite a way to go before I rival Mr. Nast."

"Not as long as you think. You've done well. Oh— you've forgotten to sign your name."

My name, she thought. *My sketch*. After reaching for her pencil, Elizabeth hesitated.

She knew from her experiences at the hospital that not all men were as charitable toward women working outside the home as David had been. He was convinced her drawing would benefit his article, encourage sympathy for the children. She wanted to help him, but fearing the name *Elizabeth* could be a hindrance to them both, she decided upon her initials. The moment she scrawled them, she heard him chuckle. The laugh was not as vivacious as his brother's, but it was pleasant nonetheless.

"You and I think quite alike," he said.

"How is that?"

"E. J. Martin is exactly what I would have written if I were you. Sometimes it's wise to keep information close to the vest until you are certain how it will be received."

Well said, she thought. Though thoughts of full disclosure still plagued her mind, Elizabeth kept silent. Trudy appeared in the doorway just then, announcing it was time for supper.

As soon as the coffee was finished, David forced himself to leave. In reality he did not wish to go, but lingering any longer would be more than unwise. It would be foolhardy. His article on the slave children still had to be written, and he could barely think straight now as it was. One more hour with Elizabeth would drive all creative reason from his head.

Remember why you are really here, his mind told him. *It is your duty to look after her, to encourage her, to help her find her place in this world. You must do this for her sake—not for yours.*

With her sketch in his hand, he walked back to the Barnum Hotel. Darkness was falling over the city, and one by one the gas lamps were being lit. David entered the front door of the crowded hotel lobby, snaked his way through the well-dressed gentlemen and ladies, who were on their way to the dining room, then arrived at his room.

Time to get down to business.

Laying Elizabeth's drawing on the writing desk, he promptly discarded his coat and tie. He loosened his collar, rolled up his sleeves. *That's better. Now I can think.* He sat down and, after taking a few moments to review his notes, picked up his pencil.

The words would not come.

David drew in a deep breath. He flipped through his notes again and readied the stack of paper before him, only to once again stare at the blank pages.

What to say? How to start?

He took to his feet. He rehearsed several opening sentences out loud, but nothing sounded right. His frustration was growing. For the life of him, he could not produce one clear coherent thought for his article. His thoughts on Elizabeth, however, were plentiful.

Finally, in desperation, he pinched the bridge of his nose, bowed his head.

Lord, I want to do right by her. I want to be honorable. Give me the strength to follow Your plan. I know You led us this afternoon. It was no accident that those two little boys crossed our path. I believe You want me to tell their story. Please, give me the words.

Afterward, he unrolled Elizabeth's sketch and stared at the image of Elijah and Elisha for a very long time. Then the words began to flow.

By the time Peter Carpenter opened the office the following morning, David was waiting for him.

"Well, Mr. Wainwright, by that grin on your face, I'd wager you've finished your assignment."

"I have."

The man hobbled to his desk, tossed his hat to the table behind it, then asked to see the article. David laid it before him, along with Elizabeth's sketch.

His editor blinked. "I thought you said you didn't draw."

"I don't. This is from a local artist, one who is just getting started."

He had chosen his words carefully. He didn't know what the man thought of *working women*. He wanted to make sure Elizabeth had a fair chance.

"I see." Carpenter unrolled the paper, blinked again. When he silently laid the sketch aside, David fought hard not to take it as a bad sign. His editor then picked up the article and began to read. Within seconds he reached for his pen and started to mark.

Oh, no...

The promise he'd made Elizabeth about taking the man's suggestions under advisement and trying again was a bit harder to swallow now. David had told her they were partners. He'd hate to have to tell her they were failures. Based on the look on Carpenter's face, that was surely what was coming.

"Good," he then said.

David's eyes widened. He wasn't certain he'd heard correctly. "Good?"

"There are one or two places where you get too close to editorializing." Carpenter showed him. "Watch that from now on."

David released the breath he'd been holding. "I will. Thank you."

"I want the next article on my desk first thing tomorrow. In addition to that, head over to the Maryland Institute. The National Union Party is holding a mass meeting this afternoon. Rumor is the new provost marshal will make an appearance, maybe even express support for the vote."

"I'll get right on that," David said. Then he dared to ask, "And the sketch?"

Carpenter picked it up once more, then after a moment called for Mr. Keedy. "Deliver this to the engraver," he said. He then looked back at David. "And tell E. J. Martin I'd like to see more of his work."

David wanted to smile but, instead, cleared his throat. Considering the consequences the last time he'd kept silent concerning her, he thought it best to be forthright. "Uh, *he* is a *she*."

Surprised, his editor was silent for several seconds. "Well, whatever," he said, "as long as *she* keeps up the good work."

Carpenter then reached into his lower desk drawer. Apparently he kept a bit of cash on hand for occurrences such as these, for he handed David a small sum of money.

"This is standard payment for starting artists. See that she gets it."

"I will," David promised.

The man then waved him away.

The thought of Elizabeth's face when David would tell her of her soon-to-be-published artwork carried him through a long, rather dry political meeting. David took down his notes, then like the other reporters gathered, raced off to his next assignment as soon as the event was over.

Sam Ward had set up the interview with the slave-pen guard for late that afternoon. If Elizabeth was willing, David wanted her to come along. He told himself his reasons for that were strictly professional. The moment she met him at the front door and he told her the news of her sketch, his sense of duty to her and devotion to his brother was severely tested.

She gasped. "Your publisher wishes to see more?"

"He does indeed."

Elizabeth could hardly believe her ears, nor the coins which he deposited in her hand. It must have been much more than she expected. "Oh, David, this is simply too good to be true!"

In great excitement she embraced him. As soon as she did, all David wanted to do was fold his arms around her and keep her close to his heart.

Elizabeth pulled back the moment she felt David tense. He might have lent her his shoulder to cry on before, but he was clearly uncomfortable embracing her now. A shade of crimson overspread his features. Embarrassment flooded her own face.

What made me do such a thing? How foolish of me to act so familiar with him. He is not my brother. In reality, he is not even my brother-in-law.

David was now staring at the floor, but before Elizabeth could apologize he looked up.

"It is true," he said.

The gentle smile told her the awkward matter was now over and done with. Elizabeth breathed a slight sigh. David then told her of his plans for the second article. He planned to interview a particular worker at the city slave pen, one who had been beaten recently by some rowdy abolitionists.

She was shocked by the men's unscrupulous behavior but also by the fact that David wished to shed light on it. "You want to draw attention to something like that? Won't it garner sympathy for slaveholders?"

"We have to tell all sides of the issue," he reminded her. "I should like to have you accompany me again, but we shall need to meet with the injured guard within the hour. Sam has already scheduled the interview."

Elizabeth balked. She wanted to help, but the thought of traveling to the slave pens made her extremely uneasy. The sight of those poor men and women awaiting sale would break her heart. What if her story came rushing out?

I can't have that happen, for his sake and mine. It would distract him from his purpose in being there in the first place, and it might cost me my opportunity to draw.

She didn't like to think she was doing this for the money but admitted to herself that the prospect of payment was a factor. If Mr. Carpenter would continue to buy her sketches, her mother would not need to worry about expenses. She could pay David back for the roof tiles and her brother, George, would not need to concern himself with such things when he returned from the war.

Still...

"We won't actually be going to the pens," David then said. "The worker is recuperating at his home, in the care of his mother and oldest sister."

Elizabeth was relieved to hear such. A home interview, she was certain she could handle. "Very well. I'll let Mother know."

She didn't have to go looking for her. Having heard

voices, her mother and sister both came into the foyer. "I thought I heard you talking," Trudy said, excitement lacing her voice. "Well?"

David grinned, knowing exactly what she was asking. "Elizabeth is soon to be a published artist."

While Trudy's eyes flew open wide, her mother's filled with tears. "Oh Beth, that's wonderful!" she said. "When will we be able to see it?"

"I don't know," Elizabeth said, only now realizing that in her excitement she had forgotten to ask. She looked to David.

"Tomorrow's edition," he said, smiling proudly. "I'll bring it myself."

"You had better bring more than one copy," Trudy insisted. "This is tremendous news. Everyone we know will wish to see it."

"Indeed," her mother said. "Will there be opportunity for more sketches?"

David told her of the story he wished to cover now. Mother immediately looked at daughter. Elizabeth could see the unspoken concern. David must have noticed it, as well, for he then said,

"Ma'am, forgive me. I should have asked you this from the beginning. Under the circumstances, since Elizabeth and I are not *exactly* related, would you prefer that we are chaperoned?"

Her mother looked back at him. "Oh, son, of course not. That isn't necessary. My reaction was more in response to the story itself. I simply wondered if my daughter was up for such a subject as that. The slave pens have always made her uneasy."

That was true, but her mother had no idea why. Elizabeth knew she could never undo what had been done, but perhaps she could keep it from happening to someone else. "You are right, Mother, but I would still like to help David tell the story. Perhaps it will make others reconsider their actions, prevent them from using violence in the first place."

Her mother nodded slowly. "Very well, if you think you are up to it."

Jane Martin kissed her daughter on the forehead, then sent them on their way. Elizabeth was quiet during the carriage ride. David must have thought she was nervous.

"You will do just fine," he insisted, "but if at any time this man shows even the slightest bit of disrespect toward you, I will immediately conclude the interview and we will take our leave."

She blinked. "You would forgo your story for my sake?"

"There are other stories to tell."

A rush of heat filled her cheeks. She wasn't certain if it was because of the kindness he was once again showing her or the fact that there were indeed more stories to tell. She'd witnessed firsthand what happened to slaves who dared disobey their masters. What would David think of her account of that story?

She shoved the question aside, for they had arrived at their destination, a narrow two-story structure at the far end of President Street. Elizabeth clutched her satchel and sketchbook tightly as they approached the front door. David knocked, then removed his hat when a middle-aged woman answered.

"Mrs. Tompkins?" he inquired.

"*Widow* Tompkins."

"My apologies. Good afternoon. My name is David Wainwright. I'm with the *Free American*."

"Yes," the woman said. "My son Thad has been expecting you." She then eyed Elizabeth. David was quick to explain.

"This is Miss Martin, sketch artist. She is here to take your son's portrait while I conduct the interview."

Elizabeth's knees were trembling beneath her petticoats, but she offered her best professional smile. The woman hesitated slightly, then stepped back from the threshold. "Do come in," she said.

David cast Elizabeth a quick glance. "Here we go," he whispered.

Yes, she gulped. *Here we go.*

Widow Tompkins led them to the front parlor where her son, a young man of eighteen or so, lay across the settee. He was in his shirtsleeves, his collar unbuttoned. From across the room Elizabeth could see the bruises on his chest. Both of his eyes were blackened, as well.

His mother explained who they were.

"A lady artist?" he said, obviously surprised. "Mother, fetch me my vest, will you?" He winced as he then moved to assemble himself.

"Oh, please, Mr. Tompkins," Elizabeth insisted. "That isn't necessary. I served previously as a nurse. I assure you, I am quite accustomed to the sight of wounded men."

David gave her a look that told her the statement was wisely made. Thad Tompkins seemed to appreciate it, also. He settled back to his previous position, wincing again as he pulled a homespun blanket up to his chest.

David then took the lead. He exchanged customary pleasantries and asked about the man's injuries while Elizabeth readied her sketchbook. Aside from the obvious bruising, the young man apparently had several cracked ribs. Elizabeth couldn't help but feel sorry for him, knowing he must indeed be in a great deal of pain.

Widow Tompkins went to fetch a plate of tea cakes for her guests. As David began his questions, Elizabeth started her outline. She decided for emphasis, and for the sake of propriety, to sketch Mr. Tompkins from only the shoulders up.

His blackened eyes and split lip alone are enough to convey what has happened. The rest of the details David will surely cover in his article.

David asked the young man to tell exactly what occurred the night he was attacked.

"I was just lockin' the main gate when they jumped me," Tompkins said.

"How many men were there?"

"Four. They had me on the ground before I even realized what hit me."

"Did you get a look at any of their faces?" David asked.

Tompkins shook his head. "It was too dark. One had wrestled away my lantern. Reckon that's how he was able to find the keys and unlock the pens."

"How many slaves escaped?"

"Fourteen."

Listening, Elizabeth struggled with her feelings. Part of her rejoiced that fourteen slaves had escaped. She hoped they had made it to freedom. The rest of her was sickened by how the unknown abolitionists had accomplished the feat. She couldn't help but wonder which way Thad Tompkins would now go. Would he distance himself from slavery altogether for fear of further confrontations, or would he dig in his heels, harden his heart and stoically support slave owners' rights all the more?.

David asked him, "What will you do now? After your injuries heal, that is."

"Find me a new job, I reckon."

"And why is that? Is it fair to say this altercation has caused you to consider another line of work?"

"No."

There was a long pause. Elizabeth chanced a glance at her partner. David was fingering his notes, acting as if he was searching for something, but she knew what he was really doing. Thad Tompkins's answer had shocked him. He was taking a moment to gather his composure.

Once more, uneasiness rolled through her. Trying her best to ignore it, she adjusted her grip on her pencil and returned to the business on her lap. Thad Tompkins continued. Whether his statement was directed at David or just the public in general, Elizabeth was not certain.

"Ain't nothin' wrong with my line of work," he said. "Least not when folks mind their own business. We're followin' the law. I'll be looking for new work 'cause they fired me."

David had found his voice, but it held a hint of surprise. "The slave pen fired you?"

"They say the loss of property occurred on my watch and hold me responsible for it."

Elizabeth squirmed. She hated it when people referred to human beings as property. She knew David did, as well. He made his point but kept it within the bounds of objectivity.

"There are some people who would take issue with the phrase 'loss of property,'" he said.

"I know," Tompkins replied. "I met four of 'um the other night. They didn't seem too concerned, though, about *my* personal property."

Elizabeth kept her pencil moving as David asked if the man had been robbed.

"No," he said.

"I'm glad to hear that."

Tompkins nodded. "So were my mother and sister. We got bills to pay—doctor's bills, too, after that—and now I gotta be lookin' for a new employer."

"Will you seek employment with one of the other slave traders?" David asked.

"More than likely. It's what I know. Slavery's big business here in Maryland. They're always in need of guards. At least unless people vote to put us all outta work."

She reached for her charcoal, began to shade.

"What will you do if Marylanders vote to outlaw slavery?" David asked.

"I don't rightly know."

With that, the interview and the sketch were complete. Elizabeth packed her supplies. David shook Thad Tompkins's hand and thanked him for his time. Elizabeth thanked his mother for the refreshments she'd set before them. She was confident she had managed to demonstrate a calm demeanor, but inside her heart was pounding.

David chewed silently on a peppermint drop until they left President Street. "That was more difficult than I'd imagined," he said.

"I thought you conducted yourself well."

"Perhaps with the exception of that long pause… You, however, handled yourself very well. One would think you had been dealing with this sort of thing for years."

"I have…"

David glanced at her curiously. Elizabeth's throat tightened. "What I mean is, I felt rather sorry for him. The fact that they beat him, that he now has no income with which to pay his family's bills..."

"I know," he said. "I felt the same, but what I couldn't get over was the fact that he wished to return to his line of work. I naively assumed he'd have a change of heart, that he would have seen the error in his ways and would now want nothing more to do with the institution of slavery. It is clear, though, that he sees his vocation as nothing more than a source of income, no different than what you or I are doing." He sighed. "I am beginning to have my doubts about the effectiveness of the upcoming vote."

"You don't think slavery will be outlawed?"

"I hope it is, but if we do win, I don't believe it will be by an overwhelming majority."

"But it will still be a victory."

"A partial one at best. It's the hearts and attitudes concerning slavery which must be changed. If not, the laws will simply change back and forth in regards to whichever politicians control the statehouse at the given time. People have to see for themselves that this is not an economic issue or a state right. Slavery has to do with people. People created in God's image who, if for that reason alone, deserve to be treated with respect."

He then told her of his concerns for Elijah and Elisha, how he feared the dry goods merchant would attempt to sell them off rather than see them freed. He sounded so discouraged.

Elizabeth wanted to tell him that if he would just continue reporting, he *could* make a difference for those two little boys and scores of others. That when presented with the truth, people's hearts would change.

But she didn't. She kept silent. After all, in her case, she had learned the truth too late.

Chapter Eight

David did his best not to let the interview with Thad Tompkins or Elijah and Elisha's present state discourage him. He knew he had to focus on what he could do, not worry about what he couldn't. He had spoken to Sam concerning the children. That man understood better than he who to contact and how to go about assisting them. He trusted that Sam would know how to avoid the more radical element, like the ones who'd attacked Thad Tompkins.

He wanted Elijah and Elisha to be free, but he knew they were not the only ones in bondage. Wallace himself was a captive of ignorance and hate. David had written what he hoped had been a careful, yet compelling article aimed at changing such perspectives, and Elizabeth had been part of it. Her sketch was on the front page of this morning's edition of the *Free American*.

He brought the paper over for her to view, but it was Trudy who first met him at the door. She nearly knocked him over with her enthusiasm.

"Did you bring it?" she demanded.

"I did indeed."

She grinned and held out her hands expectantly. "Then let me see it!"

David couldn't resist tormenting her, as an older brother would. "Oh, no," he said holding it well out of her reach. "You must allow your sister the first viewing."

Trudy pouted slightly. "Very well." Turning for the kitchen she called, "Beth! Come quickly! David is here!"

Elizabeth stepped into the room with a completely opposite demeanor. The expression on her face was wary, almost as if she feared her sketch had been drastically altered or, worse, not printed at all.

Wanting to set her mind at ease, he immediately snapped the paper open. She gasped in disbelief.

"It's real," he assured her.

A slow grin spread across her face. She looked happy, and that made him feel the same. Trudy craned her neck for a view. Her mother had joined them now, too.

"Oh, how wonderful!" Mrs. Martin said. "Everyone in Baltimore will see it!"

David didn't know about *everyone*, but he had come across three people perusing the paper just on his way here. He told them so. Elizabeth's smile broadened.

"I can guarantee your circulation will improve," Trudy announced. "Mother and I have told all our friends about your partnership."

David felt a flush of pride, felt it even further when Elizabeth then looked to her sister and said, "We appreciate that."

We, he thought. He liked the sounds of that.

"You tell that publisher of yours that I will keep promoting his paper as long as the two of you are featured," Mrs. Martin said.

David chuckled. "Thank you, ma'am."

Now taking the paper in hand for herself, she moved toward the parlor. Trudy followed alongside, studying it closely with her.

Elizabeth shook her head but did so with a continued smile. "I suppose I'll have to wait to read your words," she said.

"It looks that way. No matter. We are due at the Davis home within the hour."

She blinked. "William Davis? Emily's father?" she asked, referring to her friend who had married Dr. Mackay.

"Yes. Sam told me about their servants, Joshua and Abigail. I would very much like to tell their story."

The man and his wife, both in their midthirties, had once been slaves in a Baltimore household. When their owner died with a considerable amount of debt, his personal affairs had to be settled. Local lawyer William Davis had been called upon to do so. The deceased man's debt demanded that Joshua and Abigail be immediately sold. Rather than see them sent to auction, Mr. Davis had ransomed the pair. Upon receiving their freedom, the couple had asked if they could work for the lawyer and his family, as housekeeper and chief caretaker. Joshua and Abigail had been married shortly after their arrival in the Davis home.

"It's a tale with a happy ending," David said. "And though I pray the effort to outlaw slavery will pass, if it doesn't, perhaps this story will inspire more citizens of Maryland to follow William Davis's example."

She nodded slowly, pensively, her expression far from eager.

"Is something wrong?" he asked.

"No," she said quickly. "Just give me a moment to collect my things."

"Certainly."

From Mount Vernon they traveled a few blocks to a home larger and more ornate than even those in Elizabeth's neighborhood. William Davis promptly greeted them, exchanging handshakes with David and then a fatherly embrace with Elizabeth. Joshua was there, as well, and he smiled kindly at her.

"Abigail and I saw your sketch in the paper this mornin'," he told her. "It sure was a fine one."

Elizabeth humbly blushed and thanked him. Mr. Davis then led them to the parlor. It was there that both wives were waiting. They each hugged Elizabeth and congratulated her.

"Oh, how good it is to see you again," Mrs. Davis then declared. "I have missed you so, and I have much news to tell!"

"Are Emily and Evan well?" Elizabeth asked.

"Oh, yes indeed! And so blessed! My first grandchild is on the way!"

David inwardly winced. Elizabeth did her best to smile at Mrs. Davis's news but he knew her heart was pained. She and Jeremiah had wanted children right away, an entire household.

"She's done tole' everyone in Baltimore that news," Abigail said. "I 'spect the provost marshal himself now knows."

Everyone laughed, Elizabeth included, but David knew it was not without effort. *Lord, give her strength.*

"He does not know," Mrs. Davis said. "At least, not from me. But if I ever meet the man…"

"That is wonderful news," Elizabeth said. "Please, tell Emily congratulations for me."

"I will, but enough of my news. You have business to conduct. Abigail, I suppose we'd best serve the tea."

The women moved to do so. After they had finished, Mrs. Davis left the room, insisting she had other work to attend to. Abigail smoothed out her skirts and settled in beside Joshua. He looked pleased to have her beside him. David couldn't resist stealing a quick glance at Elizabeth. She was laying out her pencils, preparing her sketchbook, now looking entirely focused on what she was about to do, her grief once more pushed aside.

Thank You, Lord.

His mind relieved, David began the interview. He started first with Joshua. He asked him what his life had been like before coming into the Davis home. The man's slave masters had varied in cruelty. Some were better than others, but all had seen Joshua as subservient, ignorant and beneath God's grace.

David took copious notes as Joshua continued. He then told of his trade. The man had a vast knowledge of plants and animals, and his skills concerning animal husbandry, especially horses, were impressive.

"Where did you learn such things?" David asked.

"Some I picked up along the way, different jobs and such. Most, though, I've learned from reading."

It was against the law to teach a slave to read. David wondered if Joshua had learned upon receiving his freedom. He asked.

"I did. Mr. Davis himself taught me. Abigail, too. He started our lessons the day we entered his home."

David then turned to the lawyer and asked him a few

questions. The man politely declined answering most of them.

"Don't make this about me," he said. "This is about Joshua and Abigail."

"But you, sir, have certainly played a major role. Some people would call you a hero."

The man humbly shook his head. "I only did what any decent, God-fearing man would have done. I only did what my faith compelled me to do."

David asked if he could quote the man on that, and when Mr. Davis agreed, he wrote it down. He then turned his attention to Abigail. "Will you tell me of your own experiences?"

Sadly hers were just as disheartening as her husband's. There were beatings, often for no reason, back-breaking labor, and like Elijah and Elisha, chains and lack of food.

To think what some men will do... "And what is it like to be free?" David asked.

At that Abigail grinned a mile wide. "Freedom is the best thing there is." She looked to her husband. "Second, of course, only to love."

Without thinking, he then glanced again at Elizabeth. She had completed the image of Mr. Davis quite quickly, but Joshua and Abigail's likeness seemed to be giving her some trouble. Eraser in hand, she hurriedly wiped away what she had just laid down. David saw the frustration on her face, the hard set of her mouth.

He had gathered more than enough information for his article already but decided to linger longer so Elizabeth could have more time. He asked if the couple had any plans for the future. Were they interested in striking out on their own?

"No," Joshua said. "We're right happy here."

"We want to be here when Emily comes back to visit," Abigail added.

After a few more questions David looked over again. Elizabeth still had little more than Joshua and Abigail's basic outline. Once more her eraser was in hand.

While conversing with his hosts, now about subjects unrelated to the interview, he passed Elizabeth a page from his notebook. On it was a question circled for her attention.

Do you need more time?

When she discreetly responded *No*, he thanked the family for their time and bid them farewell.

Leaving the Davis home, Elizabeth marched a quick step. David knew for a fact she was troubled.

"Are you all right?"

A fool he was for asking a direct question, for although she said she was fine, she didn't look it. She tugged at her satchel and walked a little faster. David wondered if the comment Mrs. Davis had made about Emily being in a family way was still bothering her. He debated asking but decided against it. He figured the best thing he could do was focus on tomorrow.

"I'd like for us to visit a former bounty hunter on our next interview."

She froze. A look of fear suddenly filled her face. He wasn't certain why. Perhaps she hadn't heard the word "former." "The man has converted," David quickly added. "And he now spends his time advocating the abolishment of slavery."

Her fear faded, but only a little. "Perhaps it would be best if you went without me." She started walking again.

"If it is a matter of a previous commitment, I can re-schedule the interview."

"No," Elizabeth said. "I-It isn't that... I'd just rather you went without me."

"Without you?"

"Yes. In fact, perhaps it would be best from now on if you work without me."

His heart slammed into his ribs. Reaching for her elbow, he stopped her in her tracks. "Elizabeth, what is it? What's wrong? Are you upset over what Mrs. Davis said?"

She reddened, but he couldn't tell if the reaction was in embarrassment or anger. Whatever her emotion, he knew he had spoken of something he shouldn't.

"I'm sorry," he said quickly. "I shouldn't have asked that. I'm afraid questions are a habit."

"The interview is over, David. I'm not part of tomorrow's article."

"Yes, you are. I need you, Elizabeth. You are part of everything I write."

The words were out of his mouth before he even realized. As the color drained from her face, David feared he had just ruined not only their business partnership but everything else, as well.

I need you. Elizabeth felt an unmistakable tug on her heart the moment he said those words. All this time she had thought that he was simply being kind when he asked her to accompany him, that he was only encouraging her talent the way someone surely had once done for him.

But clearly our relationship is a true partnership indeed. He was leaning on her as much as she was on him.

The last thing she wanted was for him to think she didn't want to work with him. David's clear blue eyes were fixed on hers, and in them she saw fear and uncertainty.

Tell him, her mind whispered. *Tell him the truth.*

But the truth was a double-edged sword. What if she told him her story and he no longer wished to work with her? It wasn't the potential loss of income that frightened her now. It wasn't even the opportunity to learn more of Jeremiah. She couldn't bear the thought of David looking at her with disdain.

"Whatever it is, Elizabeth, you can tell me. You know you can."

Yes, her heart told her, *I can tell him anything.* And like a torrent, the emotions poured forth. "Oh David, I can't visit that bounty hunter! What if he is the one who took that little boy?"

"What little boy?"

"The one who was hiding in the bushes."

She knew she wasn't making any sense. She could feel herself shivering, and it had nothing to do with the cool spring breeze. The horrible scene flashed through her mind. If only she could go back… If only she could do things differently…

David must have feared for her well-being. "There's a bench just ahead," he said. "Come. Sit." He took her hand in his, but instead of placing it on his arm, he held it tight, using it to lead her to the seat.

Elizabeth settled on the bench, but it was getting hard to breathe. She drew in several short breaths. David gave her hand a comforting squeeze. "It's all right, Elizabeth. Tell me about this little boy."

"I was seven. It was just after sunset, and I was supposed to stay in the front garden, but I didn't. I was chasing lightning bugs. I wandered up the street to where at the time was still a vacant lot."

She could see him as clearly as she could David. "He was in the bushes. I was just about to cup my hands around the lightning bug when all of a sudden I noticed a pair of eyes. I looked closer. He was about my age. He had a cut across his forehead and his shirtsleeve was torn. He looked so scared. I asked him his name, but he didn't answer. Then…a man came riding up the street."

David's face darkened. Obviously he already knew where this story was going. Even so, he kept hold of her hand.

"The man quickly dismounted," she said. "He asked me if I had seen a little boy. He said it was important that he find him soon because it was getting dark and he might be sick or hurt."

"And you believed him."

Elizabeth shook her head. The memory made her sick. "He *was* hurt. I thought I was helping. I knew the moment that I told him where he was, the moment I saw his evil-looking smile, that I'd made a terrible mistake. That man wasn't there to help."

"He was there to capture him."

"Yes." It was imperative that he understand. "David, please, believe me, I had no idea what was actually happening or what that little boy would suffer. I knew almost nothing about slavery. We had Negro servants, but they were free. They were like members of our family."

He squeezed her hand once more. His touch, his words gave her strength. "I believe you, Elizabeth. What happened next?"

"I screamed, told the little boy to run, but there was no place for him to go. There were buildings on all three sides of the lot, and the only way out was past that bounty hunter. I'll never forget how that man dragged him from the bushes. He bound his hands and feet! He threw him over his saddle as if he were an animal!"

"What did you do then?"

"I just stood there. I was so shocked, so scared. Before that bounty hunter rode off he looked at me and told me to hightail it home before someone threw me over his saddle."

"And so you went home."

Shame burned her cheeks. "I ran up to my room and hid under my blankets like a coward. I should have done something… I should have at least told my mother and father about him."

"Elizabeth, you were a child. You were frightened. Besides, your father couldn't have done any more than you. Bounty hunters operated legally. The fugitive slave act was the law of the land."

"I know that now, but when I think about what that bounty hunter did to him…what his master probably did to him when he was returned home…" Tears flooded her eyes.

The next thing she knew David was pulling her close. Once again Elizabeth was in his arms, but this time it wasn't thoughts of Jeremiah that comforted her. This time it was him.

She was literally trembling in his arms. David hoped his words would soothe her. "We all make mistakes," he whispered. "The important thing is learning from them. And you have, Elizabeth. You have indeed…"

Her hair smelled like lavender water. He couldn't help drinking in the scent. It felt so good to hold her. Inevitably he longed for her to be beside him, not only continuing a working partnership but forming a true union in every sense of the word.

But she can never know that. For, if she ever does come to find that out, she will realize the real reason I disrupted her wedding plans. Then she would see our work as a ploy, a selfish plan on my part to simply be with her.

Guilt rolled through him, for he knew that motive played a part in his choices. His higher nature, however, had encouraged her not only because of her talent but for joy, for the sense of fulfillment he saw in her eyes every time she held a piece of charcoal. Above all else, he wanted her to be happy.

And I will do whatever I can to ensure that.

Releasing her, David felt Elizabeth return to her *proper* place on the bench.

He forced himself to focus on her revelations. "I understand why you don't want to accompany me tomorrow," he said, "but I hope you'll reconsider our other appointments. You can honor that little boy's memory by telling his story."

"How? I could never write about what happened."

"I don't mean words," he said. "I mean your sketches of those like him. Have no fear, Elizabeth. I'll never tell anyone what you told me today…unless you want me to do so."

She wiped her eyes with her black-trimmed handkerchief, another sign of mourning. "Thank you, David. I appreciate your kindness, your forbearance. I do want to keep sketching."

"Good. But, before we go any further, perhaps you should tell your mother what you saw. You've carried this burden alone for so long—I think sharing it with your mother would be a comfort to you."

"You're right. I should."

"Would you like me to be there when you do?"

"No. That's not necessary, but I thank you."

What made him ask his next question, he wasn't sure, but he wanted to know. He *needed* to know. "Elizabeth, did you ever tell Jeremiah about all of this?"

She bit her lip, looked down at her lap. "No."

"Why not?"

"Because I was afraid of what he might think. Of what he might do… It was already bad enough that my brother was serving in the Confederate army."

"You feared he would break your engagement?"

She nodded silently.

Though he realized then and there he had been handed an enormous opportunity, David refused to take it. He would honor his brother's memory by telling her the truth. He would set her mind at ease.

"Elizabeth, look at me."

She did, but uncertainty still darkened her eyes.

"Jeremiah would have responded no differently than me." The next words were the hardest for David to say, but he knew she needed to hear them. "He loved you. Nothing would have changed that."

Fresh tears spilled over. "Thank you, David. You don't know how much it means to hear you say that."

"I do, Elizabeth. I do."

When she returned home, Elizabeth found her mother in the kitchen peeling potatoes.

"There you are," Jane said with a smile. "How was your visit with the Davis family?"

"Well enough."

Her mother blinked. "Are you certain? You look disconcerted. Has something happened?"

Elizabeth drew in a breath. "May I speak with you?"

"Of course, dear."

Her mother promptly laid aside her knife, listening quietly as Elizabeth told the story. Jane's face paled but she immediately hugged her daughter.

"Oh, my dear. I am so sorry you had to witness that. Your father and I wished to protect you from such terrible things. That's why he didn't expose you to the horrors of slavery until you were much older."

Just before he died, Elizabeth thought. *When it was, by then, obvious that our country was headed for war.* He had taken Trudy and her to the slave pens, told them how slaves were treated. *But by then I already knew.*

"Beth, dear. You do know God isn't angry with you, don't you?"

Elizabeth felt her chin quiver. If she was completely honest, deep down she *had* thought that, all these years. She had even believed that was the reason why her prayers hadn't been answered. God wasn't listening to her. That was why her father had died, why He had allowed George to go to war and why Jeremiah was gone.

"God loves you, no matter what," her mother insisted. "You made a mistake, but He can use it to bring about something good." She paused and stepped back to look Elizabeth full in the face. "In fact, I think He already has."

"How so?" Elizabeth wondered.

"What you saw shaped your thinking. You have a clear sense of what is right and wrong because of it. With your interest in the slave vote, your drawings, God has given you an opportunity to change the future."

"That was what David said."

She smiled. "Well, he is a wise man, and dare I say, this partnership has been good for both of you?"

"I believe so."

It was true that when David had first returned to Baltimore, Elizabeth had looked upon him as a mirror image of her beloved. Even now, in certain moments, the turn of his head, or the way he walked still caused her to catch her breath. But he had become her friend, her confidante, an encourager to her faith.

Without him, I would never have survived Jeremiah's passing, and more than likely my artwork would still be only scribbles in a sketchbook.

"Are you going out tomorrow?" her mother asked.

Elizabeth told her about the scheduled interview with the former bounty hunter. Part of her still wanted to avoid it, the other wished to face her fear. The odds of this man being the same one she had encountered as a child were slim, that she knew. *Still...* "I've not yet decided what I'll do."

Her mother nodded understandingly. "Well, take some time to pray on it."

"Yes, and in the meantime, I have a sketch to finish."

Elizabeth headed off to her father's library and laid out her drawing pencils. It was as if a great weight had been lifted from her. She had no trouble completing the sketch of Joshua and Abigail Davis now.

Then, she dared draw another sheet of paper.

Slowly, reverently, she laid down the image that had been burned into her mind for so many years. The fear in his eyes...the tightness of the ropes that bound his thin wrists and ankles… With every stroke of her pencil she lifted a prayer, asking God to look after the little boy, who would now be a man, wherever he may be.

As she took to shading, her confidence grew. Perhaps David and her mother were right. Perhaps God would use what she had witnessed in the past to bring about some good. How utterly humbling and yet exalting was the thought. She could not wait to show her work to David, to thank him for his kindness, his continued encouragement.

She planned to meet him first thing in the morning.

Chapter Nine

David was more than surprised to see Elizabeth waiting for him in the hotel. In fact, he was nearly overtaken by her appearance. Elizabeth had discarded the black crepe, instead greeting him in pale gray, almost silver, silk. He had never seen the dress before, but he recognized its significance. The lighter color proclaimed a lighter stage of mourning. She still wore no jewelry, save her engagement ring. Even so, she looked like a queen.

"You look beautiful," he blurted out.

She blushed, making her look all the more so. "Thank you. I thought…well, now that we are working together, it was time. Mother made this several weeks ago actually, crafted from one of her older gowns. She removed the ruffles and redid the sleeves." She tugged at them nervously.

David was more careful this time. "She did a fine job. The dress will be most *suitable* for our outings."

"Yes," Elizabeth said. "I brought you the sketch."

"You didn't have to do that. I wouldn't have minded coming by the house. I was on my way there now."

"I thought I would save you the trouble."

David offered her a seat on the lobby couch, then claimed the place beside her and unrolled the sketch. Not only had she delivered the promised image of Joshua and Abigail, but there was a sketch of the unknown slave boy, as well. So vivid were the details, the emotions on his face, that David exhaled.

"Elizabeth, this is beyond words."

She blushed again, but he could tell she appreciated the compliment. "I wasn't certain if you would have use for it, but I felt compelled to draw it."

"I'm so glad you did. And, yes, I can use it. It will fit perfectly with the bounty hunter article."

"I'd like to go with you today. That is, if you don't mind."

Mind? Of course he didn't mind. "I'd be pleased to have you accompany me."

She offered him another smile. Her bonnet was covered in the same gray silk. Perhaps it was simply the change of color, but her eyes seemed to shine with new life. David couldn't tear his away.

"You say this man has converted?" she asked.

"Yes. He now feels it is his duty to help slaves."

"What is his name?"

"Jack Lodge."

"Is he involved with the Underground Railroad?"

"I don't know. I'm certain if he is, though, he won't tell us that. But he is actively telling his past experiences, sordid as they may be, to anyone who will listen. He openly advocates the call for a new state constitution."

"I'm happy to hear that."

"I must warn you, I'm told he's rather large and intimidating looking. He carries a scar." David gestured across his face. "Right here. A souvenir from one of his ill-fated conquests."

"Courtesy of an abolitionist?"

He shook his head. "A courageous runaway slave."

"He sounds a sight."

"Apparently, he is."

He could tell she was apprehensive, and he admired the fact that she was willing to go in spite of her fears. He felt nervous, as well. What if Jack Lodge was the same bounty hunter she'd met years ago? How would she respond? How would he?

As it turned out, David didn't need to worry. Jack Lodge was not the man, and although his height, girth, scar and foot-long straggly beard were rather frightening at first, Elizabeth took a liking to him. She laughed when he said he hoped she would be able to make him appear a bit more handsome in the newspaper.

As they later walked home, Elizabeth said, "You'd never know to hear him speak now that he is the same man who spent his life trying to recapture runaway slaves. He's so gracious, so kindhearted."

"Indeed. I don't believe I've ever met a finer example of a life changed by Christ."

"Nor have I," Elizabeth said. "I'm glad I came."

He smiled at her. She then asked about their next assignment.

"We've yet to profile a slaveholder," David reminded her.

"Have you someone in mind?"

"I was thinking of Francis Butler."

Elizabeth nodded. She thought that was a wise choice. "Mr. Butler is the biggest textile manufacturer in the city, and he owns the largest number of slaves. He, of all people, stands to be heavily affected *economically* if slavery is abolished."

"Indeed," David said. "I'm most curious to see what his future plans are, though I have heard the man does at least treat his slaves humanely."

"Have you set an appointment?"

"No. I'll let you know as soon as I do."

Ahead on the right a rather unruly hedge of forsythia was spilling out of a front garden, straining for the sidewalk. Elizabeth stopped to sniff the buttery flowers. She'd once told him that spring was her favorite season. David was thankful to see she was again finding pleasure in her surroundings.

"By the way," he then said, "Peter wishes to meet you."

Her emerald-green eyes popped open among the yellow branches. "Does he know E. J. Martin is not a man?"

"He does."

"And he is fine with that?"

David chuckled. "Apparently he is more than fine with that. He told me he would like to introduce our new artist to the rest of the staff *and* issue you your press card."

She blinked. "What is a press card?"

"It's your credentials. Your proof that you do indeed work for the *Free American*."

He fished out his from his pocket and showed it to her. Elizabeth studied it intently.

"David J. Wainwright," she read. "What does the *J* stand for?"

"James. I'm named after my father."

She smiled. "I'm Jane. After my mother."

"I guessed as much."

She handed back his press card. He slipped it into his pocket, then they continued walking.

"Do those credentials grant you access to places about the city which are otherwise off-limits to the public?" Elizabeth asked.

"Generally."

Intrigue now mingled with excitement. He could see it written all over her face. "You mean you or I could just walk right into a political meeting or even Fort McHenry and go where ever we wish? Speak with whomever we please?"

"Well, not exactly. Especially not the fort. We would have to have reason for being there—a story we were working on. And they wouldn't just let us have the run of the place. We'd have escorted access, limited at best."

"I see." She pressed her lips together.

"You seem disappointed."

"On the contrary," she said, her smile returning. "I was just imagining all the stories that we could tell."

David did not stay for supper that evening since he had to finish his article on Jack Lodge and still make arrangements for the interview with Francis Butler. He promised to return sometime the next day to escort her to the newspaper. Elizabeth was extremely apprehensive about meeting Peter Carpenter but at the same time excited. She had never seen the inside workings of the press before. *And to think that I am now a member?* It still amazed her.

That night as she was ironing her dress, her mother came into her room. She handed her a sum of money.

"What's this?" Elizabeth asked.

"It's what you earned from your latest sketch."

"Oh, Mother, I can't take this. You need it. We have expenses. Food, lamp oil—"

"Both of which we have plenty at present." She smiled.

Elizabeth was indeed grateful, but there was another matter. "Shouldn't we give it to David for the roof tiles?"

"I already tried. He wouldn't take it."

Elizabeth could not say she was surprised. His generosity, his kind attentiveness warmed her heart.

"You have given me every penny you've earned thus far," her mother said. "Therefore I insist you spend *this* on yourself. And as for future expenses, from what you told me of tomorrow's meeting at the paper, you will have many more coins forthcoming."

Elizabeth couldn't help but grin. Her mother looked just as pleased. "Why don't you walk down to Mr. Horn's shop before David comes tomorrow?" she said. "I know very well you've been wanting to commission a piece of memorial jewelry."

She had indeed. All this time she'd kept Jeremiah's hair safeguarded in the handkerchief David had given her. It would be good to give it a proper place. Elizabeth kissed her mother's cheek. "Thank you. If you are certain you don't need this, then I'll give the jewelry store a look."

"Give it more than a look," she said. "Purchase something to remember him by."

With the handkerchief tucked securely in her pocket, Elizabeth walked eagerly to Horn Jeweler's the following morning. The closer she came to her destination, however, the more her pace slowed. The store would be full of all sorts of pretty wedding bands—bands that she would never have the chance to wear. Elizabeth laid her hand on her engagement ring, feeling it beneath her glove. The little pearl was precious to her, not only because it had come from the man who had loved her but because the simple ring was the kind she had always hoped for.

Jeremiah chose exactly what suited me.

She wondered where he had bought the ring, what he had been thinking the day he did so. Had he been nervous or filled with excitement? *Did he tell the jeweler about me?*

Her heart squeezed, but forcing her feet forward, she stepped into the store. Mr. Horn, an older, heavier gentleman with spectacles magnifying a pair of kind eyes, greeted her from behind the counter.

"Good morning, miss. May I help you?"

She approached carefully. Her hesitancy now had less to do with Jeremiah's memory and more with parting with his hair. What if she turned it over and the man made some sort of mistake? What if he gave her order to someone else?

Mr. Horn must have recognized her struggle, and the significance of her clothing.

"Are you here to inquire of memorial jewelry?" he asked.

"Yes."

He first offered his condolences. Elizabeth wondered how many women like her had come into his store since the war had begun. "Were you hoping for a brooch or a locket?" he asked.

"A brooch."

He guided her to a particular section of glass case where examples of his work lay displayed on black velvet. There was jewelry carved of jet and vulcanite, others made of gold. Some were painted elaborately with scenes of angels and weeping willow trees. That which she was most interested in was constructed with human hair. A sample lock had been patterned into a wheat shaft design. Elizabeth pointed to it.

"I would like something such as this."

He nodded and quickly took out the piece for her to view more closely. It was not gold but the metalwork was tastefully crafted. The quality was good and the price was right.

"Yes," she said. "One like this, please."

He nodded. "I require half payment now and the rest when the work is complete."

Elizabeth agreed. Mr. Horn took down her name and street number while she counted out her coins. She then handed them over.

"Thank you," the man said. "Now, if you would…"

She knew what she must surrender, and fear gripped her. *But without it the brooch will be empty.* Drawing in a breath, she took out the handkerchief. Elizabeth's fingers trembled as she tried to unfold it.

There were moments—usually when she was with David, working on a story—when it seemed as though years had passed since losing her beloved. Then there were times when it felt as though Jeremiah had just died. Right now was one of them.

She tried her best to pray. *Lord, help me. Please don't let me cry in front of this man.*

Mr. Horn was waiting patiently, a kind, grandfatherly look on his wrinkled face. When she finally handed over the lock of hair, he promptly, yet respectfully, laid it in a small piece of white cloth.

"Don't you worry, miss. I'll take good care of your

loved one's hair. I've done many of these in my time, and I've never once had a lady dissatisfied."

Elizabeth nodded as she clutched the now empty handkerchief to her chest. "When will the brooch be complete?" she asked.

"Two days," he said confidently.

"Very well. Thank you."

She turned for the door. Once outside the tears flowed freely.

Elizabeth seemed a bit disconcerted when David met her at noon. Upon closer observation he noticed her eyes were red.

She's been crying. He knew how difficult things still were. Although he had put away his black suit of mourning, not a day went by that he didn't think of his brother. The heaviness in his heart remained.

He wondered also how much the pending meeting with Peter was troubling her. Even with the experience David had already had in publishing, he'd been extremely anxious meeting the man.

He tried his best to encourage her. "Remember, you're already a sketch artist for the *Free American*. This business today is simply a formality."

She breathed a sigh and managed a weak smile. "Thank you for the reminder."

"You're welcome."

She donned her silver bonnet, and, taking hold of his arm, they started for the newspaper.

"What is your Mr. Carpenter like?" she asked.

"Hmm, how to say?" He wanted to prepare her but did not wish to make too much of Carpenter's somewhat abrasive personality. He didn't want to scare her. "He is rather abrupt, certainly short on pleasantries, but over-all, I find him to be an honest man, serious in his com-mitment to truth and greatly concerned for the future of our country."

"That sounds like the way Jeremiah used to describe Dr. Mackay."

"Yes, come to think of it—I can see clear similari-ties." While he and Elizabeth had been blessed to serve under an amiable older physician named Jacob Turner, his brother and Elizabeth's friend Emily had been placed in the ward of one of the most disciplined, if not harsh officers, in the US Army.

Jeremiah had told him how Dr. Mackay eventually softened thanks to Emily's sweet disposition—a change that David had seen for himself in Dr. Mackay's kind-ness at Jeremiah's funeral. For a moment David won-dered what effect Elizabeth's presence would have on Peter Carpenter and the other men at the paper. He felt a twinge of jealousy, then immediately prayed God would forgive him for such a thought.

I needn't worry about such things, anyway, he told himself. *Her heart will forever belong to my brother.*

As they came to the paper, Elizabeth's grip on his arm tightened. While he took pride in the fact that she was clinging to him for protection, he hated the fact that she was frightened. He bent toward her ear.

"You will do just fine," he whispered. "Don't worry. I'll be right beside you."

The look she gave him nearly took his breath away. Keeping on task, however, he knocked on his editor's door.

"Enter."

David opened the door. As usual, Peter was at his

desk, poring over a stack of papers. His frock coat was tossed aside, his tie askew, his sleeves rolled. When he failed to acknowledge their presence, David made the introduction himself.

"Mr. Peter Carpenter, may I present Miss Elizabeth Martin."

The editor's head snapped up. Eyes widening, he immediately struggled to stand in the presence of a lady. "Miss Martin," he said, "I have been expecting you... My, that dress is lovely."

So I was wrong about the man being short on pleasantries, David thought.

"Thank you, Mr. Carpenter," Elizabeth replied evenly. "Mr. Wainwright has told me much about your paper. I was eager to see it for myself."

David watched as the man raked back his hair, trying to improve upon his rather disheveled appearance. He moved away from his desk, looking as though he were about to shake Elizabeth's hand. Apparently deciding that was much too masculine a gesture, he instead straightened his tie. "Yes, well, I was very eager to make your acquaintance, as well. Your sketches have been well received."

Elizabeth blushed humbly. "Mr. Wainwright said you were pleased."

"Indeed. And you have never been employed previously?"

"As an artist? No."

Peter nodded. "Then you have been employed in another profession?"

Elizabeth hesitated slightly. "I served as a volunteer nurse."

"Here in the city?"

The hair on the back of David's neck stood up. He didn't like where this was going. Carpenter had said nothing of interviewing her. He had made it seem as though Elizabeth already had the job permanently if she so wished.

"Yes," Elizabeth said. "I served here in the city."

"I see, and so you chose not to continue?"

David could see the tension building in her face. Peter saw it, as well, and sensed a story. Squinting shrewdly, he then asked, "Was there some problem with your previous service?"

Elizabeth quickly looked at David. He swallowed hard.

"Is there something I should know?" Peter asked.

The whole tone of the room had changed. David still had no idea what the man's political persuasion was, but he suspected Elizabeth's travails with the Oath of Loyalty were about to come back to haunt her once more. Immediately he tried to explain, "Miss Martin was asked—"

His editor shot him a look. "I asked *her.*"

Peter turned back to Elizabeth. David stepped alongside her, resisting the urge to slide his arm protectively around her waist. He prayed Elizabeth's job as an artist wouldn't be finished with her following words.

"I was asked to sign a second Oath of Loyalty."

"Why is that?" Carpenter asked coldly.

"Because I altered the first."

The man's eyebrow arched. "Altered?"

"I crossed out the line refusing to give aid or comfort to the enemy. You see, sir, I have a brother serving in the Confederate army."

The man simply stared at her without offering the

slightest clue to what he was actually thinking. David was certain Elizabeth was going to turn on her heel and forget the whole business. She, however, surprised him. Bravely, she raised her chin.

"Is my brother's enlistment going to be a problem, sir?"

"Not unless *you* make it one."

David relaxed just a bit as Carpenter then went on to give her the same speech he'd given him about leaving one's politics at the door. He even went as far as to give examples of newspapers, north and south, whose sketch artists had taken liberty with the truth.

"If the US Army doesn't burn a particular town, don't give me a sketch claiming they have, and conversely, if the Southern soldiers assist their wounded enemy, don't draw them with bayonets in hand, poised for the kill."

Elizabeth looked shocked. "I would never do such a thing, sir."

"Good." Carpenter then leaned back against his desk. Crossing his arms, he eyed them both. "A former Massachusetts private and the sister of a Confederate soldier… that should make for an interesting balance of perspective concerning this war."

Neither David nor Elizabeth knew what to say to that. They simply looked at one another. After a moment she turned once more to Peter.

"Am I to assume, then, sir, that you will have need for sketches from me even after the slave vote? That you would wish me to cover events concerning the war and other subjects relating to this city?"

David felt a grin tugging at his mouth. *Bravo! That's my girl!*

Evidently, Peter Carpenter was impressed, as well.

His hard expression softened almost to a smile. "That is correct, Miss Martin. Come. Let me show you about."

Elizabeth received the same tour as David had when he first began his work. He watched the response of his fellow reporters as they met the female artist. Young Mr. Keedy looked positively smitten. Ross, Russell, and Detwiler appeared surprised but generally accepting. Only Collins, the gray-headed business manager, showed cold indifference to her introduction. Elizabeth responded politely nonetheless. She seemed to take much pleasure in the fact that Peter was providing her with workspace and supplies.

"We'll put you right here, next to Mr. Wainwright," he said.

"Thank you." Elizabeth gave David a quick grin, then looked back at her editor. "I shall be most comfortable."

Carpenter stuck out his hand. "Welcome to the *Free American*, Miss Martin. I think you will fit in quite nicely here."

David smiled to himself. He thought so, too.

When Mr. Carpenter had asked about her work at the hospital, Elizabeth was certain her time as a professional artist was over before it had even really begun. Strengthened, however, by David's protective presence, she'd drawn in a deep breath and told the newspaperman the truth.

The whole thing struck her as some sort of test of character, of bravery, for the moment she passed it, Mr. Carpenter had returned to his previous conciliatory tone. He wasn't as friendly as David, but he seemed a fair man. He issued her press card, then laid out her duties for the rest of the week.

David was to report on the local textile manufacturer, Francis Butler, in the morning. Since that man had been featured in a separate story some months back, the *Free American* already had an engraving of his likeness on hand. Her artwork would not be needed. Mr. Carpenter said if she liked, she could simply wait until Wednesday's vote to begin her first full day of work. She appreciated that for it would give her the opportunity to return to the jewelry store.

"Thank you, sir. I will see you, then, on Wednesday."

David was seated at his own desk, quietly observing the world like he usually did, only this time there was a much more contented look on his face. Mr. Carpenter turned to him.

"Would you kindly explain to Miss Martin that I have never served in the army?" He then lumbered back to his office and shut the door.

"What was that all about?" Elizabeth asked David.

"You keep calling him 'sir.'"

"Yes?"

"He prefers Mr. Carpenter or Peter."

"He doesn't seem as though he would."

"No. He doesn't, but you'll get used to him."

He wasn't the only thing she would have to get used to. She had thought working in the hospital wards would be the extent of her interactions with coarse men. Apparently newspaper reporters were just as vulgar as hungry soldiers. Mr. Detwiler and Mr. Russell seemed not to mind a lady's presence, but they were not very quick to remember their manners.

Sack coats tossed aside, legs propped upon their desks, they shouted back and forth, firing off the latest political gossip. As Elizabeth stocked her workspace with art supplies, she wondered how she would ever get any actual work done. *How can anyone concentrate with all this chatter?*

Nearby, Mr. Ross was much quieter, but he was steadily puffing on a cigar, wholly oblivious to which way his smoke was traveling. David noticed, however, and spoke on her behalf.

"Ross."

"Huh?" the man said, looking back.

"Open a window, will you?"

Realizing what he'd done, Mr. Ross quickly stood to do so. "My apologies, Miss Martin. I'll watch that from now on."

"Thank you, Mr. Ross. That would be most kind."

Young Mr. Keedy was quiet and courteous. He repeatedly asked her if she had need of anything. The only man who seemed put out by her presence was Mr. Collins. He glared at Elizabeth every time he came into the room. Again, David noticed.

"Don't pay any attention to him," he whispered.

"I get the impression that he thinks I should be at home, or at the very most back at the hospital nursing wounded soldiers."

"He looks that way, but I have never heard him say such. If, however, he speaks inappropriately to you or treats you in any way that is disrespectful, you let me know."

"I will, but don't worry. I've dealt with temperaments like his before. If he simply does his job and I do mine, it shouldn't be a problem."

David offered her that delightful, comforting smile. "You kept a ward full of discontented soldiers in line," he said. "I have no doubt you can manage the same here."

He had completed his own tasks by the time her supplies were in order, so they walked home together. The streets were relatively quiet that evening. The air smelled of rain, but for now the setting sun cast a soft pink light upon the city.

"So now that you have seen it all," David said in a particularly jovial tone, "what say you, Miss Martin? Will you swear your loyalty to our fledgling press or will you seek artistic glory somewhere else?"

The thought of partnering with any other reporter, especially given what she had observed today of their personalities and habits, was not exactly appealing. When she told him that, he laughed. "I think, then, I shall take that as a compliment," he said, "although I am not quite certain."

"I meant it as one."

He smiled at her. That familiar twinkle was in his eyes, and in that moment Elizabeth couldn't help but think how different her life would be if things had gone according to her and Jeremiah's plans.

I'd be married now. I may even be carrying a child. Though it saddened her to think of what she had missed out on, it saddened her even more to think that she would have missed the opportunity to do this. *I would not be an artist. I would not be working with him.*

She asked David about the upcoming vote. "Are you anxious?"

"A little. I keep thinking of Elijah and Elisha."

"So do I. I have been praying for them."

He stopped square, his expression a mixture of delight and surprise. Elizabeth couldn't help but think him a handsome man in his own right.

"Yes," she said, "I've started praying again."

"I'm pleased to hear that. May I ask what has changed?"

"My perspective, I suppose. I've been reading Jeremiah's Bible. I had forgotten just how many stories there are where it appears, at least at first, that God has vanished."

"And later on you see His hand at work."

"Yes. Sometimes people's prayers were answered in the way they hoped. Other times they weren't. Some chose to keep following, others fell away from the faith."

"Indeed."

"I want to keep following. I must admit, though, when I think about this war and all that could still happen with the slaves, my faith isn't very strong."

"Well, I can relate to that."

As always she appreciated his honesty. "All I know for certain is, I'm happy when I sketch. I pray that God will make good use of my drawings, that He will take your words and use them to help little Elijah and Elisha, and all the others like them."

"Thank you, Elizabeth. I appreciate those prayers. But no matter what happens with Wednesday's vote or in the future, don't stop praying."

She promised him she wouldn't, but she had no idea what difficult days lay ahead or how much their newly knitted partnership was about to be tested.

The following morning Elizabeth dressed quickly. She saw to breakfast for her mother and sister and was at the jewelry store by the time Mr. Horn opened.

"Come in, my dear," he said as he slipped the front door key into his vest pocket. "I finished your piece last night. I hope you approve."

Holding her breath, she walked toward the counter, whereupon he presented her with a small box. Mr. Horn opened the lid. With one glance Elizabeth's fears of a jeweler's mistake vanished. There in the center of the brooch was Jeremiah's hair, crafted into the wheat pattern she had requested. Tiny green leaves had been painted delicately around the sheath. Scrolled metalwork framed the scene.

"It is beautiful," she said. "I will cherish it always."

The master jeweler smiled humbly. "I am pleased that you approve." He paused. "If I may ask, dear, was it the war?"

Genuine sympathy laced his words. Though her eyes grew cloudy, Elizabeth felt compelled to share. She wanted him to know something of the wonderful man she had loved.

"Yes," she said, "but it wasn't the battlefield. He was a steward in the hospital and contracted pneumonia. He fell ill before we could marry."

Mr. Horn shook his head sadly. "I am sorry to hear that. Many a poor soldier's been cut low by that enemy."

Elizabeth nodded. "I was a nurse at the West's Buildings where he worked. That was how we met."

Something sparked in the old man's eyes. "A pearl engagement ring?" he asked.

"I beg your pardon?"

"Did your young man give you a pearl engagement ring?"

Elizabeth's heart quickened. Could it be that Jeremiah had bought the ring here? "Yes." She quickly tugged off her glove, held out her left hand.

"Ah, yes," he said, smiling. "That's one of mine. I remember your sweetheart. He talked about you. He said you were the prettiest nurse, the finest woman in all of Baltimore."

Elizabeth hungered for more details. "What else did he say?"

"Oh, he talked a blue streak. Nervous, he was. He wanted to find you the perfect ring. The poor boy looked over each of these cases, trying desperately to decide."

She smiled, though it was now through a veil of tears. Jeremiah had stood at this very spot, poring over each and every ring, all because he loved her.

The man chuckled. "He just couldn't choose."

"How did he finally come to a decision?" she asked. "Did you suggest the pearl?"

"No," Mr. Horn said. "His brother was with him. He seemed to think it would suit you."

His brother?

"Your sweetheart gave it a bit of thought and decided he was right. I must say, he made the right decision. It does suit you."

He *made the right decision, meaning David, not Jeremiah.*

Like the postponement of their wedding, her ring was a choice her beloved had not fully made on his own.

David had chosen it. Understanding that, Elizabeth did not know what to think. Was she disturbed because he had once again involved himself in his brother's affairs? Or was it the fact that Jeremiah *couldn't* make the decision without his assistance that disconcerted her?

She told herself it would not have made much difference had *the jeweler* suggested the ring. An excited bridegroom was bound to be a little nervous, wanting to choose what his bride would like best. But how was it David knew exactly what she would have chosen had Elizabeth the opportunity to make the selection herself?

A year spent working alongside a person is bound to yield insight, she supposed, but she couldn't shake the thought that on the day her engagement ring was purchased, her would-be brother-in-law knew her better than her own fiancé did.

And what of now?

So much had passed between them since the funeral. David knew not only her dreams but her doubts, her past secrets, as well. *He knows things about me that Jeremiah never knew. I always imagined the man who married me would know me inside and out, better than anyone else, for isn't that the essence of love? Knowing both the good and bad of a person, choosing not only to celebrate the former, but bearing with the latter?*

Sadly, she realized, perhaps for the first time, just how little her fiancé had known her, how little she knew him. *I didn't even know his middle name.*

Mr. Horn was still waiting, and recognizing such, Elizabeth paid him what was due. He boxed up the memorial brooch and handed it to her.

"May God comfort you with the memory of your sweetheart," he said.

She thanked him for his kindness and turned to go, but Jeremiah's memory brought less comfort with each passing day.

Chapter Ten

The morning of April 6—the day of the vote—dawned crisp and clear. Elizabeth would have liked to have said she was fully focused on the monumental day, but she wasn't. The business with her engagement ring was still gnawing at her. She knew it shouldn't. No matter what the circumstances, the ring had been a token of Jeremiah's love and devotion.

As for David's part in it all, surely he was only trying to be helpful to his brother and considerate to me. I should not be troubled by the fact that he had such insight into my preferences, for I have certainly noticed his.

He was a man with a hearty appetite, but he never had more than a cup of coffee to start the day. He only sat down to eat a full meal after he had gathered all his notes. He also had a habit of crushing peppermint drops between his teeth whenever he was deep in thought, and he rubbed his whiskers bashfully whenever she paid him a compliment.

Yes, she thought. *We know each other quite well.*

A sudden twinge of guilt stiffened her stance in front

of the looking glass. Why did it feel wrong to be so familiar with him? They were to have been family, she reminded herself, and although they may not legally be such, Jeremiah would certainly wish for her to still think of him that way.

She pinned her memorial brooch to her collar and tried to marshal her focus.

I have work to do today. The citizens of my state are about to decide whether or not to rewrite their constitution. The end of slavery may finally be near.

Determined to remember such, she put on her gloves and turned for the door. David was waiting in the foyer when she came down the staircase. For one quick moment she was tempted to bring up the ring but decided against it. Trudy was with him, and Elizabeth didn't know exactly what she would say about the subject, anyway.

"I'm sorry to have kept you waiting," she said instead.

"You've not. I've just arrived. But we had better leave quickly, for Trudy is insistent that I have breakfast." David turned and grinned at her.

"Would you believe he refused?" her sister said. "He claims a reporter always works better on an empty stomach."

"That's so he will remain hungry for a good story." As soon as the words—ones she had heard David say many times—were out of her mouth, that twinge of guilt returned. This time it was accompanied by a rush of heat to her cheeks. She felt as though she had said something she shouldn't, especially when David looked at her and grinned.

Family, she reminded herself, but no family member had ever made her feel the way he did. When he looked at her, she felt as though she was the most beautiful, most capable woman in the world.

"I thought we would first visit the polling places, then later, city hall," David said.

Elizabeth nodded, focusing on the business at hand. "The results will be posted there, correct?"

"As they are counted, but given that this is a state-wide vote, it is going to take some time."

"How much time?" Trudy asked.

"Two or three days, more than likely," he said.

Trudy frowned slightly, her nose wrinkling. "It will be hard to wait that long to find out the results."

"Imagine how the slaves are feeling," Elizabeth said.

"Indeed," said David. And there was that look again. Elizabeth inadvertently touched the memorial brooch, grounding her thoughts and emotions.

They bade Trudy a good morning, then started off for the polls. David walked with a quick step while chatting about the historic day. Elizabeth could clearly hear the excitement in his voice. He predicted record turnout, but upon reaching their first destination, that did not appear to be the case. Optimism waning, he immediately took to counting citizens. She noticed something equally distressing.

Federal soldiers were stationed at the ballot boxes. Their coats new and blue with brass buttons gleaming, their stance was quite intimidating. Elizabeth observed the fear their presence provoked on the faces of her fellow citizens. She felt it herself and cringed at her own stupidity.

Fool that I am. What was I thinking?

David laid his hand over hers. "Something has frightened you," he said. "What is it?"

The only thing more shameful than her mistake was the fact that her fear was palpable enough for him to once again notice. She gestured discreetly toward the soldiers. "I should have known they would be here."

"I don't understand. Why should they be of concern to you?"

"The color of my dress…"

He looked her over. "It's silver," he said, innocently.

"It is *gray.* I should not have worn it. It may cost you."

"Nonsense. Your dress could hardly be considered an endorsement for the rebel army."

His tone was all too casual. Clearly he did not understand the seriousness of the situation. "David, *you* have been seen with *me.* All it will take is for one soldier to assume I am a Southern sympathizer. Not only could they deny you access to cover the event, but they could arrest you, as well. They've arrested men on far less before."

"Elizabeth," he said firmly. "I appreciate your concern, but you need not worry. No one is going to brand me a traitor because of what you are wearing. No one is going to trouble you, either."

"How can you be so certain?"

The look he gave her at that moment was enough to quell all her anxieties. "Because I won't let them."

The appreciation in Elizabeth's eyes was unmistakable. David tried to ignore the effect it was having on him. The only way he managed to do so was by focusing on that memorial brooch pinned at her collar.

This day is not about me, he reminded himself. *It isn't even about her. It is about something so much more important.*

He glanced about once more. The US Army's presence was indeed strong, but David had thought nothing of it at first. The provost marshal's office had issued a statement prior to the election insisting that troops would be in place to safeguard the polls and insure protection for the ballot boxes. Thanks to Elizabeth, he now saw the situation from a different perspective.

He suddenly wondered how many Maryland men, perhaps loyal in their own standing but with relatives or friends having chosen secession, would fail to approach the polls today because they feared the potential consequences of doing so.

"You raise a valid point," he told her. "One indeed worth noting. The presence of the army could have a bearing on the voting results."

"Do you think it will be this way at every venue?"

"I hope not." He of course wanted slavery abolished, but he didn't want to see anyone denied the right to vote because of fear. David tried his best to remain positive. "Given that this is Mount Vernon, the provost marshal's office may have thought it prudent to station more soldiers here because of past sympathy. Let's watch for a while. See what happens."

They claimed a low stone wall, just opposite the ballot boxes, where they could view the entire scene. Elizabeth spread out her pencils, took off her gloves. Within a matter of minutes, she was completely absorbed in her work, sketching the faces of the voters. David noted some of the men looked confident, others hesitant. The expressions of the soldiers and those of the election judges were stone cold.

He then began interviewing those who were exiting the polls. Many men refused to talk to him. Among those who would, David discovered a near equal split. The lines were not drawn between proslavery and abolition, as he had expected. The division concerned the army. Half welcomed the boys in blue, and others, if they had the power, would have sent them marching.

"Lincoln's lackeys," one man was bold enough to say. "They got no business being here."

David didn't divulge he'd once worn blue himself. "Are you sympathetic to the South?" he asked.

"I wasn't to begin with, but I daresay we might have been better joining them, now that those *Unconditionals* have gained control of this state."

"What makes you say that?"

The man, aged sixty or so, squinted. "Don't get me wrong. I'm all for Negro rights, but you mark my words, this ain't about slavery. It's about giving more control to Washington. You watch and see. Those *Unconditionals* only used this issue to get themselves elected. Now that they're in office they'll soon take away the rights of anyone who doesn't think just like them. They've already restricted the sale of firearms." He then eyed David suspiciously, "And they've shut down much of *your* competition."

The man walked off but not before telling David he had voted against rewriting the state constitution and had encouraged all his friends to do the same.

Heart heavy, David walked back to where Elizabeth was seated. As his shadow fell over her, she looked up. She knew right away something was wrong.

"You are discouraged," she said.

He knew he shouldn't be, but it was hard. "This isn't going to be a simple straight up or down vote to end slavery."

"What are people saying?"

"The man I just spoke with thought slavery should be outlawed, but he didn't vote that way because he feared a new constitution would limit the rights of others."

A knowing look filled her face. "He worries the delegates will try to silence those who don't think Washington should use whatever means necessary to win this war."

"Yes." He sat down beside her. Pulling out two peppermint drops from his pocket, he handed one to her, then popped the other into his own mouth and bit down hard.

"People are afraid," Elizabeth said. "They are afraid because of what happened here."

"You mean the riot on Pratt Street."

She nodded.

At the beginning of the war the Northern papers had painted the citizens of Baltimore as bloodthirsty traitors who had deserved to be shot for what they had done to Union soldiers. Part of him understood why they had taken that stance. After all, four men from his own state had died and many more were wounded. *But men from Baltimore died, as well, and adding fuel to the fire, Washington sent the same Massachusetts troops who had fired upon the civilians back as an occupying force. Any citizen who stepped out of line was immediately—and harshly—dealt with.*

The soldiers were eventually replaced by regiments from other states, yet suspicion and sometimes outright disdain of Northern men still remained. Even David and his brother had felt the sting when they later arrived in town. In their blue uniforms, they were often looked upon with contempt.

"I'm not saying our citizens should have pelted those

men with rocks," Elizabeth said, "but when the Sixth Massachusetts fired their muskets, innocent people paid the price. Sam and Julia were nearly trampled to death as they ran for cover. They certainly weren't at the station to start a riot. She and her brother Edward were only there to meet Sam's train."

David listened as Elizabeth continued with the account.

"A boy on a ship in the harbor was killed by a stray bullet, and another man down by the tracks was shot in cold blood just because he shook his fist at the train when the Yankees rolled out of town."

Even now he could hear the fear in her voice. He had witnessed its effects just moments ago. The realization that she was wearing a hue that the Northern soldiers may find offensive had drained the color from her face. David had felt the tremble of her hand as she'd clutched his arm.

He knew his focus should remain on today's assignment, but he couldn't help himself. "Elizabeth, I have often wondered something."

"Yes?"

"You once told Jeremiah that your brother went to war because of what happened on Pratt Street."

"That's true."

"Then how was it you came to fall in love with a Massachusetts man?"

He shouldn't have asked, for he certainly wasn't prepared for the answer she gave.

"It was because of you."

"Me?" His mouth went dry, and for a moment he was certain his heart had ceased beating.

She nodded. "When the wounded began arriving in

Baltimore I, like my other friends, volunteered at the hospital to make certain the Confederate soldiers would receive proper care."

"You feared we *wouldn't* treat them?"

Shame colored her cheeks. "Yes," she admitted, "or at least that you would give them negligent care. But as I watched you, worked with you, I realized that fear was unfounded. You tended to your *enemies* with dignity and respect, and you were always so kind to me. *You* made it possible for Jeremiah to win my heart."

David died inside. It took everything he had within him to keep his emotion hidden. *So it was my very affection for her that turned her heart toward my brother.* He couldn't help but wonder how different life might have been had he only found the courage to tell her what he felt when he'd had the opportunity. Now it was too late.

Elizabeth touched her memorial brooch, blinking back tears. She had just poured out her heart to him. He knew he had to say something. "Thank you, Elizabeth. I shall take that as the dearest of compliments."

Her tender, timid smile was like the twist of a knife, but he forced himself to be true to what he had just said. He *would* take her confession as a compliment, for he knew it was not Elizabeth's *intention* to wound him.

After Elizabeth had finished her sketch, she and David traveled to several other locations. He had been right about the federal army's presence. It was much stronger in Mount Vernon than in the other voting districts. Even so, voter turnout continued to be low.

David's discouragement seemed to grow worse with each passing hour. Elizabeth's heart ached for him. She knew he was worried about the vote and especially for little Elijah and Elisha. She was just as concerned. Wishing to do something to help him, she prayed, but beyond simply asking for help on his behalf and for the two little boys, Elizabeth didn't know what else to say.

They continued with their tasks. He gathered his notes. She wore down her charcoal sticks. Today the work brought little peace. Elizabeth felt the same sense of foreboding she had when she first noticed the federal soldiers, only now it was much worse. For some reason she could not get Elijah and Elisha out of her mind. A chill ran down her spine when at one point David turned to her and said, "You may think me mad, but I have this sudden feeling that we need to stop what we are doing and visit the dry goods store."

She immediately closed her sketchbook. "I don't think you mad. I have been thinking the same."

"You have?"

"Yes. It's almost as if I feel something is about to happen." She wasn't exactly certain her earlier prayer had anything to do with this, but she told him about it, anyway.

"You prayed for *me*?" he asked.

"Yes, and for Elijah and Elisha."

"That's all the convincing I need," he said. "Let's go."

They soon reached Light Street. Much to their surprise, Sam and Julia were at the dry goods counter. Wallace, the merchant, did not look pleased to see them.

"I have told you a hundred times before," he said, "they are my property. I will not hand them over to you, no matter what you offer!"

The sharp tone and the man's fierce expression made Elizabeth instinctively reach for David's arm. As they approached the counter, their friends cast them only a sparing glance, as if they were little more than strangers. David said nothing to them, either. Julia looked extremely pale and worried as her husband resumed his previous conversation.

"But why not take the certain money I have to offer you?" Sam asked Wallace. "If the vote passes, you will be forced to free them, and it's possible you could get nothing in the way of compensation then."

The merchant sneered. "You abolitionists dream of that, don't you?" He then turned his anger toward David. "And you, coming in here with that accent of yours. You don't think I know where you are from? Have you Boston boys forgotten what we do to those who won't mind their own business?"

Elizabeth's skin prickled, and for a moment she feared the man had a pistol behind his counter and was about to make use of it. David must have thought the same. He immediately stepped in front of her. He'd promised her previously that he would allow no harm to come to her. She hoped he would not have to make good on that promise.

"I'm a reporter for the *Free American*," David quickly said, "and I should be very interested in hearing your story."

Wallace looked taken aback for a second or two, but when David pulled out his press card, the man then pointed at Sam and Julia. "The story is this high and mighty fella is trying to tell me what to do with my slaves. He thinks I should hand them over to him."

David opened his journal. Elizabeth still stood behind him, but she had positioned herself so that she could see what was happening. He scribbled down a few particulars, then turned toward her. "Forgive me," he said.

"This is…my *assistant*. Would you like for her to sketch your portrait?"

He was appealing to Wallace's pride, and it worked. He quickly consented, eager to have his face make the morning edition.

"See to the man, then," David told her. "*Only* him."

Elizabeth quickly obliged. She knew full well why he was foregoing Sam and Julia's likeness. It was the same reason he had introduced her as a nameless assistant. He was trying to protect each of them.

David questioned Wallace, asking him everything, from how much he'd originally paid to purchase his slaves, to what his philosophy was on keeping them. Elizabeth winced when the merchant said the children were cursed by God, fit for nothing but servitude. Anger had her gripping her pencil so tightly she feared it would snap in two.

David took extra time writing down the man's quote, then asked, "And where are your slaves at present? Are they here?"

"No. They're out on delivery. They won't be back for another hour."

"I see." He then turned to Sam. David asked him only a few questions, most importantly why he so desperately wished to purchase the boys.

"I want to ransom them," Sam said.

"Why?" David asked, although Elizabeth knew he was fully aware of the reason.

"Because Christ died to free us from the curse of sin and death," Sam said. "He cares for all of us, no matter what the color of our skin."

Wallace simply sneered. David scribbled down the quote and thanked each party for their time. Sam and

Julia turned to go, but not without one last plea for the children. The merchant refused. To quell his anger, David mentioned when the man could likely expect to see his portrait in the newspaper. Both reporter and sketch artist then stepped outside.

"I apologize for treating you rudely," David said.

"You were not rude. I appreciated the fact that you tried to shield me from danger. I don't know how you managed to keep your presence of mind in all of that. I suppose, though, that is your gift."

"My gift?"

"For getting the story."

"Not that I really know what to do with it," he said. "I certainly don't want to print any of Wallace's quotes. They sicken me. I only took them down because I felt like I was supposed to keep him talking, that I was supposed to keep Sam and his wife there, as well."

"Perhaps you or they said something that will make the man reconsider his position."

His shoulders fell with a sigh. "I hope so. As much as I want to see Elijah and Elisha free, there is another matter at stake here."

Elizabeth guessed his thoughts. "The matter of Wallace himself?"

David nodded. He removed his hat and raked his fingers through his dark wavy hair. For some strange reason, Elizabeth wanted to run hers through it, too.

"Sometimes I think I would have made a better reporter if I hadn't been a preacher's son," he said.

"You mean if you didn't care so much?"

He nodded again.

"But your faith is what makes you different. That's what made you a good steward. That's what makes you a good reporter now. You're not just out for a story. You are a man of integrity, of honor."

He rubbed his whiskers and offered her a bashful smile, but the discouragement in his eyes still lingered. "You paint much too bright a picture of me," he said.

But Elizabeth knew what she said was true. There was a quiet strength in David Wainwright. More than merely physical, it enveloped every part of his character. His life was a reflection of Christ, and in it she saw continued proof that, despite the darkness surrounding them, God did still govern the affairs of men.

David stewed over the incident at the dry goods store for the rest of the afternoon. Though he managed to pull together a balanced piece, he still wasn't all that eager to see it in print. He handed it off to Peter, however, and continued on with the rest of his work. The next morning the article had barely hit the street corners when Elijah and Elisha's master came storming into the office. He immediately demanded to see David.

"Is something wrong?" he asked.

"Wrong?" Wallace exclaimed. The merchant then rattled off a sting of curses directed at Sam Ward. At her desk, Elizabeth cringed. David quickly reminded the man that a lady was present. Peter also lumbered over with a warning.

"Sir, I suggest you gain control of yourself."

"Control? I have news for you!"

"I don't care what news you have," Peter said. "If you don't gain control, I'll have one of my men toss you out on your ear."

As if for proof Russell and Detwiler rose from their chairs, their arms crossed. Unwilling to tangle with men half his age, and surely wanting whatever this latest chapter of his story was to be told, Wallace backed down, slightly. "I came to tell you he took them!"

"Who took whom?" David asked.

Wallace was back to blaming Sam Ward, but with Russell and Detwiler still standing guard, at least his language was a little less colorful.

"He took my slaves!"

David's heart began to pound. Casting a quick glance in Elizabeth's direction, he knew hers was, as well. Her bodice was rising and falling with quick breaths.

"Tell me exactly what happened," he said, and he offered the angry merchant a seat.

"I don't know, exactly. I don't know how he did it, but he stole them boys right off the street!"

"What?" David had suspected Sam may be involved with the Underground Railroad, but he didn't think he'd be bold enough to snatch Elijah and Elisha in broad daylight, especially when Wallace knew him and his family. *What a risk he has taken!*

The merchant would have no recourse with the US Army, for they had stopped returning runaway slaves some time ago, and the local police would be too busy with other matters, yet still David worried. *A man like this will not relent. He will find someone else to handle the situation, someone who will exact revenge on Sam, maybe even his wife and child. That's probably why he's come to me now. He wants to generate publicity.*

David's muscles tightened, but he kept his composure and listened as Wallace continued. "I looked for them all over, but they ain't anywhere to be found. Just after you left yesterday, a boy showed up at my store and handed me this."

He pulled out a wad of wrinkled greenbacks. It looked to be more than enough to ransom a pair of slave children. Just to be certain, David asked if it was.

"It's more than what I paid for them," he said. "Which is how I know it was *him*."

That doesn't necessarily prove anything. "You say a boy delivered the money?"

Wallace nodded.

"What did he look like?"

As the merchant went on to describe the mysterious courier, David discovered Wallace really meant a Negro *man* had come to his shop. He asked bluntly for clarification's sake and to make a point of his own. "You mean a *gentleman* came into your shop and gave you the money?"

Wallace huffed. "He weren't no *gentleman*. Might have been a house servant. Educated, probably. Those abolitionists do that, you know."

The description he gave was as vague as his facts surrounding the delivery. "Did this person say the money was in payment for the children?" David asked.

"No. He just laid it on the counter."

"Then you didn't actually speak to him?"

"I was busy with a customer."

Your mistake, David thought. "What time did you say the slave children went missing?"

"Yesterday between three and four o'clock. They made a delivery on Charles Street, but they never made it to the one on Hanover. That's when he must have snatched them."

David's memory sparked. "Between three and four o'clock?"

"Yes."

"You're certain of that?"

"Yes."

"I was interviewing you at that time," David reminded him. "The man you're accusing was with us. So was his wife. They couldn't have snatched those boys. They were standing in your store."

Stunned, Wallace only blinked.

All this time Elizabeth had been busy—head down, pencil in hand, looking completely absorbed in the task before her. But David knew she had been listening in on every word. Both of them had felt the need to visit the merchant yesterday. David didn't know where Elijah and Elisha were at that moment, but he recognized the hand of Providence when he saw it. His and Elizabeth's presence at the store provided their friends an alibi. The news article and sketch were evidence on their behalf.

Wallace realized it, as well, and was now completely frustrated. "What am I to do?" he asked.

"I don't know that there is much you *can* do," David said. "You don't have any idea who actually took them or even if anyone did."

"Are you suggesting they ran off on their own?"

"I'm saying you have no way of knowing what really happened. Look, if it was some abolitionist, you've been paid a fair price—"

"You saying I should leave well enough alone?" The man was fuming.

"I'm saying it's very possible that slavery is about to be outlawed. You have at least been compensated."

But Wallace was demanding further satisfaction, and it was clear he would take it any way he could get it. He pointed his finger at David. "I want you to write about this! I want you to tell everyone what I told you."

"I'll report on the children's disappearance," he promised, "but I can't go accusing a man by name of being involved in it when we don't have any proof he has done anything."

"I see," Wallace quipped, eyes narrowing. "So I was right about you. You are one of those haughty abolitionists."

"Mr. Wallace," David firmly insisted, "I am a journalist. I stick to the facts. I am committed to telling all sides of a story."

"And printing it?"

Over that, of course David had no control. Having never been out of earshot, his editor again stepped forward. "I decide what gets printed, Mr. Wallace, but as Mr. Wainwright has already made perfectly clear, this newspaper is committed to telling all sides of this issue, including which way the people of Maryland vote."

Wallace stood, nearly overturning his chair. "The people of this state better have the sense to keep things as they are! A pox upon us if the abolitionists have their way!" He stormed out of the office, slamming the door behind him.

When he had gone, the staff slowly returned to their desks. Elizabeth looked pale and worried. "Where do you think Elijah and Elisha have gone?" she asked. "Do you think someone actually snatched them?"

"I don't know," David said, "but you can be certain I am going to do my best to find out."

The following day the report of Wallace's missing slaves was printed in the paper along with the results of the vote. 31,593 *for* to 19,524 *against*. Slavery would be outlawed in Maryland, just as soon as a new state constitution could be written and approved.

Chapter Eleven

David's celebration over the proposed new state constitution was tempered by several things. One concern was just what methods would actually be used to free the remaining slaves. Also preying on his mind was the whereabouts of Elijah and Elisha.

He couldn't help but wonder what their former master might now do. Although Wallace could not deny Sam Ward's presence in his store at the time of the boys' disappearance, David still smelled trouble brewing and he felt responsible.

After all, it was he who had spoken to Sam Ward in the first place, and had urged Elijah and Elisha's rescue. Had Sam arranged some plot—deliberately visiting the dry goods store at that time in hopes of keeping himself and his family in the clear—or was it possible he knew nothing at all? David wasn't sure. On Sunday morning before he and Elizabeth left church, he pulled Sam aside.

"I already know," Sam said, even before David could tell him about Wallace's appearance at the paper.

"You do?"

"Wallace told me himself."

"How?" David asked. "Did he pay *you* a visit?"

"No. I went back to see him yesterday. I offered once more to ransom the boys, hoping he'd take my money rather than bank on the state compensating him."

"Did he tell you he had already been *compensated*?"

"He did. He was adamant that it was I who had sent the money."

David couldn't help but wonder that himself. "Did you?" he asked.

"I assure you, I did not. Although I can't say I haven't thought about such a scenario." A hint of a grin showed on the man's face, one David suspected was more than just an admission of an active imagination.

He knows something. He is involved in this in some way after all. When David had made certain no one else was in earshot, he asked Sam point-blank, "Where are they?"

Surprised, the man blinked, but he offered nothing more.

"Don't give me the silent treatment," David said. "I'm asking this strictly *unofficially*. You *know* something. I know you do. Perhaps by way of a friend of a friend?"

"Honestly?" Sam said. "I don't know where they are at this point."

"At this point?"

The grin emerged again but only for a second, then it was gone. "All I'll say is pray. Pray that they reach safety."

"And where do you assume they will be safe?"

Sam didn't answer that. Instead he dangled another piece of information before the hungry reporter. "It broke Julia's heart not to be able to say goodbye, but she rejoices in the fact their future is now much more hopeful."

More hopeful? David wasn't about to let this go. He knew the story would never make it into print, but he had to satisfy his own curiosity. *And Elizabeth will want to know, as well.* "What makes you so certain?"

Sam shook his head, smiled mischievously, and turned to go.

"Wait," David said. "You can't give me any details, fair enough, but may I offer you a word of advice?"

The man made no objection.

"Watch your back. Slavery may be on its way out, but there are still plenty of people who won't take kindly to an abolitionist's intervention, no matter how inconsequential it may be."

"Particularly Wallace?"

"Exactly. I don't think it wise for your paths to cross again. You don't want to go tweaking his nose any further."

"Point taken," Sam said. "And by the way, thank you for coming to the store when you did. Thank you for that article. Please, thank Elizabeth for her sketch, also."

With that, they parted company.

David told Elizabeth about the conversation as they walked home. She was overjoyed but just as inquisitive. "So Sam and Julia *do* know what happened to the boys?"

"Apparently so, at least to some extent, but they won't speak of the particulars."

"Do you think we will ever learn what happened?"

"I'm certainly going to keep my eyes and ears open," he said. He told Elizabeth of the warning he'd given Sam, how he believed Wallace was foolish enough to take revenge on someone even if they weren't directly involved in the boys' escape.

"I have feared the same," she said. She then sighed. "When do you leave for Annapolis?"

"Next week."

The state convention was convening, and Peter wanted him to cover the proceedings firsthand. Elizabeth would be staying here. David knew time away from her would be good for him.

Ever since her revelation that *he* had paved the way for Jeremiah to win her heart, David had found it increasingly difficult to be near her. He did not like, however, the idea of leaving her unprotected in Baltimore. There was always that risk of rebel invasion, and now he had angry slaveholders to worry about, as well.

Elizabeth smiled innocently. "If it will ease your mind concerning Elijah and Elisha, then while you are gone I'll do a little investigating."

The hair on the back of his neck stood up. "Absolutely not! I don't want you doing anything of the sort!"

The look in her eyes told him she was surprised, if not outright wounded by his words. He had never spoken harshly to her before. He hadn't meant to do so now.

"Forgive me," he said immediately. "It's just I don't want you getting hurt. Wallace is a dangerous man. Promise me you'll not go near that dry goods store while I'm gone."

"I promise."

"Thank you." He tried to focus again on their assignments. "Besides, you'll be busy covering the Sanitary Fair."

"Indeed," she said, her enthusiasm returning. "Mr.

Carpenter has already said he wants me to cover the fair each day that it is open."

The event was being held in order to raise funds for the military hospitals and prisons. It was the result of collaboration between the US Sanitary Commission and the US Christian Commission. The former concerned itself chiefly with the welfare of Northern soldiers. The latter, although still under the Union banner, tended to the spiritual and physical needs of prisoners of war.

Because the generated funds would not be spent on guns or ammunition for the US Army, all of Elizabeth's friends were participating. Mrs. Emily Mackay, herself now a Christian Commission delegate, was coming from Washington to participate in the activities, as well.

"You will be attending the opening ceremonies with me, won't you?" Elizabeth asked.

A smile returned to David's face—he was pleased that Elizabeth wished for him to be alongside her. "I wouldn't miss it," he said. "I won't leave for Annapolis until the following morning."

On the day of the fair they made their way over to the Maryland Institute on East Baltimore Street. The great hall was jammed full of fairgoers. Patriotic bunting decorated the balconies. Rows of tables filled with everything from quilts to socks, hats to cigars, which were being sold for soldiers' and prisoners' relief. In addition, there was an art gallery with oil paintings on loan by the local citizens. The fire department had an exhibit and there were vast displays of farm machinery and saddlery, as well.

David and Elizabeth moved about the hall, capturing noteworthy details for the paper. When they had finished, they stopped by the home goods department to visit with her friends. Emily Mackay and Sally Hastings were busy at their booth selling socks. From the looks of things, the ladies would soon have little inventory left. A horde of customers surrounded their table.

When Emily saw Elizabeth, she escaped the crowd and came running to greet her.

"Oh, gracious!" she exclaimed. "Look at you! Don't you look official with your sketchbook and press card? Congratulations!"

Elizabeth smiled and hugged her friend. "It is I who should congratulate you. Your mother told me your news. I declare, you are practically glowing!"

David was so proud of her. The last time Elizabeth had seen Emily she was in tears. Now she was congratulating the soon-to-be mother. He knew full well her heart would always carry a scar, but it was healing.

Emily smiled happily. "Yes. I suspect I shall be quite busy come Christmastime."

David offered his congratulations. "I am certain Dr. Mackay must be quite proud."

"He is indeed." Emily glanced about. "He's around here somewhere trying to convince people what a good cause this fair is, get them to spend even more money than they already have."

Elizabeth and he exchanged glances, knowing the army physician had the commanding personality and military authority to do just that.

"From the looks of things, I'd say Evan has been very successful," Elizabeth said. "And you have, as well."

"Thank you. I had no idea when we organized that clothing and fund-raising drive for the Confederate prisoners last fall that it would eventually lead to such a grand scale as this."

Elizabeth smiled once more. "I suppose not." She looked toward the knitting table. "I see Sally, but where is Julia? Wasn't she supposed to help you?"

"She was, but at the last minute she and Sam had an opportunity to take a holiday in Philadelphia. One of Sam's colleagues offered his home. They went, but not before Julia dropped off a bountiful supply of socks."

Hearing that, David's pulse quickened. A holiday in Philadelphia was not all that odd, but the timing of it seemed suspicious. He couldn't help but think of Wallace's tirade at the paper. *Did Sam think it prudent to leave town for a while?*

Elizabeth didn't seem to think much of it, though. She inquired of Emily's parents, and of Joshua and Abigail Davis. "Did they come with you tonight?"

"Mother and Father are about," Emily said, "but have you not heard?"

"Heard what?"

"Abigail and Joshua left town last week. They decided to go north."

"North?" Elizabeth quickly looked at David.

His shock matched hers. Joshua Davis had only recently told him that he and his wife were perfectly content working for Emily's family for the foreseeable future. *Why would he suddenly leave town?*

"It was quite a surprise to me, as well," Emily said. "When I arrived home, Father told me they had gone."

"Did they say *why* they were going?" David asked, his heart beating faster with each passing moment.

"Father said they wished to strike out on their own.

I can certainly understand that, but I wish they would have waited just a little longer. They knew Evan and I were returning to Baltimore this week."

"Did they say *where* they were going?" Elizabeth asked.

"Father said he didn't know exactly, but they promised to write when they could."

Before David or Elizabeth could ask any other questions, Sally beckoned for Emily's attention. "Oh, excuse me," she said. "I'm needed back at the table. I'll let you know when I hear from them."

Emily then flew off, leaving them to ponder what she had just said. David's mind was racing. He had just profiled Joshua and Abigail in the *Free American*. Had his article stirred up some trouble for the couple, perhaps brought them to the attention of old enemies from their pasts? Were his words enough to make some slaveholder, someone like Wallace, so angry that he threatened the family?

Elizabeth knew David was worried. She could see it in his eyes, hear it in his voice.

"What have I done?"

"We don't know that anything is actually wrong," she said. "It could just be a coincidence. Sam went to school in Philadelphia. He has many friends there. It may be just a holiday."

"But Joshua and Abigail leaving town, as well?"

Elizabeth had to admit that did seem rather suspicious. "There may be another possibility, though."

"What's that?"

She stepped closer, unwilling to let others around

them overhear. "You and I both know Philadelphia is teeming with abolitionist activity. Perhaps Sam and Julia have gone there for that purpose. It could have something to do with Elijah and Elisha. Abigail and Joshua could even be involved in some way."

David exhaled slowly. "If they are responsible for taking those boys, do you know what will happen to them if they are caught?"

Of course she knew, and the thought of such made her shiver. Whether they were met by bounty hunters or officers of the law, the consequences could be just as tragic.

"I shouldn't have conducted those interviews," he said. "I don't know what I was thinking."

"You've done nothing more than your duty as a journalist," she insisted. "I read those articles, as well, you know. You wrote the truth, and you did so skillfully, not in a way that would incite anger or cause harm."

A look of turmoil was on his face. Elizabeth suddenly had the desire to throw her arms around him and embrace him, to speak words of comfort as he had so often done for her. She held back, though, not trusting her own motives. She'd been thinking of him more than she should lately, in ways that she shouldn't.

She kept her place but did not shy away from trying to encourage him.

"David, it is important that you keep doing as you are. The people of Maryland need to hear the truth, and *you* are the one to tell them. You must go to Annapolis tomorrow and write about what is happening, what will happen if slaves are not immediately emancipated."

He said nothing, but it was obvious by the look on his face now that he appreciated her words.

* * *

David left for Annapolis the following morning. Heading to work, Elizabeth promptly delivered her sketches of the Sanitary Fair to Mr. Carpenter.

"Your diagram of the exhibits will be printed in the next edition," he said. "I'd like you to return today and do a few more sketches."

More was good—more sketches meant more payment. "Is there anything in particular you want featured?"

"Whatever catches your eye. Whatever seems to catch the visitors' eyes. Mr. Ross will be stopping by to cover a few specific stories later on today, but your work and his don't have to coincide. We want to cover as much of the fair as possible."

"I understand." She was pleased she wouldn't have to actually accompany Mr. Ross about the fair. He'd probably spend most of his time at the cigar table, anyway.

"In addition to your sketches," Mr. Carpenter then said, "I want you to gather the daily attendance figures and sales tallies when they are announced."

"Very well." Thankfully, he only wanted numbers, not words in paragraph form. Elizabeth was not a writer. That was David's talent.

He had barely been gone a day, and yet already she missed him.

Elizabeth wished she could have gone to the state convention, as well, but due to propriety's sake, as well as the paper's limited funds, Mr. Carpenter could send only one staff member to the capital.

Her editor had repeatedly grumbled about that. "The *Sun* will have their artists in Annapolis, but the *Free American* won't."

He was grumbling about it now. "Pity we can't have you cover the statehouse, as well as the fair."

An idea suddenly crossed her mind. Elizabeth took a chance and offered a suggestion.

"If I may, Mr. Carpenter, I traveled to the statehouse several times before the war. I am quite familiar with the appearance of the delegates' chambers."

Before the war, during the banking crisis, her father had been asked to testify in the area of his financial expertise concerning what the coming years could mean for Maryland's economy. Elizabeth had been given the privilege of viewing the proceedings from the ladies' balcony. The statehouse was beautiful, top to bottom, from its dome to the marble floor. She vividly remembered how the sunlight poured in the wide, elongated windows and spilled on to the very spot where George Washington himself had once addressed state delegates during his own time.

"I'm certain I could re-create the architecture from memory," she said. "And with delegate Van der Geld having been elected majority leader, he will surely be doing a good bit of speaking. He is the father of a friend of mine—"

"Where are you taking me, Miss Martin?" her editor said impatiently, scarcely looking up.

She hurried to the point. "Perhaps I could provide you with sketches after all. I am quite familiar with Mr. Van der Geld's face and would have little trouble replicating it. I could review Mr. Wainwright's articles as he wires them in each day and then create an appropriate scene."

Mr. Carpenter liked the idea, although you would never know it by that furrowed forehead and still irritated tone of his voice. "Yes, yes," he said. "Mr. Keedy is responsible for gathering the wires. Have him give them to you first."

"Thank you. I will do so."

With a smile, she hurried off. There was something special about being the first to read David's words. She eagerly awaited his wire.

David shifted uncomfortably in his Windsor chair. He and the rest of his fellow journalists were seated at the back of the chamber, beneath the ladies' balcony, watching the proceedings. Already a week had passed, and the delegates seemed more interested in voting their pay and arguing the positions that had brought about war in the first place than actually writing the provision that would forever end slavery in Maryland.

The minority members, led by delegate Harold Nash, repeatedly professed loyalty to the Union but always in the context of states' rights. They did not like martial law or the hardships it imposed on the people of Maryland. The majority, rallied by Theodore Van der Geld, insisted national allegiance should supersede state allegiance. Of the ninety-six delegates assembled, roughly two-thirds of them pledged unconditional loyalty to President Lincoln, insisting he had the authority to use whatever means necessary for the good of the nation. Most of them had won their campaigns on the promise of abolition. David hoped they would indeed make good on that promise soon.

When they finally did get around to addressing the subject, some members argued slave owners should be compensated and that Washington should foot the bill. David took note of an interesting argument from Mr. Brown of Queen Anne's County. He thought, rather, the state should give something to the *slaves*. David quoted him as saying that otherwise they would be helpless "paupers of emancipation."

"That is preposterous!" said Theodore Van der Geld, and he insisted the counties rather than the state should and could care for the local poor.

As expected, the idea of apprenticeship was proposed. "Free the adult slaves, but keep the children until they came of age," one delegate offered. "Teach them a trade, to read and to write…"

While instituting literacy had merit, David couldn't help but think of little Elijah and Elisha. He seriously doubted a man like Wallace would have done anything to prepare those boys to take their place in the world.

What of all the other children still in bondage? Will they have their freedom denied, their backs continually burdened until they come of age?

The Unconditionals demanded the new state constitution free all slaves immediately and require an oath of loyalty be administered to every man wishing to vote. Anyone who had expressed Southern sympathy at any time, even if they had now relented, should lose their rights of citizenship.

David thought immediately of the man at the polls who had insisted the slavery vote was simply a way for the Unconditionals to rewrite the constitution so as to control the outcome of future elections. *How many people will vote against the new constitution if measures such as this are included?* His heart sank. *At this rate, the slaves will remain in bondage for quite some time.*

Each day he completed his articles, then went to the telegraph office and wired them to Peter. Afterward he sought supper at one of the local establishments. It was then that he felt most lonely. He missed Elizabeth. He wondered what she would say of the convention proceedings if she were here beside him.

David had written her family twice but had addressed the letters to all of them together. He knew it would be unwise to write Elizabeth exclusively. He would be tempted to say things he shouldn't.

He picked at the crabs on the table in front of him, but he wasn't all that hungry. A group of fellow reporters was gathered at a table across the way, puffing steadily on their cigars and discussing the day's events.

"Hey, Wainwright," one of them called, "when are you going to give up writing for that two-bit press and go to work for a real news organization? One that would put a few more coins in your pocket? You know nobody is reading what you write, anyway."

A round of raucous laughter followed. David simply smiled at them and nodded as if their gibes had no effect, but they did. His spirit sank a little lower in his chest. *Am I really accomplishing anything here?*

Elizabeth's words came back to him. *"The people of Maryland need to hear the truth, and you are the one to tell them."*

While he appreciated her confidence in him, he knew for a fact it was undeserved. With a country at war and a legislature much the same, he wondered what good he, one idealistic yet seriously flawed reporter, could actually do.

David wired in every afternoon, but according to his reports, the work in Annapolis was progressing very slowly. Elizabeth was growing restless both because of that and because there was still no word on Elijah and Elisha. She decided to see what she could find out for herself. She had assured David that she would stay away from the dry goods store, but that didn't mean she couldn't still do a bit of investigating.

Elizabeth paid a call to Julia's parents late one afternoon. However, Dr. and Mrs. Stanton were not home, so Elizabeth decided to visit Sally Hastings instead. She was Julia's closest friend. Perhaps she knew something.

"Yes, I have heard from them," Sally said. "Julia wrote to tell me that Sam has taken a temporary teaching post at the seminary there, an exchange of sorts. A Philadelphia man has come to teach in his place here in Baltimore."

"Did Julia say when they would return?"

"Not until late autumn."

So long? That didn't sit right, and Elizabeth was now inclined to think as David did, that the Ward family had left town because of some sort of trouble. "Sally, does this teaching post have anything to do with the dry goods merchant or little Elijah and Elisha?"

Sally nodded. Her expression was grave. "I believe it does."

"How so?"

"Well, a few days after the boys disappeared, Mr. Wallace came to church."

"Church?" Elizabeth blinked. He certainly hadn't struck her as a churchgoing man.

"Yes. You see, Sam and Julia were serving at the bread table. Mr. Wallace came up to them, once more accusing Sam of interfering with the boys. Sam insisted he had nothing to do with their disappearance, but the man wouldn't believe him."

"What happened then? Did he threaten Sam?"

"Worse. He threatened Julia and Rachael."

Elizabeth gasped. "In what way?"

"He told Sam he might want to keep an eye on his wife and daughter. That someone might carry them off someday."

Elizabeth's blood chilled. *Someone as vicious as the bounty hunter I met as a child, no doubt. Some men will do any despicable thing if you pay them enough.* "Did you hear this personally or did Julia tell you?"

"I was standing not five feet from the bread table when it happened. I've never seen Sam look more frightened."

I can imagine. "No wonder they left town."

"Yes. They thought it prudent to do so until things calmed down. I only hope and pray they do."

Elizabeth then asked her about Joshua and Abigail.

"I'm sorry," Sally said. "I wish I could help you, but I am just as puzzled by their departure as you. I do hope Emily hears from them soon."

"Indeed."

The conversation then turned to their friend. Sally smiled. "Emily did such a wonderful job with organizing the Sanitary Fair. The proceeds gathered from the sales far exceeded anyone's expectations. The funds will be a great help to the wounded soldiers and prisoners."

Elizabeth knew it was a cause close to Sally's heart. Julia's brother, Edward, was one of those prisoners, and although he had never encouraged any romance before the war, Sally only ever had eyes for him.

How patiently she waits, Elizabeth thought. *What kind of love that must be.* She wondered then what it would feel like to be loved like that. She did not doubt Jeremiah's sincerity, but their romance had barely had time to blossom, let alone stand the test of time. They had courted for only three weeks before he proposed. They had been engaged a bare two months before his death.

Elizabeth pushed the thought aside as Sally asked if she would care to stay for tea.

"Oh, I wish I could, but I would like to visit Emily's parents today, as well, see if they know any more of Joshua and Abigail."

Her friend smiled once more. "I'd say you've taken to your work as well as Emily has to hers."

Elizabeth couldn't help but feel a twinge of pride. "I was rather terrified by it all at first, but thankfully, David was there to help me."

Sally's smile widened. "I'm happy for you. When I hear again from Julia, I will let you know."

"Thank you. I would appreciate that."

Elizabeth went then to see Mr. and Mrs. Davis. The couple immediately welcomed her inside. Emily's mother hugged her and insisted she join *them* for tea in the parlor. As Elizabeth took her seat, Mr. Davis inquired as to how things were faring at the paper.

"Oh, well, sir, thank you."

"And how is young Mr. Wainwright?" Mr. Davis asked. "I've been reading his articles on the convention. Good grasp he has of the situation."

Elizabeth smiled. Coming from an attorney who specialized in constitutional law, he was giving David quite the compliment. She would be sure to write and tell him at first opportunity. Perhaps it would encourage him. She could tell by his letters that he was disheartened.

Mr. Davis continued, "If the Unconditionals insist on limiting voters' rights, they're going to lose support for freeing the slaves. I was speaking to my colleague Reverdy Johnson just yesterday, and even he said those men were playing with fire."

And it's the slaves who will suffer the burn, Elizabeth thought, for if a staunch pro-Union lawyer like Reverdy Johnson thought the proposals excessive, surely the more moderate citizens would, as well.

"Oh, enough of that, William," Mrs. Davis gently chided. "Elizabeth didn't come here to discuss the slave vote."

"Actually, ma'am, I did."

"You did?" Her eyes widened. Mr. Davis only chuckled, surely thinking Elizabeth was a woman of the world much like his daughter Emily.

"Well, in a manner of speaking, that is," Elizabeth said. "I was wondering, have you heard from Joshua and Abigail?"

Husband and wife exchanged glances. She recognized immediately there was information to be had. Excited as she was by that, Elizabeth tried not to let it show. She knew she must be patient. David had once told her pressing a subject rarely worked and usually failed.

She quietly sipped her tea.

"Are we speaking off record?" Mr. Davis asked.

"Yes. Most definitely. I am simply concerned, as is Mr. Wainwright."

"You needn't be concerned about the article and sketch if that's what this is about."

"I needn't be?"

Mr. Davis shook his head. "No. In fact, your work was most beneficial."

Beneficial? "If I may ask, sir, how so?"

He smiled, then simply said, "Perhaps you should speak with Mr. Lodge."

Elizabeth blinked. "The former bounty hunter?"

"Yes." He left it at that, asking her about other assignments on which she was working.

"Since the fair is over, I am mostly covering the constitutional convention, as best I can from a distance." Elizabeth was unable to resist returning to the former subject. "If I may, sir, how do you suppose Mr. Lodge could be of help?"

He smiled once more. "Again, my dear, I think it best that you and Mr. Wainwright speak to *him*. I believe you will find the discussion quite interesting, the time well spent."

Indeed? Elizabeth forced herself to take another sip of her tea. She was grateful for what Mr. Davis *had* shared but was still a bit frustrated. She wondered if this was how David felt when he was seeking information and it was not quite forthcoming.

"Very well, sir," she said to Mr. Davis. "We will do so. Thank you for recommending him. "

"It is my pleasure, dear."

And with that, Elizabeth took leave, eager to learn just what Jack Lodge had to say.

Chapter Twelve

April stretched into May. The dismantling of slavery was nearly overshadowed by the question of voters' rights as the legislators pressed for measures intended to keep Maryland secure. The fighting in Virginia had resumed, and Lee and Grant were hacking their way through the wilderness at a devastating cost. In a month of campaigning, the South had lost thirty thousand men, the North, fifty thousand.

Each morning the state delegates took time to remember the fallen. Every evening as David walked to the telegraph office to wire in his articles, he noticed an increasing number of black armbands and widows' veils.

May God have mercy on this land.

Elizabeth and her family were always on his mind. If her brother was still alive, he was most certainly in the thick of things. General Ewell, George's corps commander, had been turned back at Spotsylvania courthouse. David had written the Martin family faithfully during the federal advance, offering his prayers for George and his hopes that in spite of the present difficult situation, the ladies were in good health.

They each answered his letters promptly. Jane always expressed thanks for his petitions for her son and promised prayers of her own for David. Trudy told of increased vigils at church. Elizabeth wrote that she was discouraged by the length of the casualty lists and the lack of expediency on the part of the Maryland legislature for the slaves.

> This fighting weighs heavily upon my heart two-fold, for I know that more soldiers on both sides will fall, and because of that, there will be an increased concentration on the war, not on securing freedom for the slaves.

David then learned she was creating accompanying sketches to his statehouse articles.

> Mr. Carpenter is quite pleased with the results and says we make a wonderful team. But then, we already knew that. Didn't we?

His heart warmed at that comment, even though he knew their present collaboration was providing little positive news. Still, David continued with his work. Every time he sent a wire, he thought of how Elizabeth was the first to read his words.

That made him smile.

The following week the Unconditional delegates succeeded in defeating the opposition's attempts to include any form of apprenticeship or compensation to the slave owners in the new constitution. David rejoiced in that until it became clear they were determined to include a voter's oath of allegiance in the document, as well.

As the death toll for Union soldiers mounted, tempers flared. Some delegates demanded Southern sympathizers be banished from the state entirely.

There's hardly a man in Maryland who doesn't know of someone with at least some bit of sympathy toward the South. Who will possibly vote to free the slaves if it means sending friends and relatives into exile? If measures like this are included in the new constitution, the vote for emancipation is sure to fail.

David trudged back to his hotel room that night, even more discouraged than usual. Thankfully, a letter from Elizabeth was waiting for him. The sight of her hand-writing alone lifted his spirit. He read hungrily of a visit with Mr. and Mrs. Davis and then an attempted one with Jack Lodge.

Do not worry. Your article did not give our friends any trouble. Mr. Davis said that the work had actually been a help. When I asked him what he meant by that, he just smiled and said that we should speak to Mr. Lodge. He wouldn't tell me why. I am eager to find out just what the man knows, as I am certain you are, as well.

David chuckled to himself. *She's not only an artist. She has the makings of an investigative reporter.* Elizabeth continued:

I tried to pay the man a call, but he was unavailable. However, listen to this! His housekeeper told me he is in Annapolis! He is hoping to speak with some of the delegates before they break for summer recess. Oh, David, is this not the guiding of

Providence? I've no doubt you'll be able to find him and discover the truth.

His blood was pulsing. *Indeed I will*, he thought. After a month of discouragement, he was in need of good news.

Elizabeth then closed the letter by saying she was praying for him.

Let us know when you are due to return. Mother says she will have supper waiting. Trudy and I will meet you at the train station. I have missed you so.

That simple sentence alone was life to his bones. The state legislature would begin summer recess in two weeks. Surely he could locate Lodge before then. David quickly found pen and paper. He wrote to thank Elizabeth personally for the news and tell her when she could expect his arrival.

In the days that followed he searched for Jack Lodge on the statehouse grounds, canvassed the local inns and taverns. Finally late one afternoon, David located him on a harborside bench. The formidable, scar-faced former bounty hunter was feeding stale bread to the gulls. He recognized David at once.

"Mr. Wainwright," he said, smiling and immediately extending his hand. "Good to see you again. Are you in town covering the convention?"

"I am, and I've been informed that you are here on similar business, as well."

He offered David a place on the bench and tossed the last crumbs to the circling gulls. "Yes. I came to speak with any delegate who will listen to me. I want to tell them what I have seen over the years." He paused. "I want to tell them what I have done. The legislature needs to understand what the slaves have suffered all these years."

"I want to hear of your efforts," David said. "I believe many readers would, also."

"I'd appreciate that. Perhaps you could come with me when I meet with the delegates."

"I'd like that. Have you been granted any appointments?"

"I've managed to gain the interest of a few delegates, but I have been told I must wait until after the summer recess to speak with them. Will you be returning to Annapolis when the men reconvene?"

"I will." At least Peter had said that was the plan.

"Good."

"Mr. Lodge, there is something I'd like to ask you."

"Oh?"

David told him of Elizabeth's attempt to visit and what William Davis had said. Lodge stroked his beard but said nothing.

"I assure you," David said, "my interest in the matter, as well as Miss Martin's, is strictly personal and entirely off the record. We are simply concerned. Sam and Julia Ward are friends of ours. Abigail Davis is, as well."

"I believe you," Lodge said. He then proceeded to tell him what Elizabeth had discovered already, how Wallace had threatened Sam and his family. "That young man was telling the truth when he insisted he wasn't involved. He didn't take those boys. The only thing he is guilty of is telling you to interview me."

David's pulse quickened. "What do you mean by that?"

"You and Miss Martin are at the center of all this, you know." And then Jack Lodge spelled out the story in its entirety.

David was to arrive Friday evening on the six o'clock train. Excitement reigned in the Martin home. Elizabeth's income had fattened the family purse, and her mother intended on making David's homecoming meal a grand one. She went to the market and purchased plenty of fresh fruit and coffee. Trudy pressed her best dress, a lovely silk gown she'd not worn since before the start of the war, then even went so far as to sew some newly crocheted lace on the sleeves.

All her primping and preening made Elizabeth think of her own clothing. Although she no longer wore black, she was growing tired of gray. Going to the wardrobe, Elizabeth pulled out a beautiful hunter green gown that had once been her favorite. Delicate lace and beading adorned the bodice. She was standing in front of the looking glass holding the dress to her chin when Trudy walked in.

"Oh, Beth! Are you going to wear that one?"

Elizabeth immediately laid it aside. "No. I was just looking at it."

Trudy took it from the bed and once more held it to Elizabeth's chin. "You should, you know. It suits you. It sets off the color of your eyes."

Elizabeth did so love the gown, but it hardly seemed appropriate. "I can't. It's far too frivolous, too celebratory."

Trudy lowered the dress. "But haven't we much to celebrate? The impending end of slavery? David's return?"

Indeed. The thought of his arrival brought a flutter to

her chest, until a heavy dose of guilt quashed the sensation. *It is only natural that I be eager for his return*, she told herself. *I've missed working with him.* But, business aside, Elizabeth had to admit she had also missed those clear blue eyes, that Boston accent and bashful grin.

Her guilt grew. *It isn't David I'm thinking of...it's Jeremiah, surely.*

Trudy was still busy fingering the gown. "You know, we could remove the fancy trimmings, make it appropriate for your stage of mourning."

My stage of mourning—yes...

"It would be no trouble."

Elizabeth stared at the gown. It *was* such a beautiful shade of green. What would be the harm in wearing it, just for one night? *It isn't as though I'm wearing the dress so David will take notice of me*, she told herself. *That would be silly. He would never take notice of me like that, anyway.* "Have you any black ribbon?"

"I do."

"Perhaps we could put that in place of the lace and beading."

"Capital idea!" Trudy said, borrowing one of David's expressions. "I'll fetch the sewing basket." And she ran off to do just that.

The following evening the two sisters waited eagerly at the Camden Street station. They stood on the crowded platform, beneath the clock, waiting for the first sign of the Annapolis train.

Wheels chugging, steam puffing, it finally came into view. A parade of women in feathered bonnets, businessmen and federal soldiers soon stepped off the train. Elizabeth's heart skipped a beat when at last David appeared. He looked quite fashionable in his summer straw hat and linen sack coat.

He's home, she thought.

Trudy immediately raced to embrace him. David hugged her and gave her a brotherly peck on the cheek. Watching, Elizabeth longed for him to greet her the same way. Instead of a kiss on the cheek, however, she wondered what it would be like to have his lips meet hers.

She gasped. *What is wrong with me? Why am I thinking such things?* Immediately her hand went to her neck in search of her brooch. Elizabeth remembered all too late she had chosen not to wear it today.

David drew near. "Have I a story to tell you," he said.

Her heart was pounding, for more reasons than one. She hoped he hadn't read her previous thoughts. She would be mortified. "Did you find Mr. Lodge?" she asked.

"I did indeed."

Those blue eyes of his were full of life, of promise. Elizabeth knew right away that the news was good. Her heart leapt as David embraced her and whispered in her ear.

"They are in Canada—all four of them. They are safe and have become a family."

Was it true? "You mean, Joshua and—"

"Shh," he warned, squeezing her a little more tightly. "Yes."

Blood coursed through her veins. She wanted to shout. She wanted to dance. She wanted to remain exactly where she was. The familiar scents of coffee and peppermint drifted about her. Oh, how she had missed them. "Tell me more…"

"Not here." He released her and stepped back.

Elizabeth felt an overwhelming sense of disappointment but reminded herself they could not discuss such details at the train station. *There's no telling who might be lurking about.*

"Mother has supper waiting," Trudy said, ready to be on her way.

"Yes," Elizabeth agreed. "We should go home straightaway."

He grinned. "Well, in that case…"

Instructing a porter to have his trunk delivered to the Barnum, David called for a carriage. After assisting both sisters inside, he claimed a seat beside her. Elizabeth couldn't help but grin.

Across from them, Trudy was beaming, as well. "Just wait until you see the table," she said to David. "Mother has been in the kitchen all day."

"Is that so?"

Trudy nodded. "Mother said more than likely you've not had a decent meal since you left Baltimore."

He laughed at that. "She's right."

The meal that evening was by far the grandest and liveliest they'd experienced in quite a while. As they enjoyed it, David told the story he had learned from Mr. Lodge. The Martin women hung on every word.

"As you probably know, Joshua and Abigail were aware of Elijah and Elisha because of their friendship with Sam Ward. They were afraid Wallace would try to sell the boys because of the pending changes to the state constitution. When our interview and sketch of Jack Lodge was printed, they sought him out."

Elizabeth's jaw dropped. "They tried to hire him?"

"In a sense," David said. "They asked if he might know of someone whom they *could* hire. They wanted someone to snatch the boys so they could be free. Joshua and his wife planned to lead the children to safety."

Amazing! Elizabeth thought. "I suppose Mr. Lodge knew someone who could accomplish the task."

"Apparently so."

"Who?" Trudy asked.

"I don't know. Lodge would not tell me. He only said it was someone like him. A former bounty hunter who now wanted to do something to benefit those he had once harmed." David smiled. "Lodge laughed and said it was someone who could now put the skills of planning, sneaking and snatching to a good cause."

"Then it was this unnamed man who absconded with the children?" Mrs. Martin asked.

David nodded. "While they were in the middle of one of their deliveries."

The very moment you and I were in the dry goods store, Elizabeth thought. "Did Mr. Lodge know anything about the money that was delivered to Mr. Wallace? Did he know who the person was?"

"It was Joshua Davis."

"What?"

"He told Lodge he wanted to pay the man what was due him under the present law."

"So Joshua Davis himself just walked into the store and laid the money on the counter?"

Again David nodded. "Wallace assumed he was just an ignorant slave settling a bill for a master. He was settling a bill all right, but he was the master."

"What happened next?" Trudy asked.

"He didn't give me all of the details, but what I do know is those little boys were delivered on a certain night, at a certain secluded spot outside the city. Joshua and his wife were waiting for them when they arrived. They explained what they had done and offered to take the children and raise them as their own if Elijah and Elisha so wished."

"What did the children think of that?" Mrs. Martin asked.

"They were skeptical at first, but when the couple explained they knew Sam Ward and his wife, they became far more trusting."

"How did Abigail, Joshua and the boys get to Canada?" Elizabeth asked. "Did Mr. Lodge escort them?"

"No. He took them as far as Philadelphia where an association of unnamed abolitionists then assisted them in their journey north."

"Do Sam and Julia know of this?" Elizabeth asked.

"Yes, they do now—though they had no idea what was happening at the time. Jack Lodge told them everything. They were in Philadelphia when word arrived that the four had safely crossed the border."

Elizabeth sighed with contentment as she held David's gaze. *What a happy ending!* She knew he was thinking the same. She could feel his joy all the way across the table.

Trudy and their mother offered their own satisfied sighs and smiles. After a few moments they then moved to put away the dishes. David stood to assist.

"Oh, no, son," Elizabeth's mother said. "Trudy will help. Why don't you and Beth retire to the parlor? I'm certain you have much more to discuss."

He smiled pleasantly. "Indeed. Thank you."

When David offered his arm, Elizabeth slid her hand into the crook of his elbow. Comfortable and secure, she followed him to the parlor.

"It is so good to have you home," she said.

"It is good to be home."

"Did you like Annapolis?"

"On the whole it was a pleasant town," he said, "but I missed Baltimore."

"I'm glad you did."

He chuckled warmly.

They settled on the settee. Elizabeth adjusted her hoop and smoothed out her skirt.

"Your dress is lovely," he said. "That fabric suits you."

She blushed. Elizabeth didn't know exactly how to respond to his compliment, but she loved the fact that he had paid her one. "Trudy convinced me it was time to put aside the gray," she said, "that there was much to celebrate."

"I believe she was right."

"I can't help but marvel over it all," she said. "To think what has come about! Joshua and Abigail had no children of their own. Now they are the proud parents of two young sons."

"Indeed. One wonders what they will grow up to become."

"You played a large role in all of this, you know."

Now he was the one turning red. He rubbed his whiskers. Elizabeth felt such a closeness to him tonight, a sensation she couldn't fully describe. It was simply a pleasure to be near him.

"I really didn't do anything," he said.

"Yes, you did. It was your article on the possibility of apprenticeship which made Joshua and Abigail take notice in the first place."

"It was your sketch that sent them to Jack Lodge."

When he grinned at her, she recognized at last what she was feeling, and it shook her to the core.

I am falling in love with him.

David talked on about his time at the statehouse, but in actuality Elizabeth heard very little of what he was saying. Her thoughts were in a panic. Her heart was racing.

How could this have happened? How is it even possible?

She prayed David hadn't realized. She couldn't bear the thought of him addressing the issue. She could just imagine what he would say.

"Elizabeth, you were to be married to my brother..."

Yes, she reminded herself. *I was in love with Jeremiah. I still am! I am only assigning David's face to his memory. That's all. My respect and admiration for him, along with his resemblance to Jeremiah, are simply playing tricks on my mind.*

She told herself that repeatedly over the next few weeks, but it was all to no avail. History was repeating itself. A man was filling her heart, and once again Elizabeth found herself pleading for his life.

The headlines of the *Free American* and every other newspaper in the city spelled out the danger. The Confederate army was marching on Baltimore.

Chapter Thirteen

Alarm bells rang out, and the entire city held its breath as Southern forces crossed the Potomac. Much of Maryland's defenses had been stripped to replace the huge losses General Grant was sustaining in Virginia. Only a few units remained in Baltimore, leaving the city perilously vulnerable.

In hopes of counteracting the rebel assault, commanding officer General Lew Wallace shifted what remained of his small force and met the enemy in a little crossroads called Monocacy Junction. He was outnumbered and outgunned, but David prayed the Union general would somehow win the day. If he didn't, little stood between the rebel army and Elizabeth's family.

She was standing in the corner of the telegraph office, sketching the worried looks on the reporters' faces while they anxiously paced about. David felt the blood drain from his face when news of the battle's outcome finally came. The Union troops had been defeated. The rebel army was advancing.

His colleagues immediately bolted, rushing to get the news into print. Elizabeth hurriedly secured her sketchbook and took hold of his arm. She was trying to look brave, but he could tell by the quiver in her voice she was scared to death.

"What will the city leadership do now?" she asked.

What David had feared, what had compelled him to return to this city in the first place, was actually happening. In spite of that he did his best to keep an objective tone. He needed to be strong for her sake. "More than likely, the leadership will call for volunteers to man the barricades, but try not to worry. What the South really wants is Washington."

She nodded, but she knew as well as he that the rebels had their eyes on Baltimore, also. They raced back to the newsroom. Peter was waiting at his office door.

"Well?" he asked.

"They're advancing."

Immediately their editor issued a string of commands. "Detwiler, go tell Bowman to change type. Scratch the entire front page! Keedy, find Collins and have him prepare for extra copies!" Peter then looked at Elizabeth. "Give me what sketches you have whether they are completely finished or not." To David, he then said, "Get your notes in readable form as quickly as possible."

Elizabeth scurried for her drawings while David flew to get his words into print. Responsibility weighed heavily upon him. In such a time of fear, he knew his words had the power to either calm or incite further hysteria.

God, give me wisdom.

By the time David had finished his article, Peter had sifted through Elizabeth's sketches. After choosing the ones he wanted to feature next, he told them, "I want the two of you to head over to city hall. Find out what the local leadership intends to do."

On the street the crowds had begun to gather. Rumors of the latest wires and dispatches circulated. Desperate for news, people were creating their own. Some confidently proclaimed the city's defense was sure, that the Confederate army would not dare make a move on Baltimore, thus putting so many of its own supporters in jeopardy. David hoped that would indeed be the case.

Surely the South will not risk an attack on Baltimore. They would not endanger their wives, sweethearts, their own children. The Army of the Potomac isn't about to let go of the waterways, rail lines and industry of this city without a fight. Soldiers would be lost and citizens, both loyal and secession supporting, would die with them. No one could possibly want that.

Elizabeth said not a word but kept a tight grip on his elbow as they snaked their way through the throng. When they arrived at city hall, she claimed a spot in the corner of the room where she could fully observe the proceedings. The chamber was packed. Every member of the press, public official and concerned business owner who could manage his way in had come to find out what measures the city intended to take to keep its citizens safe.

David wrangled his way to the front, ready to take down everything that was said. The mayor of Baltimore stepped to the podium and addressed the group.

"Gentlemen, I regret to inform you that we have just received disturbing word. Rebel cavalry has been sighted in Carroll County."

A collective gasp rose throughout the room, for the county mentioned was only a day's march from the city.

The mayor continued. "They have burned bridges along the Western Maryland Railroad. We do not know exactly how large the force is that is advancing against us because the Westminster telegraph wires were cut before we could receive such information."

David's heart was pounding. *They mean to strike us from the west.* He glanced at Elizabeth. Her eyes were fixed on him. Her face was extremely pale.

"We are working closely with the war department," the mayor insisted, drawing David's attention once more. "Rest assured we will shore up the area defenses. We have already wired Washington requesting additional troops. Orders have been issued locally for the impressment of horses for use by the army, and for the time being, the sale of alcohol is restricted. To maintain proper order, the board of police commissioners will deputize any willing loyal volunteer. There will be no time for uniforms, of course. Badges and ribbons will denote the men's special status."

"What about the rumors surrounding the civilian defense force?" David asked. "Is it true you have called upon all men, slave and free, to defend this city?"

The mayor nodded. "We have called on all loyal men."

"Will you issue arms to the negroes?" Another reporter asked.

The mayor hesitated for a second before answering. "We will issue arms."

A murmur rippled through the crowd. Clearly some did not like the idea of slaves or freedmen carrying guns.

The mayor dismissed the assembly, and the room immediately cleared. David returned to Elizabeth. She had sketched the worried citizens' faces, and those of the leadership who were trying so hard to appear confident and in control. She looked much the same.

"This could all be just a false alarm," he told her. "The

Confederate forces that were sighted may turn out to be just a few cavalrymen."

"But what if it's more than that?" she asked. "What if it is infantry? What if George is on his way here right now?"

David inwardly shuddered. That was a very real possibility. "Try not to think that way," he said. "It won't do any good to speculate. We have to stick to the facts."

He'd said those words for his benefit as well as hers, but he realized they were of little comfort to either of them.

Elizabeth's voice quivered. "D-do you think we might be able to check on Mother and Trudy?"

"Of course. We'll go now."

David had been mulling over ideas of where the ladies might best take refuge until the danger had passed. He didn't want them remaining in Mount Vernon. *If Lee's army gets within striking distance, the local secessionists are likely to take up arms.* And if that happened, then the guns at Fort McHenry, which were pointed directly at Monument Square, would fire such a salvo that there would be nothing left of Elizabeth's neighborhood.

Sketchbook clutched tight, she stayed close to his side. The crowd milling about outside was thicker than it had been previously, and by the looks of things, growing more anxious by the second. David hoped their high levels of emotion would not lead to any rash actions, for the volunteer police had yet to take to the streets, and soldiers were few to be seen.

The closer they got to Mount Vernon the more apprehensive David became. Some homeowners had taken to hanging out the Stars and Stripes, surely an effort to convince the authorities they were indeed loyal to the

Union. Other citizens had decided to flee. Their carts and carriages were piled high with necessities as they sped out of town.

"David, do you think—"

He heard not the rest of Elizabeth's question, for her words were drowned out by the sound of shouting, then gunfire.

Elizabeth crashed hard into a brick wall as David fell against her. He had pushed her into a narrow gap between two buildings, then shielded her body with his own. She could not breathe, but her heart and thoughts were racing. *They've come! They've come! The Confederates have come!* Any second now she expected more shots and screams. Instead, David turned her about.

"Are you all right?" His eyes quickly scoured her looking for any sign of a wound. "Your face..."

He reached out. She followed his fingers with hers. She must have scraped her cheek against the brick. It stung, but it was nothing compared to what could have happened had he not acted so quickly. A chill then ran through her as she thought about what could have happened to *him*.

"It's nothing," she said quickly. "Are you well?"

"I'm fine." David glanced over his shoulder.

The gunfire had stopped, but Elizabeth could hear the sounds of panic still coming from the street. "The army—"

"That's not musket fire."

"What is it, then?"

"Stay here. I'll find out."

There was no telling who or what was out there. It may not be the Confederate army, but there were still many in this city who might do harm to a man who spoke with an obvious Northern accent.

"No, David! Don't go!"

"I have to, Elizabeth. I have to find out what is happening. It's my duty."

"But we are partners," she reminded him. "Your duty is mine. I'm coming with you."

He clearly did not like her plan, but he realized leaving her alone was no more safe than taking her with him. "All right," he said, "come on." Taking her hand, they made their way to the street. People were running in all sorts of directions, some with wild looks in their eyes. David grabbed a paperboy as he sped past. "What happened?" he asked.

The young boy's mouth ran fast. "That man over yonder tried to pull down an American Flag. A Yankee up and shot him!"

"What Yankee? A soldier?"

The boy shook his head. "No. The owner of the house!"

Elizabeth gasped. "Citizens shooting *each other*?"

"Yes, miss. I'm afraid so…"

David let the boy go, and the two of them hurried over to where a group of locals had apprehended the alleged gunman. With his hands now helpless behind his back, two derringers lay at his feet. He was steadily cursing those who had subdued him and the scoundrel who'd dared to touch his flag.

"Do you recognize him?" David asked her.

Elizabeth gave the man a good long look, but she did not know him or any of the other men around him. She shook her head, then turned. Just a few feet from them was another crowd. A pair of legs peeked out. The cobblestones around them were stained with blood.

"David, look!"

He turned, as well, then immediately flew to the wounded man.

Elizabeth's hands were shaking, but the instinct to assist outweighed her fear. She tried to press her way through the crowd. One of the men stopped her. "You don't wanna be seein' this, miss. This ain't no place for a lady."

"Let me go!" she demanded. "I was a nurse—perhaps I can help."

Reluctantly the man released her. Elizabeth wiggled in to where the victim lay. David was already bent over him. Still alive, the man was writhing in pain, yet those about him had done nothing to assist. Kneeling alongside David, Elizabeth realized she recognized the wounded man.

Mr. Wallace!

"Call for a surgeon!" David quickly commanded the crowd.

"Already did," someone said, "but it ain't no use— not with a chest wound like that."

"That might indeed be the case, but we can't just let him die." David quickly drew back Wallace's saturated shirt. The wound was worse than Elizabeth had expected.

Oh, dear Lord, please... "W-what sh-should we do?" she asked.

"Let him alone," one man from the crowd said. "He's a traitor. He deserved what he got."

David ignored him. "We've got to slow down the flow of blood."

He'd already pressed his handkerchief to Wallace's chest, but the blood was soaking through. David's hands were turning crimson. Elizabeth promptly tore the bottom portion of her outer petticoat into strips, then placed her hands alongside David's. Though pale and growing weaker by the moment, Elijah and Elisha's former master recognized both of them.

"You…" he said to David, "you write this. You tell 'um what happens when *Unconditionals* have their way…tell 'um they'll pay…they'll pay…"

"That may be, old man," one of the onlookers said, "but I'd rather this land be laid to waste than give it over to the likes of traitors like you."

Elizabeth chilled at such a statement. David responded in exasperation.

"Enough!" he shouted. "Get back!"

Mr. Wallace's eyes remained fixed on his, a defiant look filling them. "You tell 'um. They'll be sorry. They'll pay…"

"Wallace," David said, "listen to me. You don't have much time. God—"

"You tell 'um…"

"Wallace…"

Elizabeth's heart was pounding. She knew David was trying to speak of eternity, yet the wounded man's only interest was in condemning all those around him.

David continued to try. "Wallace, can you hear me? Listen to me—"

"They'll…pay… They'll all…"

The physician had arrived, and upon his orders, she and David backed away, allowing him room to work. He was too late, however. With a curse and a final threat, the dry goods merchant breathed his last.

"He's the one paying now," the agitated shooter sneered. A few others around him laughed.

In the wake of such callousness, such hatred, Elizabeth was about to give into tears. One glance at David, however, kept her from doing so. That lost look was in his eyes, the same one she had seen the night Jeremiah died. She desperately wanted to comfort him.

Very quietly she took his hands in hers, then wiped them clean with what remained of her makeshift bandages.

"I should have done more," he said.

"You did your best. Even the doctor—"

"No. Before that. I should have done more. I was so focused on Elijah and Elisha that I lost my focus here. Wallace is dead. I did nothing to tell him about Christ. He said those boys were 'cursed by God.' I treated him just the same."

Elizabeth didn't know what to say to that. The sad truth was they could do nothing about Mr. Wallace now.

Elizabeth felt as if they were trapped in a nightmare, one from which they could not escape. The odor of gunpowder, sweat and blood permeated the air. Neither of them said anything for the longest time.

When David finally did speak, his thoughts were of her. "We are closer to the paper than your home. I'll take you there, then I will see to your family."

As scared and as sickened as she was by what had just happened, she did not want to separate, especially now. "Let me come with you."

"No. You'll be safer at the office."

A squad of federal soldiers had arrived. They quickly took the gunman into custody and saw to Wallace's body. David led her back to the office. Mr. Carpenter was standing in the middle of the newsroom when they arrived. He took one look at their soiled, tattered clothing, and his eyes flew open wide.

"What happened?" he asked. "Are you all right? We heard the shots. I sent Russell and Detwiler to investigate."

Elizabeth's stomach rolled at the thought of what she'd just witnessed, but she was determined to keep her composure. *If I give in to tears, David will worry about me, and he doesn't need anything else to trouble him now.*

Dutifully, he helped her to her desk. Then the two men headed into Mr. Carpenter's office and shut the door behind them. Only then did Elizabeth realize how badly she was still trembling.

Her coworkers noticed it, as well. Mr. Keedy brought her a glass of water. Even Mr. Collins showed concern. "Shall we call for a doctor, Miss Martin?"

"No. That's not necessary, but thank you."

The staff let her be as Elizabeth picked up her pencil. With quick lines, she sketched, hoping the task would settle her nerves and help her process all that she and David had just witnessed.

She was so grateful that her closest friends were not in town. Sam and Julia were still in Philadelphia. Julia's parents had gone only this week to visit them. A letter from Emily had come yesterday. Evan had been granted a few days liberty, and they and the Davises had gone to the seashore. Sally Hastings and her father had left for several days' respite from the summer heat on their family farm north of the city. Rebekah was in Annapolis.

But what of my own family? Elizabeth couldn't help but wonder. *What of David? What will become of us all if the Confederate army invades Baltimore?*

Three years ago she would have rejoiced to learn they were advancing upon her city. Now she shuddered. *Those men will not bring liberty to Maryland. They will bring about its destruction.*

"I will never leave thee nor forsake thee..."

Even as the verse passed through her mind, Elizabeth could not shake the feeling of impending doom that was surely about to fall upon them all.

David apologized to Peter for being so befuddled.

"There is no shame, man. You aren't the first former soldier whose hands shake at the sight of blood. Although I daresay, it may have been Miss Martin's close proximity to the danger which troubles you more."

Wallace's murder disturbed him deeply, but just as terrible was the thought that Elizabeth could have met that very same bullet had the gunman's aim gone awry.

If the local citizens insist upon turning on one another, what will happen if the rebel army arrives?

He'd been determined to defend her should it come to such, but he realized now what little he could actually do to protect her. He wanted Elizabeth and her family out of this city, immediately. He told Peter the situation. "Miss Martin was once engaged to my brother. It is my duty to make certain she and her family—her mother and sister—are safe. They have no other living male relatives in town."

Great concern flashed through his editor's eyes. "Go," he said immediately. "See to their safety at once."

"Thank you. If you don't object, then I'll bring the ladies here for now," David said, "until I can determine a better place for them."

"My mother and father have a home on the York

Road, just north of the city. The ladies could lodge there. I was planning on riding out there myself to make certain they have all they need in case travel in and out of the city becomes restricted. I could escort Miss Martin and her family there personally."

David would rather put them on the train for Boston, but he knew the women would never be willing to go that far. So he agreed with Peter's suggestion. The home would at least be away from the most volatile neighborhoods and out of range of Fort McHenry's guns.

The moment he stepped out of the office, Elizabeth caught his eye. She looked as pale and as troubled as she had when he'd first returned to Baltimore. "I'm going to get your family," he promised.

The look she gave him made him dare to believe for just a moment that her feelings were more than concern. "Please, be careful," she whispered.

"I will."

David hurried off to the Martin home. The shutters were closed up tight. When Mrs. Martin peeled back the door, worry lined her face. Trudy was close to her side. "Where is Elizabeth?" they both asked.

"She's at the paper, finishing her sketches."

Her mother shut the door behind him and locked it once again. "People have been roaming the streets for hours," she said. "Some look to be up to no good. Is the situation as dire as it seems?"

"I'm afraid it is."

Trudy noticed the stains on his coat. Her jaw dropped. "Is that blood?"

"Yes." He told them what had happened, giving as little detail as possible. He then told them of Peter's offer. Trudy seemed most eager to accept. Her mother, however, hesitated.

"I don't know. Please, tell your Mr. Carpenter I *am* grateful for his offer, but for now I think perhaps we should remain in our own home."

David suspected he knew the reason why. "Ma'am, respectfully, I do not believe that wise. It's not safe here. If George does come, there will be no joy-filled family reunion."

"The guns, Mama," Trudy added, sounding like a frightened little girl. "Remember what the commander at Fort McHenry once said? If there was any trouble in this city, they would fire upon our neighborhood."

At that, Mrs. Martin was persuaded. She told Trudy to gather her things and Elizabeth's, as well.

The women wasted no time. David was glad, for the streets were growing rowdier by the moment. When they reached the paper, Elizabeth met them and immediately embraced her mother and sister. When Peter came to speak of the arrangements, David pulled Elizabeth into the editor's office. He wanted to tell her himself what was going on.

"I want you to go with Peter. You and your family will be safe at his parents' home."

She shook her head. "No. I want to stay here. You'll need the sketches to—"

"We've already enough sketches to run the rest of the week."

"But I want to stay with you."

His heart stirred, but he would not be swayed by sentiment. David would do what was best for her safety. "Elizabeth, you remember what happened here with the riot."

"Yes."

"Such things could very well happen again—and much worse. We've seen the beginning of it just now. I want you to go with your family."

"Where will you go?" she asked.

"To the civilian defense force. More than likely I shall be working all night."

Her eyes grew wide with fear. "Working how?" she asked. "With a pen or a musket?"

"Excuse me?"

"Will *you* take up arms to participate in the defense of the city?"

She looked literally sick. He felt very close to it, as well. "God forbid it come to that, Elizabeth, but if this city is invaded, I will defend it. I will defend *you*."

Her green eyes flooded with tears. As she broke down completely, David pulled her close and wrapped his arms around her tightly.

"Ah, my girl, don't cry. Pray. Pray for this city—pray for your brother's army, as well."

"It isn't George I'm thinking of," she said. "It's you."

His heart was pounding, his ears thudding. When Elizabeth looked up at him, searching for hope, for comfort, David did not respond with words. Instead he did what he had longed to do from the moment he first met her. He pulled her into a kiss.

Chapter Fourteen

All thoughts of what had just happened to Wallace and the impending attack vanished from David's mind the moment his lips met hers. There was only him. There was only her, and they were together. When they finally parted, Elizabeth was breathless and blushing like a bride.

My bride. David could not hold back any longer. The words he had vowed to keep to himself came spilling out. "Elizabeth, I love you. I have loved you from the moment I first laid eyes upon you."

The flush on her cheeks faded. A look of confusion took its place. "The moment you first laid eyes upon me? You mean...*at the hospital?*"

He realized what he'd just done. He swallowed hard. It was too late to turn back now. "Yes," he admitted. "At the hospital."

"Before Jeremiah?"

"Yes."

The joy she'd shown vanished completely. Stunned wasn't word enough to describe her expression. As he knew she would, she quickly put the details together.

"You told Jeremiah you feared he'd be sent to the battlefield—"

"That was true."

"But that wasn't the whole story, was it?"

For a moment he was tempted to lie, but he knew that would only make things worse. The damage had been done. "No," he said. "You're right. It wasn't the whole story."

"My engagement ring…"

He blinked. *How do you know about that?*

"Our partnership—"

"Elizabeth, you are a talented artist—"

"And you encouraged me on that basis alone?"

He didn't answer. He didn't have to. The truth had revealed itself with his kiss and now in her response.

It was not me she was so eagerly embracing.

For the longest time, Elizabeth just stood there, her eyes swirling with emotion. David wished she'd say something, anything, even if it was to rail at him in anger. Her silence was killing him. He felt lower than a worm.

I have betrayed my brother. I have dishonored her. I had no right to touch her. Forgive me, God. Please, forgive me for everything.

Before David could apologize, the door flew open. In stepped Peter. Realizing he'd just intruded upon a very awkward moment, he froze. Elizabeth immediately flushed crimson and looked down at the floor.

"Rail service will be suspended shortly, Miss Martin," Peter then said in that matter-of-fact tone of his. "We must be on our way."

She raised her eyes, looked at David for one brief second, then turned to Peter. "Y-yes. Of c-course. Thank you." And with that she went to join her family.

David stood for what seemed like an eternity alone in that empty office. What did he do now? What should he do?

Before David could decide anything, Collins stuck his head in the door. Apparently Peter had appointed him as acting editor during his absence.

"There you are," he said. "I've been looking for you. Detwiler and Ross are still out investigating your slain dry goods merchant. Russell is headed out to find out what he can about the approaching rebel cavalry. I want you on the barricades."

Forcing himself to focus on his present assignment, David grabbed his journal and left. The crowd from earlier had either taken shelter indoors or had gone to volunteer their services to the civilian defense force. The streets were deserted, yet at every barricade David came upon men standing shoulder to shoulder, prepared for whatever may come. Commanding officers forbade him from taking down any detail on location or strength of the fortifications, lest the information become known to the enemy. He was, however, able to confirm that guns had indeed been issued to all loyal men, regardless of the color of their skin.

David hoped they would not have to use them.

As evening fell, all travel in and out of the city was suspended. Trains were grouped together in a secure location within the city and guarded by soldiers in hopes of keeping them out of the hands of the rebel army. Alarm bells continued to ring, and all of Baltimore waited anxiously to see which flag would be flying over the city come morning.

With notes enough to spare, David returned to the office. Peter struggled in at the same time as he. His limp was more pronounced. Judging by the strain on his face, he was in pain. "I managed to catch the last train," he said. "It was standing room only."

David followed him to his office. He wanted to ask about Elizabeth and her family, but he didn't have the opportunity. Russell and Detwiler had also returned.

"What did you find out?" Peter asked them as he carefully lowered himself into his chair.

Both men pulled out their journals. Russell read from his first. "The alleged gunman's name is Albert Neely. He's an Unconditional, and he voted in favor of freeing the slaves. Wallace was passing by as Neely was putting up his flag. They exchanged words."

"What kind of words?" Peter asked.

"The fighting kind," said Russell. "According to one witness—Mr. Roger Fox—Wallace said the flag should be removed, that it no longer represented the land the forefathers had intended but had instead become a symbol of tyranny. Neely responded back by saying Wallace was a traitor."

Detwiler then spoke. "Wallace then shouted something else, but none of the witnesses Russ or I interviewed could agree on exactly what. Some said it was about the rebel army. Others claimed it was about slaves. That's when he tried to pull down the flag."

"And that's when Neely shot him?" Peter asked.

Detwiler nodded. "Point-blank. Right in the chest. Just as Wainwright said."

David's stomach turned, for he vividly remembered the damage that had been done.

"The reb army and slaves…" Peter said, thinking out loud.

Again Detwiler nodded. "That's what some of the

witnesses said, but as I mentioned before, no one was exactly certain what he said."

David clearly remembered what Wallace had said to him. *"You tell 'um this is what happens when the Unconditionals and abolitionists have their way..."* He told Peter about it.

"That doesn't surprise me, given all he said when he visited us." Peter then issued the follow-up assignments. "Russell, you and Detwiler dig into Neely's past. Find out who his friends are. Find out his enemies. Wainwright, you do the same with Wallace. I wouldn't be surprised if this is tied to the fact that his slaves were taken."

With that, David went cold. He told himself Wallace had instigated the confrontation by addressing Neely in the first place, by attempting to remove his property, but he again wondered if he wasn't the one ultimately responsible for all of this. *I encouraged action on behalf of Elijah and Elisha. That which followed was the direct result of my articles.* He had known about all this since Annapolis. *And what did I do with the information?*

As soon as Russell and Detwiler left the room, David spilled the entire story to his editor. The only thing he left out were the specific names of Jack Lodge and Joshua and Abigail Davis.

Peter was furious. His face turned beet-red. "You should have told me about this before!"

"You're absolutely right. I should have. I see that now."

"Why didn't you?"

"I wasn't acting in *official* capacity when I was investigating the issue. It was strictly personal."

"It stopped being personal the moment that dry goods merchant showed up here! I warned you not to turn my paper into some two-bit abolitionist press! You are off this story for good. I'm pulling Miss Martin's sketches off it, as well."

David was just as angry with himself as Peter was. Once again Elizabeth suffered from the consequences of *his* actions. He had come to Baltimore wanting to make a difference. This was not what he had intended.

"Don't take this out on her," David said. "It isn't her fault. I pulled her into it. It was my mistake."

Peter crossed his arms and stared at him shrewdly. "If you spent half as much time concerning yourself with your assignments as you do trying to romance *her*, perhaps you wouldn't have made such a mistake."

His editor's rebuke was strong but not undeserved. David offered no response. Evidently Peter did not appreciate that, either.

"Get out of my office," he commanded. "Finish your work on the defense measures. See if you can't turn out an article that will make me consider keeping you on my staff."

Peter Carpenter's parents immediately set out to make their unexpected quests feel welcome in their home. Elizabeth's mother and sister tried to make the best of a dreadful situation by drinking tea and discussing the things people normally do when war is not on their doorstep. Trudy took an immediate interest in Mr. Carpenter Sr.'s life. Evidently he'd been a newspaperman, as well.

"You spent twenty years with the *Baltimore Sun*?" she asked.

"I did," the man said with a proud smile. "I saw the paper's inception. Then I witnessed the birth of a soon-to-be rival when my son started a publication of his own."

"Did younger Mr. Carpenter work with you?" Trudy asked.

"He started as a pressman. His fingers were always black from the ink."

Mrs. Carpenter chuckled. "All of our boys spent time at the paper in some form or another, but it was Peter who really took to it."

"How many children have you?" Elizabeth's mother asked.

"Four," said Mrs. Carpenter. "Peter is the second, having an elder sister who is married and now lives in California. We have two younger sons, but neither Daniel nor Matthew are here at present."

All of this Trudy and her mother seemed to find quite engaging, but Elizabeth could not focus on the conversation. Her mind was back in her editor's office. Every vivid detail ran through her memory. David taking her in his arms. Telling her he loved her, that he had loved her *before* Jeremiah had.

At that discovery Elizabeth hadn't known what she felt more, anger or affection. She still didn't know.

"Beth, Mr. Carpenter asked you a question."

Her mother's voice brought her back to the present. "Forgive me," Elizabeth said. "My thoughts were—" she searched for the appropriate words, knowing full well everyone in the room could see the color in her face "—elsewhere."

"That is understandable, given all you have witnessed today," Mr. Carpenter said. "Our son told us of the shooting. I'm so thankful you and Mr. Wainwright were not harmed."

Elizabeth shuddered as a different set of thoughts now rushed through her mind. *Mr. Wallace has been killed in cold blood! My city is preparing for war, and my brother could be marching into town at this very moment!*

All she could think of then was who might be manning the defense barricade and what might happen to him if volleys were exchanged. *What if today was the last I shall ever see of David?*

Tears were gathering in her eyes, but she forced herself to focus on what Mr. Carpenter senior was now saying.

"I don't know if you have any sketches to finish, but if you do, you may have the use of my study while you are here."

"Thank you, sir." Elizabeth managed. "You are most kind. I do have several assignments to finish."

"Then by all means, let me show you…"

Elizabeth eagerly set aside her teacup. *Perhaps work will clear my mind, calm my heart.*

"Beth has always been a scribbler," she heard Trudy explain to Mrs. Carpenter. "She draws even when she doesn't have an assignment. It's her way of praying."

"And at this present time, there are many people in need of such prayers," the lady said sadly.

Mr. Carpenter showed Elizabeth to the room. A pair of long windows behind the desk filled the space with comforting light. She immediately stepped into it. It might have been early July, but a chill had plagued her since she'd left the paper.

After her host saw her settled comfortably, he left her alone. Elizabeth spread out her pencils and charcoal sticks and looked at her sketches. Various unfinished scenes lay before her, ones she had begun on her journey here. She had captured the worried faces at the train station, the soldiers and civilians at the perimeter barricades.

Only a few of the faces had been completed. The rest were still in outline form. Picking up her pencil, she started with the sketch of the station. Graphite had barely made contact with paper, however, when she noticed one particular citizen she had drawn. A summer straw hat, linen sack coat, chin whiskers… "Oh, dear," she gasped.

She flipped to the sketch of the barricade. She'd drawn David there, as well, only this time in military clothing. *Have I done this before?*

Quickly searching through her published sketches, she was mortified to find that she'd drawn him at the Sanitary Fair and a host of other venues along the way. It wouldn't have been obvious to anyone else, for David was never the featured subject. He was only somewhere in the background.

Still…

All this time she'd told herself any connection, any spark she'd felt with him was only a memory of Jeremiah, but she hadn't sketched her late fiancé all over Baltimore.

It was no secret to her that she and David had become close. But when exactly that had first begun, she could not say. They had worked together for a year at the hospital. He may have been a man of few words, but even then he had still been a comfort to her, an encourager in the dark times.

She remembered one particular day when he had found her crying in the supply closet after the death of an unknown soldier. He could have told her to pull herself together and get back to work, that the remaining wounded needed her. Instead, with a look of sympathy and understanding on his face, he'd handed her his handkerchief.

He was telling me then in his own bashful way, "I'm here if you need me." He has always been in the background. I just never realized it until now.

The time spent with him had made more of an impact on her heart than she wished to admit, and a question now begged to be asked. If David had approached her first, would she have fallen in love with him instead of Jeremiah? Today when he'd kissed her so fervently, she'd not been thinking of his brother. She'd been thinking only of him.

No! No! This cannot be. I will not let my heart go there! I can't!

She reached for her eraser. Wiping away his face from the sketch, she then did her best to replace it with another. The task was impossible. No matter how hard she tried, she could not get the image right. The only face she could clearly envision was his.

Pushing her work aside, she decided she'd finish the sketches in the morning.

That night, Elizabeth climbed into the bed she was sharing with her sister, feeling exhausted, hoping sleep would quickly claim her.

"Were you able to finish your sketches?" Trudy asked.

Elizabeth wrestled with the blankets, wishing her sister would put out the lamp. "No. I'll see to them in the morning."

"I shouldn't wonder you are having trouble, especially considering all that happened today."

There was something in the tone of her voice that told

her that Trudy was not referring to what had happened to Mr. Wallace. Elizabeth turned toward her.

"What happened between you and David?" her sister asked. "I saw the look on your face when you came out of the office this afternoon. Did he kiss you?"

Heat crept up her neck and overspread her face. When Trudy grinned, Elizabeth knew she couldn't deny the kiss even if she'd wanted to. "Yes," she admitted.

At once, her sister sprang to a sitting position, clapping her hands with delight. "So he found his courage at last? Oh! How wonderful!"

"Wonderful?"

"Yes! I have seen the way he looks at you. He has looked at you like that for quite some time. Did he declare himself?"

David had not proposed marriage, but Elizabeth knew he was not the kind of man to proclaim his devotion and then not follow it up with a lifelong commitment. *Surely that was what was coming had I not interrupted him.*

Trembling with emotion, she told her sister everything, even the story behind her engagement ring.

"Oh, Beth!" Trudy sighed as if the entire tale were a romance lifted from the pages of a Jane Austen novel. "I thought it happened when you started working together at the newspaper, but to think he loved you all that time, and he stood beside his brother as the two of you planned your wedding."

"He convinced Jeremiah to postpone it," Elizabeth reminded her, but she knew full well she'd said the words for her own benefit. If she could hold on to anger, perhaps she would not give in to the other emotions she was feeling.

"That is true," Trudy conceded, "but he didn't do it

maliciously. He was concerned for you. What did you say when David told you he was sorry?"

Elizabeth blushed once more, this time in shame as she thought of how she had responded. "I didn't say anything. I was so shocked by it all, and then Mr. Carpenter came walking in…"

"I can certainly understand that. An interruption at that moment would have been disconcerting. How exactly did you part?"

The moment haunted her. *The look on his face…* She knew she had wounded him deeply. "He was standing there looking at me, and I…"

"Yes?"

"I simply…left."

Eyes wide, Trudy blinked. "You *left*? You mean, without telling him one way or the other how you felt?"

"Without a word." *Why didn't I say something? After what he said about failing Mr. Wallace, why didn't I at least tell him that God forgives? That despite our failures, He will remain faithful to us? Had I been the one troubled, he would not have hesitated to comfort me.*

The answer hit her square between the eyes. She couldn't tell him that because she still didn't fully believe it herself. If she did, she wouldn't have walked away from David.

"I don't understand," Trudy said. "Are you saying you *don't* care for him? I'm not sure I believe that. I have seen the way you look at him. It's different than the way you looked at Jeremiah."

Tears clouded Elizabeth's eyes.

"Oh, Beth, I'm sorry. I shouldn't have said that…"

"No. That isn't why I'm upset."

"What is it, then?"

"You're right. It is different."

"Then, you *do* love him?"

Elizabeth shook her head. To do so was to make herself vulnerable, again. "I *cannot* love him. I've already lost one man to this war. I cannot bear the thought of losing another."

David had given Peter his article on the civilian defense measures. Whether it was the result of good writing solely, he wasn't quite sure, but his editor's anger toward him had abated.

"About what we discussed earlier..." Peter said.

"Yes?"

"You made a mistake. Now learn from it. The next time you have a story, whether you think it was obtained *unofficially* or not, you let me in on it. There are enough secrets in this city already. I won't stand for any of them in this newsroom. Understood?"

For one brief second the words *yes, sir* threatened to come out of his mouth. David bit them back. "I understand."

Peter nodded and, after a pause, said, "I'm not one for being *religious* as some folks are, but I do know there is a God, and He is the only one capable of delivering truth, perfectly, all of the time."

David was struck by the comment and waited to see what, if anything, his editor would say next.

"You had a duty to protect your source," Peter said, "and the way I see it, an obligation to protect those children, as well. Did that couple who took them go about things in the best way? I don't know. Could you have done a better job with the information entrusted to you?

Probably, but even if you had, I seriously doubt it would have changed Wallace's outcome."

"What are you saying, exactly?" David asked.

"The point is, we do the best we can with what we have. When we do wrong, we try to make things right, but in the end, we have to trust the outcome to someone greater than ourselves."

David suddenly had the feeling Peter Carpenter wasn't just talking about slaveholders, missing children or newspaper articles. *Elizabeth*... More than anything he wanted to make things right with her, but he had no idea where to even begin.

His editor returned to journalism. "Keedy just brought in some wires from Annapolis. See to them."

David went to his desk.

Throughout the night he and the rest of the staff continued to work. Coffee flowed and, thankfully, so did words. Sometime in the wee hours of the morning, however, David escaped the war. Even Elizabeth slipped from his mind. He heard the sound of bells, a call to worship. He was back home in Boston, racing his brother up the front steps of his father's church, hurrying to claim a pew before the service began.

A hand then fell to his shoulder.

"Wake up!"

Recognizing his editor's commanding voice, David lifted his head from his desk. The story he had been working on last was nowhere to be seen. "Where's my article?" he asked groggily.

"At press."

Then I must have finished it.

Across the way Ross stirred at his own desk. His collar and vest were unbuttoned, his paisley-patterned suspenders showing. David's head was aching, the product of too much coffee and too little sleep. Last thing he remembered it was three in the morning. Now it was dawn.

I still hear church bells. Then he realized it was not the sound of worship. It was a cry of alarm. Fully awake, he bolted upright. "Have the rebels attacked?"

"The city? Not yet," Peter said, "but their cavalry has lit up the countryside. Two trains have been burned at the Magnolia station and several Union officers have been captured. The railroad bridges on the North Central Line have been destroyed and Governor Bradford's house is in flames."

"What?" David cried. The Governor's house was on North Charles Street, only five miles from the city. The other places were all north of the city, as well. "It was almost certain they would hit us from the west."

"I suppose that is what they wanted us to think," Peter said, his face grave. "A source just informed me that rebs have been spotted at a tavern in Towsontown. A federal patrol is on its way up the York Road as we speak to meet them."

The hair on the back of David's neck stood up. "*The York Road?* That will lead them right through—"

"Govanstown."

Heart racing, David snatched his coat. In attempting to protect Elizabeth and her family, he had put them directly in harm's way. "We have to get to them!"

Peter had already started for the door. "I've secured two horses. They are saddled and ready to go."

David wondered how the man had managed that when all the horses had been impressed into military service, but he did not take time to ask. They hurried for the street. In the alley, Keedy was holding a pair of mares.

They weren't much to look at, but that just might be a blessing. *If we meet up with any Union troops, perhaps they won't want them.*

There was even more to worry about than the potential confiscation of their horses. David and Peter would be riding *toward* rebel activity, and although they were both carrying press cards, they could still be accused of spying.

Peter seemed more concerned about meeting the rebel army. Taking a pistol from one of the saddlebags, he handed it to David. "I assume you know how to use one of these."

"I do." As much as he detested the thought of doing so, he secured the weapon in his waistband. He had to get to Elizabeth. He didn't know what he would say to her when he saw her, but he would figure that out later. Right now the safety of her and her family was all that mattered.

He helped Peter into the saddle. "Will you be able to ride the distance?" David asked.

"Ride? Yes. Walk? No. Let's do our best to keep our horses. Shall we?"

David nodded and mounted his horse. Already the sun was rising.

"You are a praying man, aren't you?" Peter asked.

"I am."

"Good, because I believe we are going to need divine intervention to make it to our destination."

Chapter Fifteen

Elizabeth felt she had barely closed her eyes when she heard the sound of her mother's pleading voice. "Girls! Girls! Wake up! The army has come."

"Which army?" she asked, still in a state of sleep.

"Both of them."

That jolted her awake. Trudy rose, as well, and blankets were quickly tossed aside.

"Hurry now," their mother urged. "We must get to safety."

Elizabeth snatched her morning robe and fled downstairs with her family. She could hear the sound of shouts and approaching hoofbeats. It seemed a cavalry battle was about to commence in the Carpenters' front yard. Fears raced through her mind. What was to become of her and her family? Would she ever see David again?

Mr. and Mrs. Carpenter were already in the kitchen. He urged the women toward the larder. "This way, ladies! Quickly!"

They hurried toward the narrow closet packed with jams and cheeses. On the floor was a small opening leading to the root cellar. The sound of gunfire sent them below with great haste. Mr. Carpenter shut the door behind him.

Panic ripped the breath from her lungs. Beside her, barefoot on the damp, dirt floor, Trudy shivered. Their mother gathered them close, and the three huddled together for warmth and security. The thunderous hoofbeats were getting closer.

Mrs. Carpenter lit a lamp while her husband took to nailing planks across the small window at his head. He covered it completely, but not before Elizabeth caught sight of a federal cavalry officer reining back his mount and shouting for his men to turn and engage. Shots met with the clanging of sabers. Terror ran through her.

Oh, Lord, please, don't let George be out there...

She could not bring herself to pray for Union victory, but she did not wish for Confederate glory, either. If the Southern men were spared, they would surely ride on to Baltimore, trampling the defense barricades and shooting those who manned them.

Elizabeth's heart was ripping in two. *Oh, Lord, please... please, save him...*

Finished with his task, Mr. Carpenter now moved to comfort his wife. Suddenly there was the sound of shattering glass. Everyone realized the house was taking fire. Elizabeth continued to pray for her family, for David. She prayed for those soldiers outside, as well, although she could not help but wonder how many of them would litter the ground when the fight was over.

How long they huddled together in the cellar, Elizabeth could not have said, but at some point the snorting horses, piercing commands and smell of black powder faded. A silence, even more eerie than the cry of battle, fell like a shroud.

"Is it over?" Trudy asked hopefully. "Have they all gone?"

Mr. Carpenter rose slowly, and crept toward the covered window. He removed one of the boards and peeked through the slats. "I don't see anyone," he said.

"Are there any wounded?" Elizabeth asked.

"Not that I can see from here."

She breathed a shallow sigh. At least that was something.

"Is it safe, then?" Mrs. Carpenter asked her husband. "May we leave the cellar?"

He shook his head. "I think we should wait a little longer, make certain they are all gone for good."

The wait was agonizing. Just when Mr. Carpenter announced he thought they could leave the cellar, a door slammed open on the floor above. The women all jumped with fright. Eyes wide, Mr. Carpenter laid a finger to his lips, encouraging silence.

The footsteps were fast, frantic. Was it a deserter? A looter? Someone even worse?

To Elizabeth's horror, a second set of footsteps sounded above her. These were heavier, uneven, and they were coming straight toward the larder.

A voice then called, "Mother? Father?"

Mrs. Carpenter brightened immediately. "Peter! Oh, Peter, down here!"

Light spilled through the entryway as the door opened. Heart in her throat, Elizabeth watched her editor, flushed and leaning heavily on his cane, navigate the narrow stairs. Relief washed over her like a wave. David was right behind him.

* * *

They were huddled like chicks on the hard, dirt floor. They were shaken and shivering, but they were blessedly unharmed.

O Lord, thank You. Thank You.

Peter's mother quickly hugged her son. The Martin women rose, as well. Trudy flew to David, immediately embracing him with sisterly affection. Mrs. Martin stepped forward to embrace him, also. Elizabeth, however, held back. He scolded himself for thinking her response might somehow be different.

"I am so pleased to see you are well," Trudy said.

"I am pleased to find you are, too."

He could feel Elizabeth's eyes upon him, studying him, making certain he was not injured in any way. David allowed himself a glance in her direction. She, like the rest of the women, was barefooted and dressed in her morning robe. Her red hair hung long and loose about her shoulders. As beautiful as she was, he forced himself to look away. He could feel the tension between them. The last thing he wanted was for her to think he was staring at her.

"Tell us," her mother said, "what has become of the city? Have there been many battles?"

"Not within the city," he said, but he told them what he and Peter had learned about the railroads and the governor's residence.

Mrs. Martin gasped. "Why would they burn Governor Bradford's home?"

"It was most likely done in retaliation," David said. "The home of the governor of Virginia was burned recently."

"Did you meet up with any soldiers?" Trudy asked.

"We stayed away from the main roads, only meeting one patrol on the edge of town."

"Federal or Confederate?" Peter's father asked.

"They were in blue." David was grateful the troops had not been wearing gray, but for several moments he'd thought he and his editor were in just as much trouble. Peter explained what had happened.

"They stopped us and demanded our horses. When we told them why we needed them and where we were headed, they then accused us of being spies."

"Oh, no!" both Mrs. Carpenter and Mrs. Martin cried.

"But as Providence so willed," Peter said, "one of the officers was none other than Robert Williams."

"Your old schoolmate?" his father asked.

"Indeed. He recognized me. Thanks to that and this fellow's Boston accent, the officer in charge believed our story."

"And so they let you go?" Trudy said, wide-eyed.

"Not only that—" Peter smiled at her "—he let us keep our horses."

Elizabeth finally spoke. "What has happened to the Confederate cavalry?"

"According to my schoolmate, they've turned back."

"For the Potomac?"

"It looks that way."

David again dared glance in her direction. She refused to meet his gaze.

"Let's get you all upstairs," Peter said. "You can get dressed and settled. Then afterward, I'd like to know exactly what went on here."

Upon leaving the cellar, the ladies each went off to don appropriate clothing for the day. The elder Mr. Carpenter told his son and David what details he could of the battle.

"It was cavalry, and from best I could see before I boarded the window, not that many on either side. It may have been only a skirmish, but the clamor still shook the house."

"The front parlor window and one in your study have been broken," David said.

"I am not surprised." Mr. Carpenter wished to see the damage for himself. They first went to the study.

Shards of glass littered the desk. Elizabeth's unfinished sketches lay beneath them. When David first saw them, he feared Elizabeth herself had been sitting here when it had happened. He knew now, thankfully, that had not been the case.

After funneling the glass into a nearby wastebasket, he gave the sketches to Peter. He wanted to deliver them to Elizabeth personally but knew that would be unwise.

Peter's father was leaning out the open window, surveying the damage to his property. "The vegetable garden has been trampled," he said. "The back fence is down, and we'll need to check the well."

David hoped it would be filled with nothing but water. Soldiers had been known to toss the bodies of their enemies down innocent civilians' wells.

"It appears, though, we are very fortunate." The older man turned to his son. "Did you notice any damage to our neighbors' homes?"

"From what we saw riding in, it is about the same as it is here."

Peter's father drew in a breath. "It could have been so much worse. I'm so thankful none of us were hurt. I don't know what I'd do if your mother..."

He left the rest unsaid, but David understood completely. If something had happened to Elizabeth, to her mother or sister, he would never forgive himself.

Soft footfalls and the rustle of petticoats turned his attention to the door. Now wearing a simple cotton work dress, Elizabeth stepped hesitantly into the room. Her focus was directed solely toward Peter.

"I left my sketches here," she said.

He handed them over. "I'd like for you to complete these as soon as possible," he said, "and anything else you have seen today."

"I...didn't see much."

"But you did see *some* of it, and you heard the rest."

She nodded quietly, but David could tell she was not all that enthusiastic about the assignment. He hoped that was only the result of fatigue and shock, not that she was reconsidering her position at the *Free American*.

Lord, please, don't let my foolish behavior keep her from what she loves doing.

Without further word, she left the room. David longed to go after her but knew that would only make things worse. Clearly she did not wish to speak with him. *And if she doesn't, how can we possibly continue working together?*

Peter was thinking of the next edition and the condition of his neighbors. "Let's visit the other houses," he said to David. "We can make certain the families are all right and hear what they have to say. The telegraph office appeared to still be operating when we rode into town. If that is indeed the case, we can wire our reports back to Collins. Then, if you don't mind, I could use your help around here."

"I don't mind."

David was glad Peter hadn't told him to hand deliver the reports. The rebel army may be in retreat, but he wasn't going anywhere until he was certain they had crossed the Potomac and Elizabeth's family was once again settled in their own home.

Then, after that, she can be rid of me.

Elizabeth's mother, sister and Mrs. Carpenter were out trying to salvage what they could from the trampled vegetable garden. Peter, his father and David had gone to assist the other nearby families, while Elizabeth tried to complete her work.

As difficult as the task had been the previous evening, it was even harder today. Her mind was far too distracted, her heart much too heavy. She knew she had no hope of completing the sketches until she talked to David, and she dreaded doing so. The look on his face when he'd found her in the cellar was one of relief and unmistakable love.

Her first thought had been to run to him, to throw herself into his arms. She'd refused, however, to allow herself that privilege. He was safe, this time, but that was no guarantee he would be in the future.

What am I going to say to him? If things had happened under different circumstances...? If only there was no war...?

She could not give him her heart. She knew all too well how painful it was to have it broken.

Leaving the desk, Elizabeth went to the window and sighed. If she looked beyond the broken glass and trodden garden, she could see a different world.

Summer sunshine painted the grass in a shade of warm gold. Birds were once again chirping.

David was making his way across the yard, carrying a coil of rope, headed for the well. Elizabeth watched as he took off his coat, secured the rope to the well and climbed over the edge.

"Mr. Carpenter was going to see to that, but David insisted he be the one to do so."

Elizabeth quickly turned. Her mother was standing behind her. She had not even heard her approach.

"I am not surprised," Elizabeth said. "David is a thoughtful man."

"Indeed he is, and he loves you very much."

Surprise and a host of other emotions rushed through her veins. "Trudy told you?"

Her mother smiled gently. "She didn't have to. You don't think I know when my daughter is struggling with matters of the heart? I have known about this for quite some time."

Elizabeth sighed once more. "Oh, Mother, I don't know what to do."

Jane kissed her forehead. "Trust your heart, Beth. Better still, trust the Lord with it. He made it. He knows how to take care of it."

With that, she quietly walked away, leaving Elizabeth to ponder her words. Turning back to the window, she watched David emerge from the well. If Elizabeth was to do what her heart was telling her now, she would walk out there and tell him she loved him. She would bravely face whatever horrors this war continued to bring.

She watched as he rested for a moment against the stones, fanning himself with his hat. He was hot. He was tired. Undoubtedly he had been up all night working, and yet once again he had come to make certain she was cared for and protected.

The least I can do is take him some water, she thought.

Going to the kitchen, she filled a glass from a bucket Mr. Carpenter had drawn before the skirmish. David was making his way to the door as she stepped outside.

"You looked thirsty," was all she could think to say as she held out the water.

"I am. Thank you."

His fingers brushed hers as she handed him the glass. His very nearness had once made her ache for Jeremiah. Now her breath caught in her throat for a far different reason. Elizabeth did her best to speak.

"Has the well been poisoned?" she asked.

"No. It's fine."

He took a swallow. The awkwardness between them was very apparent. Elizabeth hated the fact that it existed at all.

"Were you able to finish your sketches?" he then asked.

"I…uh, no. Not yet."

There was a long pause. The tension was getting thicker by the moment.

"Elizabeth, I'm going to speak to Peter."

"About what?"

"About leaving the *Free American*."

Her heart slammed into her ribs. "Leaving? You can't do that! Your work is so important."

"*Your* work is important, and I do not wish to hinder it any longer. I don't want to cause you any more discomfort by my presence."

My discomfort? It could be no worse than what I caused you when I was engaged to Jeremiah!

Regret coursed through her. She could not, would not, let him sacrifice his position for her. "No, David. You are needed so. The slave issue has yet to be fully resolved, and after all of this, when the convention reconvenes, goodness knows what provisions the Unconditionals will try to make. You have a job to do."

"So do you," he said. "As much as I wish to go back to the way things were between us, I know we can't. I can't take back what I said."

She didn't want him to take it back. That was one thing of which she was certain. Her hands were shaking. Her heart was pounding. If only she could make him understand. She tried. "David, I…you…Jeremiah—"

He stopped her cold. "Elizabeth, I'm very sorry. I never meant to hurt you or my brother. I know you loved him." He paused, his jaw tightening. "You love him still."

No! No! You don't understand! Inside, she was screaming. *It isn't that I don't love you. I cannot bear the thought of something happening to you!*

But before Elizabeth could get the words out, David turned on his heel and walked away.

It wasn't much of an apology, but it was the best he could do for the moment, under the circumstances. She did not love him. He was a fool to think she ever would. The time they had spent together, the work they had shared was just that—business. He had succeeded in helping her as an artist, and for that she was grateful, but she was not *his girl*. She never would be. Her heart would forever belong to his brother.

David spent the rest of the day avoiding her. He helped Peter and his father fix the fence and board up the broken windows. When the house was secure once more, he pulled his editor aside.

"I need to go back to Boston," he said.

Peter blinked. "Are you worried about trouble with your own family?"

"No. It's not that…" What could he say? He knew he needed to explain, but he didn't want to go spilling details. Elizabeth would still be working at the paper, or so he hoped.

Thankfully, he didn't have to spell it out. The seasoned newspaperman recognized the story. "Miss Martin," Peter said with a knowing look.

"Yes. You will keep her on staff, won't you?"

"Of course. She's invaluable."

Indeed she is. "I'm ever so grateful for the opportunity you gave her, as well as for the one you gave me."

Peter shifted his weight from his weak leg and eyed David shrewdly. "There's no chance I can convince you to stay?"

David shook his head. "I think it's better for everyone if I don't."

His editor nodded slowly. "I'll need you to finish out the week. Can you do that?"

It would be difficult, but he owed the man that much. "Yes."

"Good. I appreciate that. I'll be happy to give you a reference."

David thanked him for that, but at this point finding a new position was the farthest thing from his mind.

When morning came, they escorted the Martin family back to the city. After making certain their home was secure, David and Peter left for the newspaper.

Elizabeth stayed behind, clearly relieved that her house was still standing, and apparently further relieved that for the time being, her editor had granted her permission to complete her sketches from home. David could not blame her for making the request. In a way, he was glad she had. Sitting across from her in the newsroom would be just as unbearable for him as it would be for her.

For the next several days he covered the damage done by the skirmishes, interviewed witnesses who'd encountered the rebel army and did his best not to think of her. His effort on that account was fruitless. Elizabeth was constantly in his thoughts.

On the day before he was scheduled to depart for Boston, Peter called him into his office.

"I've one last assignment for you," he said.

"What's that?"

"I want you to head over to the provost marshal's department. I have it on good authority they're holding a couple of Confederate prisoners. They may turn out to be only deserters, but they could be part of that crowd who tore up the countryside. See what you can find out."

David gathered his journal and hat, then started out. Blue-clad sentries stood guard at the entrance to the provost marshal's headquarters. David showed his press card to one of the grim-faced men and asked to see the officer in charge. He was promptly escorted to a waiting area on the second floor. A lieutenant colonel soon met him.

"I understand you are holding a couple of Confederate prisoners," David said. "May I have a look at them?"

"Not until I'm through with them," the lieutenant colonel said. "Then you can question them all you like."

David blinked in surprise. He hadn't expected to be granted that much access. "You'll let me interview them?"

"As long as you make it clear in your article that they'll be heading to prison forthwith. Let the rebel sympathizers of this city know what comes of their treasonous schemes."

At that moment a door to the right opened. Encouraged by a bayonet-wielding guard, a pair of ragtag prisoners crossed in front of him, then disappeared into the room opposite. David did his best not to falter when he saw them, but he was certain he recognized one of the Confederates.

It was Elizabeth's own brother.

Chapter Sixteen

Elizabeth struggled to lay down the scenes of the skirmish in her sketch pad but couldn't stay focused on her task. David was leaving town in just a few days. He'd told her so when he escorted her home. The look on his face haunted her. He had acted as a gentleman as always, but Elizabeth knew she had hurt him. She hated the fact that she had. She wanted to confess everything. She *had* loved Jeremiah, but she loved *him* more. Elizabeth, however, dared not say such words.

Things will settle in time. Once he returns to Boston and becomes absorbed in another newspaper, he will forget all about me.

But Elizabeth knew full well she would never be able to forget about him. She would never again be able to pick up a drawing pencil or a stick of charcoal without being reminded of what they had shared.

And of what I let slip away...

Reason told her she was doing the right thing. She was protecting herself from a painful future, yet already her heart was aching at the thought of his departure.

But it must be this way, she argued. *For if he were*

to stay, it would only hurt that much more when something happens...

And she had convinced herself something would inevitably go wrong. The recent skirmish was her proof. War still raged, and disease and destruction were still part of this world. They always would be.

Yes, her heart whispered, *but you have survived, and look at what you've learned, what you've experienced in the process...*

She forced herself to focus on her work. *Mr. Keedy is due to arrive shortly. I must finish this assignment.*

Somehow she managed to complete her task with only moments to spare.

"Thank you for coming to claim the sketches," she told the young man.

"It was my pleasure, Miss Martin. Mr. Wainwright said you were busy tending to things here at home, what with the rebel scare and all."

Rebel scare? David had apparently told the rest of the staff she was needed at home, not that she was hiding here until he left town. *Bless him*, Elizabeth thought.

He was protective of her until the last. How much Elizabeth appreciated that, how much she wished she could tell him.

But I can't... I can't give in...

Mr. Keedy had no sooner walked away when again a knock sounded. Thinking he had forgotten some manner of business, Elizabeth quickly opened the door.

To her surprise, there stood David. Her heart immediately lodged in her throat.

"I know you probably don't wish to see me," he said, removing his hat, "but I've come across some news you must know."

"N-news?" she stammered.

"Yes. Your brother is here in Baltimore."

"My brother?"

Trudy rounded the corner. Mother was not far behind. "You've seen George?" they both said. "Where? When?"

"He's currently being held at the provost marshal's department. He's been captured."

Elizabeth's head was spinning. *He's alive? He's been captured? He's here in Baltimore? Can this really be true?*

"You've seen George personally?" her mother asked. "Is he wounded?"

"I have and no. He's a little worse for the wear, much thinner than that tintype you have of him on the mantel, but he's uninjured. And I am positive I recognized him. It's George."

"Did you speak with him?" Trudy asked.

"I tried. But neither he nor his fellow soldier would offer a word. To my knowledge, he hasn't spoken to anyone since his capture."

"Why?" Trudy asked.

Elizabeth was still struggling to find her voice, but she was certain she knew the answer. She looked to David. "He's trying to protect us, isn't he?"

The depth of emotion in his eyes cut her to the core. "I believe so," he said. "The lieutenant colonel in charge seems to think both men were either scouts for the would-be assault on Baltimore or they came here trying to warn their families of the impending danger."

"Then we must let him know we are well," Mother said. "We mustn't let him worry."

Elizabeth understood her mother's eagerness, but she knew that George would not be allowed any visitors, and even if he were, it would be very dangerous for them to claim knowing *him*. "What will they do with him, now?" she asked David.

"They are moving him to Fort McHenry this afternoon. After that he'll be transferred to the prison camp at Point Lookout."

Prison. Elizabeth's heart squeezed. *Where he'll be held for the remainder of the war.*

Her sister realized that, as well. "Then there is no telling when we will see him! To think he is this close and we can't go to him." Tears filled her eyes. Mother was dotting her own with her handkerchief.

Elizabeth couldn't stand to see them in pain, especially when she might be able to ease it, even if only a little. She was cautious, however, in making her request. "David, perhaps I shouldn't ask you this, but…will you take me to see him?"

He looked at her as if she had lost her mind. "Elizabeth, the sister of a Confederate soldier can't just waltz into the provost marshal's office."

"Indeed, but a sketch artist could. You could say we've come because of your article. I know my brother will recognize me."

"That's exactly what I'm afraid of! If those soldiers realize who you are, they will hound you and your family until they get whatever information they are seeking, maybe even worse. They could accuse you of being a spy—"

"But I'm a member of the press, and I'd be with you, a former federal soldier."

When David raked his fingers through his wavy hair, she was certain he was going to tell her no. He had every right. If the soldiers grew suspicious of her, he would be in danger, too, for bringing her. There was no reason for him to put himself at risk for her after she had refused him. Guilt consumed her.

I shouldn't have asked him. It was selfish of me to even think of asking such a favor of him.

David sighed. "We may be able to catch a glimpse of him before they move him to Fort McHenry."

Elizabeth blinked. "You'll take me?"

Before she could thank him, he placed his hands on her arms and looked her square in the eye. Elizabeth tingled from his touch, from the fierce look of protectiveness on his face.

"I want to make certain you understand the severity of this situation," he said. "You must stay beside me at all times, and if I sense even the slightest threat, we are leaving immediately."

"I understand. I trust your judgment."

He looked at her as if he were about to say something else, but Trudy had already brought her sketchbook.

"Before you go," her mother said, "let's pray."

They did, and then David and Elizabeth turned for the door.

"So you're back?" the lieutenant colonel said. "You want to try again? Think you'll get more out of them than I did?"

David was careful in his response. "No, sir, but without much to go on, I could use a sketch." He didn't say exactly what he was going to use the sketch for, though. This was one likeness that would never make it into the newspaper.

The lieutenant colonel nodded, then looked to Elizabeth. "You the artist?"

"Yes, sir." She handed him her press card.

David held his breath as the lieutenant colonel gave her the once-over.

"Don't get too many ladies in here," he said, then evidently deciding she was no threat, he handed back the card and called for a guard.

A pockmarked private escorted them to the holding room David had previously visited. Elizabeth tensed the moment she saw her brother. David hoped that would be the extent of her emotion on display. A second guard stood watch only a few feet from them.

George was at the back of the cell, seated on the floor, knees folded to his chest. He hadn't even bothered to look up when they had entered. His comrade did, though, and immediately stood, eyeing Elizabeth with intrigue.

"She's here to take down your likeness," David explained.

George then lifted his head. Recognition and shock sparked in his eyes. The guard noticed and glanced at Elizabeth. David quickly covered. "She gets such looks all the time," he said to the man in what he hoped was a casual tone. "Evidently few fellows have met a lady artist."

"I know I haven't," the guard said.

Under his watchful glare, George moved forward. Elizabeth hurried to busy herself with her sketchbook, capturing his image. David wondered just how much she'd actually be able to put down. The grip on her pencil was as tight as the set of her jaw.

"My sister likes to draw."

Elizabeth froze at the sound of her brother's voice. The guard was completely taken aback, as well. "You've more power here than the lieutenant colonel, miss. Those are the first words he's uttered."

Elizabeth ignored him. Her eyes focused solely on George. "Does she?" she asked.

He nodded. "I'm right proud of her. Always have been. I miss her very much."

Her chin twitched. David prayed and watched as she then adjusted her grip on her pencil and kept sketching. "I'm certain your sister misses you, as well," she said.

"I pray for her," George said. "I pray for all of my family."

Before her emotion could get the best of her, Elizabeth wisely shifted her attention to his comrade. "What about you? she asked. "Do you have any family?"

The man grinned. Vain as a peacock at Elizabeth's attention, he brushed back his hair and posed gallantly against the wall. "None as pretty as you."

David took offense at the caddish remark, as did Elizabeth's brother. When George's fists tightened, David knew it was time to leave. Any moment now, the guard was going to realize who she was. How he hadn't already noticed the family resemblance was beyond him.

"Have you enough to go on?" David asked. She had her brother's face down but nothing else.

Elizabeth nodded slowly. Her face was ashen. "Yes. I can complete the rest from memory."

"Good," he said. He eyed the nameless soldier with a purposeful look of disdain, as if his impudent remark was the sole reason for their departure. "Then I think we are through here."

She closed her sketchbook, moved toward the door. David knew it was killing her, but she did not look back. He did, however, just long enough to notice her brother's eyes were following him. The look in them told David that George appreciated what he had just done.

Elizabeth had never been more thankful for fresh air in all her life. The room in which George was being held had been stale smelling and stiflingly hot, but she knew her discomfort had more to do with the emotions she couldn't show than the actual physical conditions.

She hadn't seen her brother since the war began, hadn't even heard from him in almost a year, and then there he'd stood, inches from her, only iron bars between them. Where had he been all this time? Why hadn't he written? Why was he really here in Baltimore?

She didn't know, and she wouldn't until this war ended and he returned home. The thought of having to wait until then was such agony that it was all she could do to keep back her tears. But she knew that she could not let her distress show. That guard could have arrested her and David on the spot.

So she'd prayed. She'd prayed for strength. She'd prayed for safety for David, for George and for herself. She'd prayed for the courage to walk out of that room and for the faith to believe that her brother would be all right.

And she had been granted those requests.

When they were far enough away from the provost marshal's sentries, David asked, "Are you all right?"

Oddly enough, she was. Despite what she had just witnessed and all that had recently happened between them, Elizabeth felt an unmistakable peace.

"I know it may sound strange, given the fact that my brother is on his way to a prison camp, but I believe God has answered my prayers."

David glanced at her curiously. "How so?"

"I now know what has become of George. He isn't dead. He isn't lying wounded somewhere. And as dreadful as prison is, at least he's out of the fighting."

David offered her a sympathetic smile. "Well said, Elizabeth. I believe that's the way to look at it. God has not forgotten him."

"I will never leave thee, nor forsake thee..." Faith rose like a tiny bubble inside her, for she realized God had been with her brother all along. He had been with her, as well. Her prayers hadn't always been answered as she had hoped, but God had comforted her, provided for her and loved her every step of the way.

He had given her the opportunity to see her brother and the ability to sketch his face so her mother and sister could catch a glimpse of him, also. He had given her the chance to answer her brother's prayer—to see her safe and well. He had given her an avenue by which she may earn income doing what she loved. He had given her the will to go on living when she had wanted to die.

Oh, Lord, you have been so good to me...

As a child Elizabeth had known God as Creator and Savior. Through grief, she had learned something else. God was also a Father, and even though she hadn't recognized His presence in her life, she knew now for certain He had always been there.

And You sent a good and honorable man back into my life to show me that I was capable of loving again.

Elizabeth had no idea what tomorrow would bring, but God did, and knowing that, she could face the future without fear. She wasn't certain how David would respond to such news, given all that had taken place, but she had to tell him.

Beside her, David was walking, munching on a peppermint drop, deep in thought.

I have to tell him. It may make no difference now, but I can't allow him to leave without letting him know how I truly feel.

They were nearing Monument Square. Elizabeth asked if they might stop for a moment.

"Of course," he said.

They claimed the bench beneath the shade tree, the very one they had occupied on their first day of working together. Elizabeth's heart was pounding.

"David, there is something that I need to explain—"

He stopped her at once, lifting his hand. "Elizabeth, you don't have to—"

"I love you."

His eyes widened with a look of surprise. "*What* did you say?"

"I love you."

"Then why did you—?" His surprised expression settled to a look of gentle understanding. "You're afraid, aren't you? Because of what happened before."

He knew her so well. He always had. "Yes," she admitted. "I couldn't stand the thought of something happening to you as it did to Jeremiah, but David, I don't want to let fear rule my life anymore. I would rather have five minutes with you, if that is all God has ordained, than to not love you at all."

Moving closer, David took her hands in his. A look of devotion, of certainty filled his face. "Elizabeth, I would like nothing more than to be able to promise you that I will love you and be with you for the rest of your life, but I can't. I can only promise you that I will love you for the rest of *mine*."

Coupled with God's promise, that was enough. Tears of joy filled her eyes. "Then you will stay?"

"Of course I will stay. I want to marry you. You know that, don't you?"

A giggle escaped her throat. She couldn't help it. She felt so happy. "I figured as much when you kissed me."

David chuckled, also. "Oh, you did, did you?"

Turning serious, Elizabeth then drew back her hands. She removed the pearl ring from her finger and held it out. "You chose this for me," she said.

"How did you learn that? Did Jeremiah tell you?"

"No." She explained what had happened the day she claimed her memorial brooch. "The jeweler said you thought the ring would suit me. You were right. You know me better than anyone else."

"And you, me." As he took the ring from her, there was a hint of sadness in his eyes. "I loved my brother," he said. "I wanted him to be happy, but I so badly wanted to be the one to put this on your finger."

"Will you?"

The most handsome smile she had ever seen emerged on his face. It reached all the way to his eyes. "Nothing would make me happier."

Her hands were trembling, but this time it was not in fear. David slid the ring on her finger, then sealed the moment with a tender kiss. Elizabeth could feel the beating of his heart. It matched the rhythm of her own.

Epilogue

November 1, 1864

"You may kiss your bride."

When Reverend Perry said those words, David did not hesitate. Lifting Elizabeth's veil, he planted a kiss on her lips, all to the cheers of their family and friends.

Sam and Julia Ward had returned from Philadelphia in time for the ceremony, and David's parents, sister and brother-in-law had come from Boston. The staff of the *Free American* was on hand, as well. When David led his wife down the aisle, he received a fair share of back slapping from his fellow newspapermen.

"You'll now have new stories to tell," Peter said.

David couldn't help but grin. *Indeed*, he thought. He and Elizabeth had covered a host of events in the preceding months. Many of which had been a test of faith.

After the failed invasion, the rebel army had retreated to Virginia. Elizabeth's brother had been transferred to a prison camp in southern Maryland, and the city had slowly shifted its focus from defense back to politics. The state convention had reconvened. David returned to

Annapolis, and Elizabeth churned out sketches based on his wires. The Unconditionals had succeeded in drafting a new constitution that would immediately emancipate all slaves in Maryland, but the document prohibited all those with less than impeccable loyalty from voting in future elections.

When the complete proposal was brought before the people, it passed by the narrowest of margins. David didn't know what the future would bring for Maryland and her people with divided loyalties, but at long last, the slaves were finally free. The new constitution had taken effect today.

How fitting that we are beginning our new life together on the very day when the former slaves are beginning theirs.

Elizabeth squeezed his hand, as if she knew what he was thinking. The light in her eyes nearly stole his breath.

"Peter is going to have to issue you a new press card," David told her.

She let out a laugh. It was the most beautiful sound he had ever heard. "He already has."

"He has?"

"I asked him to bring it over to the house this morning."

"You did?"

She nodded. "I was eager to see *Elizabeth J. Wainwright* printed out for myself. Besides, it might come in handy on our honeymoon."

David blinked, curiously. "You think we might run into a story while visiting art galleries in New York City?"

"You never know." She smiled, mischievously. "After all, we are partners."

"Partners, you say?"

"In work and in life."

David grinned, pulled her close. "That's my girl."

* * * * *

Dear Reader,

Thank you for choosing *Second Chance Love,* the third book in my Civil War series. By 1864 many Maryland secessionists were beginning to reconsider their support for the Confederacy and for slavery. Just as many battle-weary unionists were entertaining ideas of compromise with the South, in hopes of ending the fighting. When I first wrote this story I had simply intended to tell this part of Maryland history. Little did I know, however, as the manuscript entered the review process, I was entering one of the darkest and most discouraging periods of my life.

My family and I experienced a devastating loss. My Christian upbringing told me God had a purpose in the suffering, and that He was still in control. Yet, the more I tried to press through the pain, the more I wanted to keep moving forward, the more I hurt. Prayer seemed pointless. Like Elizabeth, for a time I had to rely on the faith and intercession of others. Eventually, though, I found joy again.

I still don't have answers, but I do know that God loves me. He proves it time and again, not by giving me what I asked for but by carrying me through the storm. I can say with certainty that what the Bible says is true. No matter how desperate our circumstances, or how weak we may become, God will *never* leave us, nor forsake us.

If you are going through a difficult time, may I encourage you to hold tight? Continue to spend time with

God, even if all you do is cry. He understands. He feels every pain, and He alone has the ability to take our ashes and turn them into something beautiful.

By His grace,
Shannon Farrington

COMING NEXT MONTH FROM
Love Inspired® Historical

Available September 1, 2015

WOLF CREEK WIDOW
by Penny Richards
Still healing from emotional—and physical—wounds left by her late husband, widow Meg Thomerson turns to Ace Allen for help running her business. Promising to remain at her side while she recovers, can he also mend her bruised heart?

HIS PRECIOUS INHERITANCE
by Dorothy Clark
Newspaper editor Charles Thornberg is an expert at running a business, not raising a toddler. He desperately needs reporter Clarice Gordon's help caring for his little brother...and learning how to become a father—and husband.

A HOME FOR HIS FAMILY
by Jan Drexler
Cowboy Nate Colby journeys west for a fresh start with his orphaned nieces and nephew. Maybe fellow newcomer and beautiful schoolmarm Sarah MacFarland will be the missing piece to their fractured family...

THE MATCHMAKER'S MATCH
by Jessica Nelson
Lady Amelia Baxley is known for finding perfect love matches—for everyone except for herself. She agrees to help Lord Spencer Ashwhite find a wife...but can she follow through after she begins falling for the reformed rake?

LIHCNM0815

REQUEST YOUR FREE BOOKS!

2 FREE INSPIRATIONAL NOVELS
PLUS 2 *FREE* MYSTERY GIFTS

Love Inspired® HISTORICAL

SPECIAL EXCERPT FROM

Love Inspired HISTORICAL

*Still healing from emotional—and physical—wounds
left by her late husband, widow Meg Thomerson turns
to Ace Allen for help running her business. Promising to
remain at her side while she recovers, can he also mend
her bruised heart?*

Read on for a sneak preview of
WOLF CREEK WIDOW,
available in September 2015 from
Love Inspired Historical!

"Look at me, Meg," he said in that deep voice. "Who do
you see?"

"What?" She frowned, unsure of what he was doing
and wondering at the sorrow reflected in his eyes.

"Who do you see standing here?"

What did he want from her? she wondered in confusion.
"I see you," she said at last. "Ace Allen."

"If you never believe anything else about me, you can
believe that I would never deliberately harm a hair on
your head."

His statement was much the same as what he'd said the
day before in the woods. It seemed Ace was determined
that she knew he was no threat to her.

"Elton used to stand in the doorway like that a lot.
For just a moment when I looked up I saw him, not you.
I…I'm s-sorry."

"I'm not Elton, Meg."

LIHEXP0815

His voice held an urgency she didn't understand. "I know that."

"Do you?" he persisted. "Look at me. Do I look like Elton?"

"No," she murmured. Elton hadn't been nearly as tall, and unlike Ace he'd been almost too good-looking to be masculine. She'd once heard him called pretty. No one would ever think of Ace Allen as pretty. Striking, surely. Magnificent, maybe. Pretty, never.

"No, and I don't act like him. Can you see that? Do you believe it?"

Still confused, but knowing somehow that her answer was of utmost importance, she whispered, "Yes."

He nodded, and the torment in his eyes faded. "You have nothing to be sorry for, Meg Thomerson. That's something else you can be certain of, so never think it again." With that, he turned and left her alone with her thoughts and a lot of questions.

Don't miss
WOLF CREEK WIDOW by Penny Richards,
available September 2015 wherever
Love Inspired® Historical books and ebooks are sold.

LIHEXP0815

JAN 1 1 2016